BIG FOOT

Blues

a novel

also by pamela foster

BIG FOOT Blues

a novel

pamela foster

RADIANCE

RADIANCE

An imprint of Roan & Weatherford Publishing Associates, LLC
Bentonville, Arkansas
www.roanweatherford.com

Library of Congress Cataloging-in-Publication Data
Names: Foster, Pamela, author
Title: Bigfoot Blues/Pamela Foster | The Bigfoot Trilogy #1
Description: Third Edition. | Bentonville: Radiance, 2025.
Identifiers: 978-1-63373-112-7 (hardcover)
ISBN: 978-1-63373-113-4 (trade paperback) | ISBN: 978-1-63373-114-1 (eBook)
Subjects: | BISAC: FICTION/Romance/Romantic Comedy | FICTION/Women
Fiction/Romance/Contemporary

Radiance trade paperback edition June, 2025

Cover & Interior Design by Casey W. Cowan
Editing by Gil Miller

For Mica, Joshua, Isaac, Riley, and Noah.

foreword

MY FAMILY SETTLED in Humboldt County in the 1800s. I grew up in a little Pierson House behind Fort Humboldt. When I was forty I married a Vietnam Veteran, a man who outran his PTSD by changing scenery as often as possible. We spent twenty-five years living mostly in the tropics, punctuated with a few years in the high desert of Arizona, as well as in the hardwood forests of the Arkansas Ozarks.

I've come home now, back to living in Eureka. But, *Bigfoot Blues* was written when I lived in Panama and was so homesick I ached, when I woke from dreams of dense fog, the quiet of a redwood forest, or the blessing of salt spray on my skin. In a way, *Bigfoot Blues* is the story of my longing for Humboldt County.

My desire was to write a book about a young woman raised within a belief system different from that of the society around her. I wanted this young woman to be loved and cherished by family and by believers within that group. I could have set this book in a religious cult, a group of fanatics of any particular persuasion. But those people have no sense of humor whatsoever. Bigfooters, however, are mostly good ole boys and girls who love nothing more than stomping around in the deep woods communing with a creature that may or may not exist. My kind of folks.

Besides, there is a family connection to Bigfoot. Grandpa had an encounter when he and Grandma lived up past Peckwan. I was staying with them that summer. This was fifteen years before Patterson snapped his famous footage along Bluff Creek. You know the film— the bigfoot known as Patty striding fast, looking over her shoulder at the man with the shaking camera. I was three, submerged to my flat chest in the warm soapy water of a metal wash basin when Grandpa returned to the cabin to say that the equipment for his logging road had been strewn about. Cement culverts tossed down an embankment, an earthmoving cat pushed sideways, footprints of huge bare feet left in the muck.

So, when I sat down to write this novel, a collection of warm, loving, decidedly odd Humboldt County Bigfooters seemed the perfect collection for the story of a young woman finding her own path in the world without disrespecting those who raised her. And, since family legend says that during prohibition my Aunt Mandy was a madam at a house of ill-refute on the Eureka waterfront, it was obvious that Samantha, my main character, would live in a bar inherited by her family from her working girl Aunt.

Those decisions made, all I did was sit in front of the computer and let the story tell itself.

Bigfoot Blues was first published in 2012. This new edition is in preparation for the next book in the series which is scheduled to be released in January of 2017. I hope you both enjoy this first novel and that it leaves you happily anticipating the second, *Bigfoot Mamas*.

Oh. And, one more thing. While I tried to stay true to the spirit of Bigfoot Country, the book is in no way meant as a guide to Humboldt or Trinity County. In the interest of the story line, I moved entire mountains, altered the course of rivers, and misplaced whole city blocks in Eureka. Any reader attempting to find bigfoot using this novel as a guide is likely to end up hopelessly lost in the rainforest of the Pacific Northwest.

—Pamela Foster

Eureka, California

June 7, 2016

acknowledgements

WITHOUT THE ASSISTANCE of everyone at Roan & Weatherford Publishing Associates, this book would not have been re-released. Thank you Casey Cowan, Gil Miller, and the whole publishing team, for believing in me when my confidence faltered.

I owe a huge debt of gratitude to my loyal fans who took the time to let me know how much they enjoy my work, and who encouraged and prodded me to get my butt in a chair and continue the tale of Samantha, and Hawk, and Bubba.

one

"TELL ME THIS here, then. How come nobody's ever found a body? A skull or a tooth even?"

Distorted by the shimmering campfire, Lefty's face flickers in and out of shadow. He takes the bottle from Bubba. The liquid amber is down an inch when he wipes his mouth on his flanneled sleeve, passes the bottle to Hawk.

Dense fog, heavy and cold with the rainforest's lifeblood, wraps itself around me, renders me invisible. From where I'm hunkered down, just outside the campfire's glow, I can hear something scratching around behind me in the leaf mold at the edge of Bluff Creek. A skunk or a raccoon. I'm hoping raccoon. Sooner or later I'll stand up, walk into the light of the campfire, and let the boys know I'm here. I'd just as soon not have them smell me before they see me.

My hesitation at joining them, my need for an extra moment of solitude is borne, partly, on the shoulders of my sex. As the only woman of the group, and the joint owner of the bar in which two of them spend every evening, my place is guaranteed. Yet, lately, I find myself pulling back from these childhood buddies, yearning for some separation from the good-ole-boy lifestyle that is my heritage.

Hawk passes the flat bottle to Bubba without taking a swallow. His right hand slips into the pocket of his denim jacket and I know he's fingering the talisman of his two-year AA chit.

In the fire's blue center, a chunk of wood burns through, sends orange sparks into the black night. The brief flare of light illuminates the dark, striated feather woven into Hawk's braid at the base of his neck, a prayer aimed into the night sky. The fecund smells of Bluff Creek, still too low for the salmon run, and a musky odor I can't place are momentarily infused with the bite of wood smoke.

"This here is the way I see it." Bubba passes the bottle to Lefty who appears to be planning on bogarting what's left in the pint. "If I can't see a thang and I can't touch it, then I ain't likely to waste my time worryin' about it none."

I shift my position to ease the strain in my thighs, grin at the accent that earned Mr. Robert Lee Johnson of Noisy Creek, Georgia, his nickname the first time he ordered a shot at VD's. In the five years Bubba's been hanging with us, the edges of that drawl have been smoothed some. Until he gets excited. Emotion thickens his speech to a muddy roux of moss-draped live oak and honeysuckle nights. I grin into the darkness. Booze'll draw out the southern redneck too. Oh yes, it will.

"So, what I hear you saying," Hawk's soft voice is just audible above the crackle of the fire and the rustle of whatever nocturnal critter continues to move around behind me, "if you'll allow me to put a label on your thinking, is that you are an empiricist."

Lefty's voice is already slurred around the edges. "Call it whatever you want, Professor. I'm with Bubba on this one. The day I see one of them Bigfoots, that there is the day I'll believe in them."

I contemplate chucking a few rocks toward this philosophical little group.

Out near Weitchpec, where the reservation wraps itself around the stumped remains of ancient forest my ancestors cut less than a hundred years ago, Hawk and I huddled together last spring break while something threw stones as big as goose eggs at the side of the pockmarked Airstream we borrowed from his cousin Bobby Whitetail. Hawk, more Indian in these situations than Professor of Anthropology, believed Bigfoot was saying hello. As the daughter of a longtime Bigfooter, I am fully aware that chucking rocks is well-documented Bigfoot behavior. Still, I suspected the rocks were thrown by a wannabe girlfriend of Hawk's, unhappy with his bringing to the reservation a girl whose skin is, alas, as white as a frog's belly.

"When's Sam getting here anyways?" Lefty asks.

I've known Lefty for twenty years, since he was my boyfriend for two weeks in Mrs. Moulex's fourth-grade class at Alice Birney Elementary School. It's not my company he's missing.

When I step out into the firelight and call out a loud and friendly greeting, Lefty startles, nearly toppling from the old maple log on which he's perched and Bubba actually squeals. Only Hawk doesn't flinch, which, stoic Indian or not, means he knew I was there.

"What the hay'ell girl?" Bubba drawls.

Lefty rights himself and demands, "Where's the beer?"

"I am just as happy as a pig in shit to see you too, Lefty," I tell him. "The cooler's in the truck back up on the road. You want it, you go and get it."

"Nice to see a barmaid set some boundaries," Hawk says with a straight face.

I touch the bottom of his boot with the toe of my tennis shoe. "Hey. Anytime you want out of the business our dads left us, just let me know. I can run VD's just fine without your educated input."

Truth be known, I would miss Hawk as my business partner, but the one thing I'd do if I owned the bar outright is to change the name and get a new goddamn sign out front. Until I can convince Hawk otherwise, or buy him out, I'm stuck with scrolled neon flashing Victor & David's into the night, the V and D pulsing deep orange and the rest in silent muted silver.

"No way," Hawk says. "The first thing you'd do is take down that poster my Daddy painted with his own two dago hands."

"Yeah. A tragedy," I agree. "I'm sure business would drop substantially without the hand-painted offer of *Fresh Local Crabs* directly below all that neon."

Once Lefty and Bubba return with the case of beer, minus the six cans they drank on their way from the truck, I decide to entertain myself with a little experiment.

Hawk has built a lovely Indian fire. Huddled around the warmth, except for the denim and Carhartt, we could be any small group of hunter-gatherers in the last ten thousand or so years.

Pushing my back against the log, I tuck my hands under my bent knees, stare into the flames and mention casually, "I can't believe you set up camp here."

"Ain't nothing wrong with here," Bubba says. "This more Bigfoot bull?"

This close I can smell Lefty's recycled beer belches and could rat out Bubba's old hound for sleeping on his coat. Instead I stay focused.

"Nothing at all wrong," I say, "unless you don't care for the idea of sleeping on the very spot where Mary Sue Foster chopped her five children to death with a hatchet pretty near exactly like that one over there embedded in the stump of that piss fir."

"You're full of...." My look stops Lefty. He knows the rules. I can cuss any goddamn time I want. They, as potential gentlemen, have to watch their language around the girl. Well, not any girl. Just the one who pours their drinks and brings their beer.

"Hey, you don't have to believe it. I'm just saying. I'm surprised you decided to sleep here. Hell, the baby wasn't even a year old. My great-great grandpa Victor Senior himself found the bones from the four-year-old's hands not six inches from where you're sitting, Lefty. I believe the child's name was Jason. They all had *J* names those kids. Jason, Jimmy, Johnny. Mighta been a Jethro. I think the baby was Jennifer."

It's not that difficult to fool rednecks when they're half in the bag.

"How come there ain't no sign of a house here?" Lefty shifts on the log, scratches his chin and cuts his eyes out into the black all around us.

"That's right, girl. There ain't no rock fireplace, not one single corner stone." Bubba's head nods in agreement, but he looks to Hawk, waiting, I assume, for confirmation or denial.

"The way I always heard it," Hawk's low voice forces us all to lean forward, strain to make out his words, "the other white eyes carried off every single scorched pot or pan, dug up every stone, smashed or broke up what they could and the rest they hid in the woods around here."

Bubba bites. "I'm not getting this. Why would a mama kill her younguns?"

Somewhere in the forest at our backs an owl screeches victory, proclaiming that some small rodent who, moments before was going about its ordinary life, is now dinner. Hawk places another log on the fire, adjusts the burning wood with two thick pieces of kindling employed as makeshift tongs.

"I can totally see how it would happen," I say.

All three men shift their butts, put a fraction more distance between them and me.

"Her husband had died of pox or dysentery or working himself to death trying to keep food on the table for a wife and five babies. The closest neighbor would have been the Kerrs, whose original cabin is a good two miles from this spot here. My grandpa said the poor woman's horse and cow had died. How was she going to get to town for supplies? How was she going to feed all those children?"

We stare into the fire some more. The cloud cover splits in one jagged tear, exposing two distant stars the names of which none of us know.

"How was this woman related to you again?" Lefty asks.

"Well, let's see." I count on my fingers like a child doing arithmetic. "Great-Great-Grandpa Vincent was Mary Sue's husband's brother. So I guess that would make the ax murderer my great-aunt twice removed. No blood kin." I cover my mouth to stifle a mirthless little laugh. "No pun intended."

The men cringe.

Lefty rolls his shoulders.

Bubba rubs his palms over his unshaven face.

"Okay," allows Lefty. "So she's desperate and not wanting to watch her kids starve and she decides to kill 'em. But why use an ax? Ain't there gentler ways a saving your babies from a slow death?"

The stars are hidden again, the night black as a shroud around us.

"Ah, yeah," I finish up. "I never said ole Mary Sue wasn't crazy as a bed bug. Great-Grandpa said when he and his cousin Merritt got here come spring, the bodies of those children were strewed over a half-mile area. They ran, those kids. Their mother right behind 'em with the bloody hatchet."

Beyond our fire's glow, we can hear something rustling through the underbrush. Sounds a little bigger than a raccoon.

Probably a deer.

"How'd she kill her own self?" Bubba asks as he pops the top on another Bud. "She cain't a hacked her own self to pieces."

"They never found her body. Ask my dad. He swears that on certain icy winter nights, Mary Sue still comes around, crying and wailing for her babies."

"I don't believe that bullshi…. that ain't true." Lefty insists.

"Well, of course that part isn't true," I allow. "Good lord, we're educated people, not superstitious old fools who believe in things they can't see or touch." The triumphant owl, or her mate, screeches into the night again. "We don't believe in ghosts or any sort of evil that could, like, permeate the very ground under our sleeping heads. Course not. Still, I wish you hadn't set up camp right here in this exact spot."

Hawk's face, across the fire from me, is all sharp angles. Strangers often comment that his high cheekbones and a nose that splits his face like a wedge are classic Indian features. They're thinking Sioux or Cheyenne. Hawk's lean looks come from his tall Italian dad not his shorter, more solidly built Yurok Indian mother.

"You get any work this week?" I ask and watch both Lefty and Bubba shake their heads.

"Doing some roofing for Mikey." Lefty rubs his knees, lets it go at that.

"I'm doin' awright," Bubba nods, which means he's still got harvest money.

The fire is mostly electric blue embers when Lefty announces, "It's colder than a witch's tit tonight. I believe I'm gonna sleep in the cab a the truck."

"I believe I'll go with you," Bubba decides. "Throw my bag under the camper shell. I been feelin' a bit peaked these last few days. Better not to take chances with my health."

Hawk and I wait until the stumbling and the cussing dies out. Then he builds up the fire and we open our sleeping bags and lay my warmer, plaid-wrapped goose-down over his heavier brown flannel. We take off our boots, crawl inside our soft cotton nest and snuggle denim to denim. I stare out into the thick, pearly fog, pondering the limited visibility of this place I call home.

"Have a bad night?"

I roll into him, slip my arm over his narrow waist.

"Not especially. I was just feeling mean I suppose. And that Mary Sue deal did happen. 'Course it wasn't anywhere near here. Was up Bald Mountain, near Snow Camp. Bubba's right. You can still find the cornerstones of the cabin if you know where to look."

I push against Hawk's length, take what comfort I can from his heat. His cold hand makes me flinch as he slides it under my sweatshirt.

"How long were you squatted over there, listening to our conversation?"

"Long enough to hear those two yahoos diss The Big Guy," I confess.

"Ah huh." His hand cups my breast. "Lord Sam, you're not even a washed-in-the-blood believer."

I slip my elbow under his forearm, force his busy hand away. "Maybe not, but twenty-eight years of listening to my dad and yours and every other Bigfooter in four states. I've been water baptized. At least. I may not have Bigfoot in my heart, but I sure as hell am not willing to discount the possibility that he's out there somewhere."

He rolls over me, forces my hands above my head, uses his weight to anchor me to the ground.

"You can't have it both ways, Sam."

His right hand slides under my sweatshirt, edges it up, brings his head down to a hard nipple.

"Make up your mind," he taunts me between licks. "Are you a true believer?"

I fight to control my breathing, catch him at just the right moment, use his own heavier weight to flip him under me.

"I can have it," I whisper into his ear, "any damn way I want it."

His earlobe is soft between my teeth. I bite down. Hard.

The fog turns to mist while we're busy under the sleeping bag. At the end, Hawk throws off the flannel covering and howls into the dark as I buck under him. Which means the inside of the sleeping bag is cold and clammy when, once we come back to our senses, we fling the cover over our heads and spoon.

Within minutes, Hawk's breathing is steady and even. I pull back the water-resistant bag, peek out to see if the weather has evolved into run-for-cover rain. Still light mist. The fire is a ring of orange embers, the night sky a soft purple-gray, the existence of the stars something I must take on faith. A breeze ruffles the coals and the acrid smoke floats toward me. I'm just pulling the cover back over my head when a rancid smell makes my eyes water and brings Hawk up out of sleep.

The first rock hits the blackened dirt less than a foot from the dying fire.

two

"WHERE YA WANT the Bigfoot butt?"

Lefty and Bubba stagger sideways into the bar, the heavy plaster cast between them.

"Set the Skookum right here, place of honor. Up on the table. Let everybody get a good look."

Dad's always been tall and lean, but now, watching him supervise the preparations, I notice the stiffness from that fall he took at Happy Camp last summer. His left leg drags just a whisper at each step. At seventy-eight, his once thick chestnut hair is now soft, snowy wisps.

We used to be a study in contrast, Dad and me. His olive skin and thick dark mane and my pale skin and white blonde hair. As a child I looked like my absent mother. With each passing year though, Dad and I are more alike. His hair lightening, mine darkening a little. Letticia swears she saw us coming into Marcelli's last month and I was gimping along, a hiccup in my gait, an unconscious imitation of the man who raised me from birth.

The heavy plaster positioned on the table to Dad's specifications, Lefty rubs his back, twists his scrawny upper body from side to side. "Tell me again why it's called 'The Skookum.'"

"Because the imprint was captured in Skookum, Washington." Dad puts his arm around Lefty's shoulder, pats his back. "Thanks for helping an old man. Packing it in from the storeroom."

Directing the arrangement of the foot casts along the back wall under the elk heads, Dad's movements are especially slow tonight, his body shaky when he bends to straighten the Blue Mountain imprint. The notion that this man is not going to live forever hits me like a blow.

Hawk and I are behind the bar, taking some inventory, doing a little maintenance, but mostly, keeping an eye on things. The meeting's set to start in ten minutes. We'll both head out once the door's locked and the service gets going.

Bigfooters, like every group of faithful on earth, take themselves seriously. Last July's meeting, there was a fistfight between a group that believes there are two species of Bigfoot in the Northwest, and those that maintain that the far north's Sasquatch and our Bigfoot are one and the same. The bi-species congregation now meets in Willow Creek at the home of their leader.

"Lord have mercy on my soul," Bubba exclaims as he peers down into the Skookum replica. "This is one heavy mutha."

He scratches his head, tips his face inches from the plaster. "I can't exactly make this here out. Whereabouts is the ass?"

David strolls over from where he's arranging the collection of young Bigfoot casts known as Littlefoots. Nothing he likes better than preaching to a non-believer. The man turned seventy-six last month. In '88 he lost the tips of three fingers on his left hand to a logging accident and he's carrying about twenty pounds more than he should be, and he's still the best looking man in the bar. If Hawk ages half as well as his dad, he'll be making women suck in their stomachs and catch their breath for a good many years yet.

David puts one arm around Bubba's shoulder, moves his right hand over the surface of the cast. "See right here now, these two rounded clefts? Well, obviously, that's his ass."

"Ain't obvious to me," Bubba says. "If that there's his ass, what's this here?"

David grins in triumph. "Why son, that's a near perfect imprint of the big guy's testicles and about two-thirds of his penis."

Bubba flinches, jerks his face up away from where his nose was nearly pressed into the plaster of Paris.

Then a grin splits his big honest face. "Well, hallelujah," he proclaims like a soul being lifted up out of the water and into the light. "That there helps some to explain those college gals what are running around out there in the tick-infested woods looking for this here fella."

I hand the inventory sheet to Hawk and call across the bar. "So, what Bubba? You think modern women are panting for some wild, hairy savage with a big dick?"

Beside me, Hawk whispers into my ear, "I'm hoping."

I bump his hip with mine, buzz his cheek, "Your doctorate just a nice bonus for the ladies?"

"A thin veneer of civilization over the savage beast within," he assures me.

Picturing him last night at Bluff Creek, naked and backlit by the fire, his arms opened in a wide welcome, chanting into the night while rocks fell all around him, I can only grin.

"You tell 'em about our little encounter?" I ask as an overdressed stranger pushes his way through the front door.

"That was a private audience," Hawk declares. "And Sam." He looks away from me, puts an inch or two more distance between us. "I, uh, I need to talk to you sometime before the meeting starts."

A nod of my head and he knows I've heard him. If he's got something to say, why not just say it? He and I have been doing well these last few months, but this man has a history of monkey wrenching himself, and me, out of being happy.

"Can I help you?" I call to The Suit. "We're not open for business. Twentieth of every month. Private party."

This guy is definitely lost. Ninety percent of our business is regulars and a clean sweatshirt is considered formal attire. The man walking across the original plank floor of my Aunt Mandy's old brothel is wearing clothes worth as much as I paid for my car. Okay, more actually, since I inherited my '78 Ford F-150 from my dad who won it off Pete Cotaldi in a game of blackjack.

The stranger's jacket is, and I'm guessing here, some kind of lightweight fabric made from the wool of lambs handfed by virgins. The tie is probably silk, power yellow with thin slanted stripes the same dove gray as the suit. He has hair the color of those butterscotch candies I love to set on my tongue and let melt, filling my mouth with soft sweetness.

I want to hate him.

"I'm aware that tonight is a meeting," he says, sliding onto the barstool directly across from me. His smile is blinding and directed at me and me alone. "I was told that this is where the monthly Tri-County Bigfooters meet. I'm hoping to talk with Victor Foster and David Morrelli."

Dad and David sit at the wooden table in the far corner. Both pretend to be busy arranging papers. Bubba and Lefty, however, walk toward the bar. Their chests expand and legs stiffen just that little bit that indicates a challenge in the testosterone-infused half of the species. Lefty is what my dad calls "a wiry little bugger," but Bubba is well over six four and built like a brick shithouse—solid and constructed to take whatever crap comes his way. I know for a fact that Lefty is the more dangerous of the two, but the gorgeous fool sitting in front of me is watching Bubba coming at him like a freight train, his Adam's apple moving under that fancy silk tie.

Hawk edges his way toward us along the bar, nonchalant, subtle as a rock through a window. "You a reporter?"

"That obvious?" The Suit reaches his manicured hand to the inside of his jacket and the four of us hold our breath, tense up just a little. When he extracts a business card, we all exhale, exchange sheepish grins.

"Mark Neilsen." He hands me a cream-colored card.

I run my fingers over its surface. Embossed. I really want to hate this guy. Which would be easier if he didn't have eyes the color of that variegated moss along a late summer river. He smells citrusy. Why would I be attracted to the smell of a fruit?

"I'm writing a book on Bigfoot," he says, looking directly into my eyes.

I can feel myself blushing under his stare, the heat flushing my chest, neck, and face as Bubba and Lefty sit, one on each side of mossy-eyed Mark Neilsen.

"Ya'll comin' down with something, Sam?" Bubba asks, "Cause your face is kind of reddish. You didn't rub up against poison oak did you?"

Beside me Hawk emits a choking sound, like a car refusing to start on a cold morning.

Still looking into my eyes, Mr. Neilsen begins his research. "So I understand this bar, Victor and David's? It has a history of its own?"

This is no secret. *The Times-Standard* does a piece on this particular local color about once a year.

"My great grandpa's sister was the town madam back in Prohibition days. Mandy's it was called back then. This was her brothel."

David stands up from the corner table, ends my historical lecture by calling across the bar. "Join us, Mr. Neilsen. My son will draw you a beer. On the house. The US of A is still rumored to be a free country. Believer or debunker, you are welcome to join us at our monthly meeting."

I rarely see the people and things I love through the eyes of an outsider. This ratty bar with frame 352 of the Patterson tape centered over the sparkling bottles of booze, the deer, elk, and bison heads hanging from the walls like visiting relatives, the mismatched metal chairs upholstered in gold glitter Naugahyde, the smell of beer and honest sweat—this is home. Watching Mark Neilsen pick his way around the scarred wooden tables, I decide I really do hate this outsider with the deceptive green eyes and bleached teeth. I hate him because his suave, sophisticated presence is like a goddamn floodlight showing me why I am filled lately with a desire for something different than this inheritance, something I can't help but label better.

And that pisses me off.

"Two months from now, October's meeting, that's the one you'll be wanting to attend," Dad tells Mr. Neilsen.

"Why is that?" asks the stranger as Dad gives me the universal signal of a raised eyebrow and cocked index finger that, in every bar on earth, means, "Bring us a couple beers, will ya, dear."

I look around for Hawk, but the man has disappeared from sight. Probably hiding in the backroom pretending to be doing some damn thing. I knew he wasn't going to be fetching a beer for Mr. La-de-freakin-da-Neilsen.

Hawk's dad leans his wooden chair back on two legs, gives his best impersonation of a man who is shocked down to his bones.

"You done much research for this book yet?" David asks. "October twentieth, nineteen sixty-seven? The Patterson video tape?" David points toward the picture over the bar. "Frame three fifty-two. Bigfoot Patty, as this particular Bigfoot female individual is affectionately known, looking back over her shoulder like a cover girl, right into Patterson's lens."

I set three drafts on the table. For some reason I stand a couple inches too close to Mark Neilsen.

"The Shroud of Turin of the Bigfoot movement," I educate him. To Dad and David I say, "We camped there last night. Bluff Creek. Right about where Bud Ryerson and Fritz Brockmueller had all that construction equipment strewn around in, was it 'fifty-seven?"

Dad raises his eyes, meets mine. "See anything?"

"Nothing unusual. A big stink and a half-dozen chucked rocks."

I leave it at that and head back to the bar.

Twenty minutes later the bar's already crowded. The veteran Bigfooters, Dad and David at their center, are clustered at the Skookum cast. The younger guys mill around swapping stories. Five women of varying ages, all in denim and flannel, muck up the works, make the men nervous. They stand out like sore thumbs among the men, cover their unease with loud talk and aggressive boasts.

"We've got a better shot at drawing him out than any of you men," a young redhead is lecturing Bubba. "We plan it right. Go when we have at least three of us on our menstrual cycles. It's the smell that draws him out. Attracts him."

Bubba appears too dumbfounded to come up with a reply to this assertion. He shuffles his boots, can't keep his eyes away from the bountiful cleavage exposed above the blue flannel.

At the bar, a guy in greasy jeans and a biker jacket, his shoulder-length graying hair tied with a rainbow scrunchy, lectures a small group of younger hunters. A cross between a Keebler elf and Charles Manson, the miniature biker has an energy field that draws into his orbit anyone missing a heavy dose of skepticism.

"They're from another dimension than ours. This is the explanation for why no one's ever found a body. Have you not noticed that many reports tell of the observer catching no more than a glimpse of one of these creatures before they appear to fade back into the woods?"

I lean across the bar and kiss his cheek. "Evening Dr. Bernstein, how was the ride up from Berkeley?"

"It was a glorious trip, dear. Thank you for inquiring."

"Anything new in the world of string theory?"

"We are on the cusp of wondrous discoveries." Dr. Rubert Bernstein, physicist and professor at UC Berkeley, gives me a mischievous wink.

I know from experience that this particular little group is headed for the Bigfoot-As-Space-Alien conversation. I do not believe I can listen to that discussion right now.

Tradition dictates that once the group is settled, the bar is closed until the meeting ends. There is no reason for me to hang around, acting like a schoolgirl, waiting on Mark Neilsen to notice me. Evidently Hawk ducked into his room because he's back at the bar wearing a new pair of jeans and a button-down shirt the color of milk chocolate.

"Want to go to Marcelli's?" I ask him.

"Shootin' or eatin'?" Bubba invites himself.

"I was thinking raviolis or chicken parmesan." I grab my jacket. "But we'll see. Maybe some shooting after dinner."

Lefty, Bubba, and I are on our way out the door before I notice Hawk is still polishing glasses, glancing around the room as though looking for someone.

I call back over the noise. "You're not coming?"

Hawk shakes his head, won't meet my eyes. "I'll stay."

I shrug, head out.

Hawk's '52 Indian Chief is directly in front of my truck. Powder blue and chrome. Just looking at the bike transports me to a world I never knew—a simpler, more honest and beautiful time. A period in my country's history when *Made in America* meant pride and craftsmanship instead of throwing together parts made around the world and slamming on an expensive price sticker.

It's odd that the Chief is parked out front. Hawk usually pushes the vintage motorcycle through the bar and into his bedroom. I have wanted to make love straddling this piece of equipment since the first time Hawk drove it home. So far, Hawk has not been persuaded.

My peculiar little fantasy is putting a smile on my face when I see her. Dark hair pulled back in a braid that hangs to her waist, nice brown eyes, though if those are her real lashes I'm Mrs. Bigfoot. Not that I care, but I wonder how long it took her to get into those jeans. Rhinestone hearts on the back pockets. This bitch is headed for VD's like a heat-seeking missile.

It's not like Hawk and I have an exclusive thing. I hate the term, but we're friends with benefits. That's all. I couldn't care less who else he sees. Or fucks. Six months ago I did my best to have the "moving on to the next stage of our relationship" talk with him.

"I might like to wear a fancy white dress one day," I told him after a few glasses of champagne at the wedding of a high school friend.

"No kidding?" He creased his forehead, twisted his soft mouth into a wrinkled prune, winked to show me he was teasing. "Myself? I've never had much desire to wear anything frilly. Not partial to veils, either."

My glare eventually ate through his patina of levity. He leaned forward, took my hand in his and whispered, "You and me. We don't want to get married, Sam. Lifelong monogamy is a lie and a trap. You know that."

He's always been honest about being more bonobo than snow goose.

I watch the sway of his latest dalliance, spike-heeled boots on pocked sidewalk. She looks like she knows exactly what she wants and where she'll find it. This must be what a sucker punch to the belly feels like.

Between gasping inhale and violent exhale, my vulnerability morphs to raw anger.

No skin off my nose if he wants to have wild, monkey sex with every co-ed at Humboldt State. Maybe she's got simian herpes and his stupid dick will rot off.

Miss Rhinestone Ass swings open the door to VD's. A smile as big as the lust that built the place lights up her over-made-up face. She spots Hawk behind the bar. I have no trouble envisioning the look on his face right this minute, fight the urge to go back inside and wipe that self-satis-fied little grin right off his handsome face. Not that it's my business who he sleeps with. God knows, he's made that abundantly clear. Crystal freaking clear. But the man could have the decency to tell me he's meeting some-one. It's not like I give a flying crap.

When I swing into the truck, Hawk's powder blue pride and joy is framed perfectly in the F-150's cracked front windshield. The redwood 12x12 bolted below the grill as a makeshift front bumper whispers to me like the answer to prayer. I slip the truck into first, depress the clutch and rev the engine until it screams. I don't know what it says about me, but if it were Hawk standing in front of the truck, I believe, right at this moment, I might let my anger have its way. But a cherry 1952 Indian motorcycle?

I slam the stick into reverse, flip a U-ey, and lay rubber all the way to Lazio's fish market where I slide onto Clark Street and head uptown. The Ford's tires squeal again making the turn past St. Bernard's Catholic Church and onto Fifth where a flashing blue light slows me down some. Rolling down my window, I wave back at Jamie Renner as he turns into the courthouse lot. Shit, piss, damn. Now, in lieu of the ticket, I'll owe him and three or four of his cop buddies a free drink or two. Another blazing example of why I'm never going to save enough money to get moved out of my childhood room at VD's.

I swing the truck into a parking place on Fifth Street, stomp into Marcelli's where a garlic-and-tomato-sauce-tinged steam instantly brings a sweat to my forehead. Bubba and Lefty sit at our usual table, the one in the far right corner. Their wide grins disappear when they see the look on my face.

"Take off your damn hats," I growl as I take a chair next to Lefty. "Jesus. Nobody ever told you to remove your cover when you're inside?"

"Y'all talkin' trash about the way my mama raised me?" Bubba grumbles as he removes his stained Braves ball cap.

Lefty reluctantly reveals his flattened hair, twists a black ball cap around in his scrawny lap so the words *Free Mustache Rides* are hidden against the slight concave of his belly.

"You don't even have a mustache!" I grouse.

The two exchange a look.

It's Lefty who gathers his courage. "Christ on a crutch, Sam. You were fine when we left the bar. What happened? And where's Hawk? Thought he was coming."

These two knuckleheads would walk through fire for me and I'd do the same for them. But, right this moment, I have a desperate need to talk to a woman.

Except I don't have any girlfriends. I blame this on being raised by my dad and growing up over a bar. But that's an excuse. A handy place to lay the blame, a justification I've used for years, but it rings hollow. I employ two bartenders and two barbacks—Stacey, Carrie, Amy, and Tiffany. All wonderful women.

Four nights a week I work side by side with them, listen to their boyfriend troubles, dreams of owning a home, trouble with their classes, problems house-training their dogs. What they know about me would fit nicely on a profession-al résumé. I admit I have, as Hawk pointed out once, and only once, "Mother Issues." Well, screw him and screw mother issues. These two yahoos are what I've got. At least they're not going to want to go to the mall after dinner.

"Hawk's not coming," I say, and if my voice skips a groove when I say the bastard's name, I can't seem to help that. "So, anything new going on with either of you?"

They remind me of school boys, caught by the ear, neither knowing which sin to confess. In spite of my mood, I grin watching the wrinkled brows and shifting eyes. That expression, "see the wheels turning" was invented just for these two.

Finally, Lefty confides, "I'm dog sitting for Caroline's puppy."

"Car-o-line?" Bubba and I ask together.

"Waitress at Marie Callender's. Cute," Lefty insists and, as though I don't know what he's doing, he cups his hands in the air twelve inches from his chest as if he's hefting muskmelons, grins at Bubba.

Honest to God, I have to find me some women friends.

Letticia's shy granddaughter, Ruthie, sets our soup in front of us and hightails it back to the kitchen. Tomato-tinged steam from parmesan-flecked minestrone rises into our faces. My blood pressure drops twenty points be-fore I've taken my first slurp.

"You ain't exactly been yo'self lately, Sam," Bubba offers tentatively when Letticia removes our empty soup bowls and sets heavy white plates of homemade raviolis on the stained Formica table.

Letticia lays her warm hand on my shoulder, "You're tense as a pussy cat at a dogfight, Sam." Every table is full tonight, but she takes the time to give me a nice motherly massage.

"You coming to the dart tournament tomorrow night?" I ask this woman who has known me since before my mom left. There were a few years, when I was eight or nine, I pushed hard for my dad and her to get together. Letticia's hands take the tension from my shoulders, bring me right back to those times when I fell asleep dreaming of her as my new mother.

She pats my back a final time and hurries back to the kitchen, calls over her shoulder, "Sad to say, Dart Night is the highlight of my week. I'll be there."

Comforted by Letticia's ministrations and the carbohydrate-rich food in front of me, I relax a little more. "I'm sorry guys. Not your fault. I'm just a mess here lately."

For a while the only sounds from our table are the occasional moans of pleasure as we dip French bread in red sauce, or trade forks of twined spaghetti with dripping carbonara, or savor eggplant parmesan.

We're spooning up the last of our spumoni before I break the silence. "Fuck it, dudes. Let's go shooting. My treat."

I wave to Letticia through the kitchen cubbyhole and we head to the backdoor which leads from Marcelli's restaurant directly into Marcelli's gun range. Our meal will go on an informal tab which, at year's end, will be just about equal to the VD tab for Letticia and her three daughters. It's an easy system with the added benefit of cheating the tax man. What could provide a warmer, more fuzzy feeling than that?

My snub-nosed Colt .38 Special is a familiar comfort against my pelvis in its custom-fitted belly pack. Bubba's first-generation Glock 17 rests under his left arm. Lefty's Smith and Wesson .38 service revolver lies in a lockbox in my bedroom where it's been since last June when he got his unfortunate DUI and lost his concealed carry permit.

Eureka may be rural, but, like it or not, we do live in the State of California. There's only so much local law enforcement can do to protect our rights against the encroachment of state-mandated, Los Angeles based sympathies. So our local district attorney doesn't prosecute for the cultivation of marijuana, allows good ole boys like Bubba and ten thousand of his buddies to raise enough cash crop to keep their heads above water. Those of us who've lived in Humboldt County for upwards of six generations, we mostly know the folks who can grandfather in our old concealed carry permits or slip in a new one here and there to the next generation of rednecks. But a DUI is a deal breaker these days and Lefty's not likely to be packing that service revolver of his anytime soon.

By the time the guys and I have burned up a month's ration of reloads, I'm feeling a little better, though I pull low all night. The silhouette targets sliding toward me, I aim for the heart and hit the crotch every damn time.

three

THE BAR IS dark when I let myself in the side door just after midnight. Before I can flip on the light, the smoke from Dad's Marlboro tells me he's sitting in the dark, waiting.

"Against the law to smoke in a bar anywhere in the State of California." I take my hand from the light switch, wait for my eyes to adjust.

"Ah yeah, I've heard tell."

"Like old times. You waiting up for me."

Using the red glow of his cigarette tip as my guide, I weave around the tables to join him directly below the head of the she-bear he shot up near Peckwan.

"How you doing lately, Samantha Jean?"

His hand is rough when he lays it over mine, rubs his thumb along my knuckles. I'd lie to him if I could get away with it. Justify it by telling myself he's getting too old for me to burden with my problems. My eyes still not completely adjusted, I breath in his Bay Rum, fight the urge to scoot my chair over and put my head on his chest, let myself pretend he can make everything all right again.

When I don't answer he puts out his smoke, reaches across the little space between us, and takes my face in his calloused hands.

"You been kicking against the traces here lately, seems like." His thumbs stroke my wet cheeks. "Wanna tell your ole dad what the problem is?"

"Don't know," I manage before he takes a soft hanky from his pocket and hands it to me. "I…I just feel like maybe there's something more out there, you know? Something I haven't seen and touched and done about a million times already. And then. Hawk. I keep thinking about that picture you and David kept behind the bar. Remember? Hawk and me, him all dark hair and eyes and skin, and me like an albino rat, both of us tucked into that old milk crate. Snuggled together under a blue and white baby quilt.

"I mean. Sometimes he feels like the safest place on earth to me and other times it's like, what the hell, Dad, just because he's all I know, that doesn't mean he's the best I can do. I don't know whether to pull him in or push him away and run like hell. And then… tonight…."

Dad scootches his chair over, gently pulls my head against the familiar smoky scent of his shoulder. He strokes my hair off my face, kisses my forehead.

"You want life to surprise you some. Nothing wrong with that, Sam. Hawk's a good man." His chuckle rumbles against my ear. "Honey. You and Hawk been in love since he stole that first kiss under the monkey bars at Sequoia Park. The boy's had his troubles with alcohol. You've gotta be a little patient."

I nod my head against his chest, blow my nose into his hankie.

"Now, Sammy, as for tonight, well, I got no excuses for Hawk. Except to remind you that sometimes we men can't seem to help mucking things up."

His hand strokes my arm. The world seems, in this moment, like a sensible place.

"I've been around the world a bit, Sam. I happen to know for a natural fact that Humboldt County is the most beautiful place in this whole big world of beautiful places. But you, honey, you've got no basis for comparison."

"Hell, Dad, I got my business degree ten miles from here at Humboldt State. Do you know I've never been south of The City or north of Portland?"

"Well, you oughta do that. Take a trip. Get out of town for a while."

"I wouldn't even know where to go. Besides I can't leave VD's."

His voice is harsh as he lights and draws on another cigarette. "Won't be much longer, you aren't going to have me as your excuse for staying around."

A sharp intake of a breath that seems to catch in my throat snaps my head up off his chest. His face is just visible in the dark, a wreath of smoke swirling upward from his mouth as he reaches across, uses his index finger to lift my chin.

"I'm going to have me one last hunt. Me and David. We're going in around Redwood Creek. Been a good many sightings there over the last few months."

Last year's trip ended when Dad slid down an embankment and fractured his hip. David and the other old timers on the hunt rigged up a travois and drug him out behind his horse, a means of transport with which the doctor in Weaverville was none too impressed.

"What do you mean, I won't have to worry about you much longer? Is there something you're not telling me?"

Outside, the Doppler sound of a siren screams into the night air. Smoke from Dad's cigarette floats spirit-like out the open window at his elbow. I lay my head back on his chest. His heart beats under my cheek, instilling a premonition of how thin the veil between this life and the next.

The siren's wail has disappeared into the night when I pull my head up, look into his gold-flecked brown eyes. "Dad? I don't want you out there in the wilderness again. Remember last time?"

He shakes his head. "Too bad. It's my life. I'm going." As if that settles the issue, he pulls away from me. "Now. What about you? What are you going to do with your life?"

A shifting wind raises the window curtain, carries the smell of the bay at low tide infused with a promise of rain.

I shake my head. "I don't know. Yet."

"Well, when you find out, you go right on out and do it. Not anybody's going to stop you." He gets up, heads for his little room behind the bar. "Right now, I'm going to bed. See you in the morning, Samantha."

I sit for a while in the thick darkness, stare into the glowing white of the plaster foot relics, wish I'd told him I love him.

The wind is battering the west-facing windows when I lock up and climb the steep stairs to my loft. Rain beats a familiar song on the metal roof above my head while I change into my sweats and pull the old cigar box from the top shelf of the closet. Sitting cross-legged in the middle of the bed, I smile, for about the thousandth time, at Dad's extravagance in putting oversized windows on all three outside walls of this tiny room. As on so many other nights, the rain builds me a sanctuary of silvery light as it finds its way down the grooves of the roof and free-falls into the rich black dirt below.

Inside the cigar box, under a childhood collection of osprey feathers, ocean smoothed jade, and the pure white skull of a badger that was Hawk's first gift to me, I find what I'm looking for.

She's laughing in the picture. Her hair as golden as the pure light on the first day of summer. The Chinese dragon robe flows around her—a glory in iridescent purple and enamel red against an onyx background streaked with threads of gold. She's caught in that moment when, her circle complete, she arrives back where she began her dance—smiling into the face of a laughing man holding a yellow-haired baby girl against his chest.

I run my finger over my mother's face, attempt to conjure her scent, the feel of her breast against my searching mouth. Stare at the fuzzy image of the little girl baby in the picture. Try to accept that this creased photograph in my hand represents the last time my mother and I lived in the same house, breathed the same molecules of air down into our lungs. My eyes squint to bring the picture into better focus.

What might that baby have done to drive this woman out of her life? The woman's shining hair is frozen forever at the apex of its rise from her neck as she twirls across the yellow linoleum. That very next morning, while I slept against Dad's chest, she slipped out and disappeared forever into a cold fog.

Cocooned in my shimmering liquid veil, I don't hear Hawk come through the bar and into his room on the ground floor until the squeals of what can only be his tight-jeaned playmate penetrate the pounding rain. I bury the photo under its childish blanket of days long spent, stomp to the closet, and return the box to its rightful place at the back of the shelf, buried behind more useful, everyday items.

There is no reason for me to care one way or the other what Hawk is doing to cause the crescendo of squeals, thumps, and downright trampy screams that float up through the ceiling in his room into my own private bedroom. We don't own each other. He's made that clear. It's not like I couldn't date other people if I wanted to. I could. I damn well might.

I step back out of the closet and stumble over my bowling ball and bag. A rage-infused idea springs full-blown into my head. The fourteen-pound ball makes a satisfying thunk when it falls from waist height to the section of my floor just above the headboard of Hawk's bed. The rapture below stops abruptly. I drop the bag a time or two more. The impact vibrates across the wood floor and into the soles of my bare feet. Feels really good. Satisfying almost.

In bed, with the rose-appliquéd quilt Letticia sewed for me when I was seven pulled up over my head, the first slap of thunder rattles the windows and instigates in me a crying jag that, eventually, lulls me into an exhausted sleep.

four

DAWN IS A smudge of silver across a swirl of pewter and lavender. Another rainy morning in Eureka. Downstairs, I turn on the heat, start the coffee, refuse to look at the door to Hawk's room. Straddle-legged over the floor vent, heated air from the furnace blows up, makes a lovely tent of warmth between my ratty chenille robe and sweats.

A familiar knock at the front door means Bubba and Lefty want their morning coffee.

"Almost ready," I tell them when I open the door.

A swirl of cold air thick with the smell of rain-soaked streets follows them inside. Halfway to the bar, I get a good look at Lefty.

"What the hell happened to you?"

His left hand is wrapped with a ragged, pink-tinged undershirt. The right side of his face looks like a misshapen eggplant, and, when he walks past me, I see that the back of his head is missing a tuft or two of hair.

"That bruise on his face is a good likeness to the Mother of Jesus, ain't it?" Bubba grins at me.

We're sipping caffeine before I get the story.

"That dog?" Lefty rubs his cheek gingerly. "The waitress's pup I got for the weekend? Didn't know what to do with him when I went out last night."

Bubba bobs his head, doing his best to hurry Lefty along in his telling of the story. I'm staring at Lefty's battered face and mangled hand, trying to decipher how a puppy could have done this much damage.

"So anyways, Caroline, she told me the dog... it's not good to leave him around windows. He gets excited is what she said. Raises hell trying to get at anybody might be walking past. So, see, my apartment, it's got those windows along the front. So I couldn't leave him in the living room and I didn't want him in my bedroom. So I figure, I'll tie him to the 'frigerator."

"You tied a puppy to the door of your refrigerator?"

"Well, see, here's the thing. She said *puppy*... but this dog, it's some kinda big mutha."

"Sonofabitch is a mastiff!" Bubba enlightens me. "I seen the bastard this mornin' when I picked up our boy here."

"You tied a dog as big as a pony to the door of your refrigerator?" The last cold sip of coffee empties my cup.

"I ain't never had a dog before. What the... what do I know about taking care of an animal? It worked fine though, the tying him to the major appliance. Till I got home. Then Rufus was so happy to see me, he just took off at a run, his big ole tail just a going."

Bubba's laugh bounces off the rain-streaked windows. He moves behind the bar to pour a refill for me, more eye-opening cups of caffeine for him and Lefty.

"I'm telling you, Sam." Lefty bounces on the hard wood of his chair, eyes bright. He's into the heart of the story now. Won't be any stopping him. "It looked like one a them movies where everything falls in slow motion. That dog was running. I was watching the slack come up off of that lead and I was racing to stop what I could see was gonna happen. My legs felt like they were about frozen to the spot. Rufus just kept coming."

Bubba puts the steaming mugs on the table.

Early morning sounds emanate from Hawk's room.

"Okay. So. Just as I get to the dog, the fridge starts to tip forward. I'm tangled in the lead and Rufus is jumping on me, you know, like a dog'll do? Okay. So. I get to the 'frigerator just as it tips past the point a no return. The door flies open and the muthaf... the thing falls on me."

"Little guy is pinned to the floor under his own refrigerator."

Bubba snorts coffee up his nose. I beat him on the back just for the fun of it.

"Okay. So. The door a the 'frigerator has swung open so's I'm actually smashed inside the thing with the weight a the mutha on top me, you know? The dog is scarfing the remains a the turkey my mom sent home with me Saturday night. I got, like, grape jelly and eggs and what's left of a broken jar of mayonnaise all the fu… all over me. 'Frigerator weighs a ton. No way in hell I can get the sumbitch off me."

I'm laughing at Lefty but my ear is cocked to the bedroom door.

"How'd you get out?"

"Was my lucky night…."

"His lucky night!" Bubba repeats, in danger of seriously injuring himself in his fist-pounding, knee-slapping glee over his buddy's misfortune.

"My upstairs neighbor heard the commotion and him and another guy was able to lift the fridge off me."

"How'd you hurt your hand?" My finger traces the top of his cotton-wrapped knuckles.

"Oh. That was after. Learned it's not a terrific idea to try and take a turkey carcass away from a two hundred pound dog."

My coffee needs more milk.

Pouring from the carton at the bar I ask, "When's Car-o-line getting back? Picking up her dog?"

"Tonight… and she better be real damn grateful, too!"

"Yeah Bro, y'all are in tiptop shape for a little a the funky stuff." Bubba simply cannot contain his joy.

I line up nine shot glasses. Three and three and three. A full clip.

"Where's the dog now?"

"Sleeping on my bed."

Speaking of dogs in beds, the door to Hawk's room opens and Little Miss Fuck-Me-Harder steps out into my bar. All the air leaves the room. Drawn, I'm pretty sure, into the open mouths of Lefty and Bubba.

"Oh. Hi." Her eyes sweep over the men, settle on me." I… I'm just… are you Samantha?"

I cannot believe this clueless bitch is talking to me.

I smile sweetly. "Ah, yeah. That's me."

Her professor is still, no doubt, cowering in his room.

"Hawk said that was you last night. That noise coming from your room? It just about scared me to death!"

"Nothing to worry about." My smile is making my jaws ache. "Just a shotgun. Found another rat." I sip my coffee. Keep smiling into her wide-eyed face. "Was just birdshot. It doesn't usually go clean through walls." I force a tiny laugh. "Or in this case I guess that'd be floors, huh?"

Finally making his appearance, Hawk, red-eyed and puffy, takes his screamer by the arm and leads her out the front door.

Scratching his belly under his old flannel robe, Dad comes out of his room and enters the fray.

"Can't an old man get any sleep around here?" He pours himself a cup of coffee.

Lefty and Bubba look near frozen in place, though Bubba has a set to his jaw I've not seen before. All humor gone from his face, he stares at the front door. The bar smells of fresh coffee, an old man before his morning shower, and rage. A goodly portion of blood-red rage with little sparkles of electric blue igniting along the edges.

Cold, wet air blows into the room along with the Indian I'd most like to scalp right now. He stands with his back to the front door, a sickly smile on his handsome face.

His voice is low, almost normal. "Any coffee left in the pot?"

The first shot hits just left of his ear, explodes against the wall at his back.

"Jesus, Sam!" He brings his arms up to cover his head when my next shot slams into a table to his right.

I don't connect until he's already turned and headed into his room.

"Goddamnit, Samantha Jean. That hurts!" He rubs his lower back, in full retreat, almost safe back in his little love nest.

The next six shots bounce harmlessly off his closed bedroom door. Five of the tiny glasses don't even break.

Dad sets my refilled cup in front of me, kisses my cheek, "Morning, Sammy. Lucky thing for Hawk. You always did throw like a girl."

five

THE MIRROR ON the medicine cabinet is fogged with steam. I'm drying roughly under my breasts when the clank and ping of pipes tells me that Hawk, directly below where I'm standing, is stepping into his own shower. My hands pause, linger for a heartbeat while my memory supplies the image of a hard flat chest, the deep clefts of a well-muscled ass, long smooth legs.

The door slams harder than I intend when I flee the warm steam of the bathroom. A turn of a knob and KRED FM, Big Red Country 92. 3, pours Keith Urban's aching voice into my cold bedroom. A dense gray dance of light is the only view from the windows, the fog obscuring bay, pier, sidewalks, and wet streets.

I suck in my stomach, wiggle into my tightest jeans. No rhinestones on the ass, but they're soft and worn in all the right places. On tiptoe, I twist around to check out my butt in the chipped mirror over the dresser. Slap my flat hands against the strained denim.

Kiss this, Hawk Morrelli!

Bypassing my usual boxy men's Fruit of the Looms, toward the back of the closet, I find the girlie T-shirt Letticia gave me for my birthday. Sky blue and deeply V'd, it's ready-made hourglass shape is a siren call this morning.

I pull it over my head, tug at the sides. Whoa. Three inches of white belly is exposed above my waistband and, from here, looking directly down, about two yards of freckled cleavage. I feel like the figurehead of a ship. Plus, my sports bra isn't going to work with this thing. I'm going to have to drag out the Wunder Bra I bought the one and only time I went mall-shopping with Stacey.

Screw this.

I return the girlie shirt to the back of the closet and pull on my forest green sweatshirt. Then I hang my head upside down and blow-dry my hair until it's a sleek curtain. Maybe I don't have my mom's golden mane, but my hair color's not bad. Tawny maybe. Pretty much anything sounds better than dishwater blonde. I toss my head, force myself to smile at the young woman in the mirror. The almost pretty one who most certainly does not look like she cried through her morning shower, and then suffered some kind of desire attack for the cheating bastard in the room below her.

Downstairs, Bubba has swept up the mess I made with the shot glasses. He holds the broom with the red dustpan clipped to the handle, on his way to return it to the closet. Dad and David, both with black-framed bifocals perched daintily mid-nose, pore over topography maps at the bar. Lefty nurses a cold cup of coffee and flips through an old copy of *High Times*.

"I gotta run to Winco and get the hotdogs and chili for tonight," I tell the men.

"Dart Night." Lefty smiles. "Damn girl. You look… good."

"Wanna go fishin' when you get on back?" Bubba drawls, "There's 'posed to be an early run a silvers at the mouth of the Mad."

I hug Bubba's neck, curtsy to Lefty.

"Thank you both. For cleaning up after me, and for noticing I actually brushed my hair this morning. I can't go, but ask Hawk if you can borrow his Whaler."

Bubba's eyes harden and he shakes his head at me.

"Better with a boat," I tell him. "The Whaler'll cross the bar no problem."

"I'd sooner drown in my waders."

I grin. "Today? Me too."

Maybe I don't need girlfriends. These two aren't so awful bad to have around.

A knock at the front door surprises us all. We don't open for business until noon and deliverymen all know to hit the buzzer in back. Bubba pulls back the curtain, peeks out the front window into the gray morning. He sucks in his gut, straightens his shoulders.

Who can this be?

Bubba opens the door Wet air follows Mark Neilsen into the morning-cold bar. The writer wears pressed chinos and a chamois shirt the same mossy green shade as his eyes. His arms are filled with delicate, pastel flowers. Pale pink and soft yellow lilies mixed with creamy sprays of baby's breath.

"Good morning," he greets the men first.

His faces changes, I want to say transforms, when he turns to me—eyes soften, mouth parts slightly.

"I brought these for you, Samantha." The fragile blooms shimmer with each step he takes toward me.

I know my blush is making my face a blotchy mess and this knowledge only makes me redden more.

No one has ever brought me flowers.

Mark Neilsen has moved so close I could reach out and touch him. My arms seem to rise up of their own volition to accept his offering, my hand touching his as we make the transfer.

"Um… thanks."

What am I, fifteen? Get a grip. He's not my type. He is definitely not my type. But, my God, he does have the most gorgeous smile, and that butterscotch-flavored, er, colored hair. Lord, it's all I can do not to reach up and touch it with my fingertips. I stand like a dunce, smash the lilies to my breast, wonder why I never realized how much I've always wanted someone to bring me flowers.

Hawk's bedroom door swings open.

His eyes sweep the little scene. Soft mouth tightens, bloodshot eyes turn hard. I know just what he's feeling. Like someone has kicked him in the gut. Like a hard jealous knot has settled into his chest cutting off his breath. Well, maybe that's not what he's feeling. But it sure as hell is how I felt last night listening to him with that little tramp he brought home.

I lay my hand on the soft chamois-covered forearm across from me.

"Thank you so much for the flowers," I coo like a little bouncy girl in one of those romantic comedies I watch sometimes late at night, alone in my childhood bedroom. "Aren't you sweet."

I can't help cutting my eyes over to Hawk as I slip my arm through Mark's.

"No one has ever brought me flowers before. They're beautiful."

Now that I've started, I can't seem to stop channeling Reese Witherspoon, Cameron Diaz, Kate Hudson.

"Can I get you a cup of coffee while I put these in water?"

My voice is two octaves higher than it ought to be. Jesus Christ. I'm chirping. When I turn around, Hawk is gone. Bubba and Lefty stare at me open-mouthed. Dad and David have left off studying their maps.

"I thought we set up an interview for this evening," David says gruffly. His glare could peel paint.

"We did, sir. We certainly did. I... ah... I came by this morning hoping to persuade Samantha to join me for a ride in the country." He turns back to me. "I thought perhaps we could meander our way to Willow Creek. Have lunch along the way."

Part of me wants to fly out of here, join this sophisticated man in a day of new possibilities. But I am rooted to my spot behind the bar. I have errands to run. Preparations to make for the dart tournament. Besides, once this man gets to know me, he'll see that the two of us are an impossible match.

Look at me! Faded jeans and a sweatshirt and I'm fooling myself into believing I'm hot stuff. Within minutes Mark is going to see that the two of us have nothing in common and be delighted to escape back to his own wider, infinitely more sophisticated, world.

"There ain't no place to have lunch 'tween here and Willow Creek." Bubba jumps into my private conversation.

"'Sides," Lefty adds his two cents' worth, "tonight's Dart Night."

"You do need to get set up for the tournament tonight," David bosses me.

My heart beats out a cadence of anger and stubbornness. This rhythm is accompanied by a little flute somewhere in the back of my head, running a riff suggesting the promise of freedom, change, a new goddamn day.

"Give me just a minute." My voice breaks. "Let me see what I can arrange."

I walk into the backroom, hit number four on my speed dial, and the cell phone chirps its annoying ring against my ear.

A croaky "hello" tells me I woke her up.

"Hey, Stacey, it's Sam. Sorry to call so early, but, can I get you to come in and do the prep for tonight's tournament?"

"Sure. I guess." Her dainty yawn fills my ear. "What's up?"

"I'm going on a drive," I whisper, "with a guy from The City."

"What guy?" I picture her sitting up in bed, rubbing her eyes, playing catch-up.

"Mark Neilsen. He's writing a book about Bigfoot. He was here last night. To interview Dad and David. But then he showed up this morning. He brought me flowers! Lilies!"

If I came equipped with a tachometer, the needle would be deep into the red zone, but I can't seem to settle myself down, ease off on the emotional accelerator.

"He's got the most gorgeous green eyes," I babble.

"Where the hell is Hawk?" Stacey asks. She sounds pretty much fully awake now.

"Just…. Can you come in early and do this one damn thing for me?"

"Yeah. Okay. Don't get your panties in a knot. So, I need to hit Winco for the dogs and the rest of it?"

"Ah, yeah. Chili and buns. The usual deal. You're in charge. I'm going on a pleasant ride in the country with a man who smells like lemons."

I flip the phone shut, stomp back into the bar where Dad shows off his plans for turning David's old Challenge Dairy delivery truck into a combination horse trailer and Bigfoot cage. Lefty peers over Dad's shoulder. In this light, that purplish bruise on his face really does look a little like The Virgin Mary.

"How you gonna get them horses to load if you got one a them Bigfoots in the truck?"

"Once we capture a Bigfoot, son, that will not be a concern. We'll stake the horses and hightail it to a phone and alert the presses."

Crowding The Flower Bearer up against the paper strewn table, Bubba asks Dad, "Why not just shoot the mutha?"

"Ah, yeah, we could. But I am opposed to the idea. Plenty of people believe this is the correct course of action. It's a fact that the scientific community would forgive the killing of such a rare creature. Once. Many of my colleagues feel that the first man to shoot a Bigfoot will be rich, the second person to do so will be spending a good long time in jail."

Mark Neilsen smiles at me, winks one mossy green eye.

To Dad he says, "So it is your intention to capture—not kill—this elusive monster?"

That wink puts a hiccup in my resolve. Was it a friendly greeting, his way to say, "I see you over there. Soon now, we'll fly down the road, just you and me. Spend the day getting to know one another."? Or was that a conspirator's wink, this stranger's way of attempting to draw me into ridicule of my own father?

"I would never harm a Bigfoot." Dad's voice is solemn. "Even our plan to capture one requires that the honest creature be returned to his home in the wilderness once proof of his existence has been established. My hope is that, in the long run, this will benefit the species by helping to preserve their special niche in our world."

Mark Neilsen glances at the glass eyes staring at us from the walls, offers his hand to Dad.

"It's nice to meet a man of honor, sir. I'm looking forward to talking more with you and Mr. Morrelli."

Another blinding smile and wink directed at me.

"Are you ready to be my tour guide?"

I run upstairs for my fully-equipped belly pack and a hoodie, wave goodbye to a room of scowling men.

Cold wet air slaps us as we step outside. Mark steps into the street and opens the passenger door of a black Infiniti coupe that seems to glow from an inner light. Money, perhaps, a power source all its own. I slide onto leather the color of that decadent real whipped cream Starbucks squirts on a venti caramel cappuccino. This is about as close to Cinderella's carriage as I'm ever likely to get.

At the push of a button the engine comes alive, sends a lovely vibration up through the seat. We pull away from the curb and I have one tiny moment of panic when I want, more than anything on earth, to be astride a powder blue Indian Chief feeling the wet air chap my cheeks, pressing myself along the length of Hawk's hard body.

six

IN THE THIRTY miles between Eureka and Blue Lake, Mark drives through mist, pouring rain, and then a pearly gray fog that absorbs the Infiniti's headlights and limits our visibility to under ten feet.

At the peak of Lord Ellis, like magic, we break through the coastal fog, enter a land of cerulean sky above mountains of fir, each dark green branch tipped with this year's paler new growth.

"It's like driving into a different world." Mark smiles.

"I always feel like Dorothy landing in the colorized world of Oz."

Even his laugh is civilized—a soft chuckle that makes his eyes crinkle at the corners.

"Dad said you sold municipal bonds for like, what? Eight years? And now you're writing this book?"

His hair is a zillion shades of blond in the sun. Honey. Amber. Butterscotch....

"In Sacramento, yes. Bonds were a decent living. But, when my dad died, I inherited enough money to fool myself into thinking I could take the risk. Be a writer."

Gold flecked. Sun-kissed. Platinum....

"So how long have you been writing?"

A rust-pocked Dodge Ram Diesel is riding our tail. In the rearview mirror I catch a rainbow flash of sun off one of the barrels cradled in the gun rack. Mark pulls over at a wide shoulder and the full throated roar of the truck passes us by.

Maybe he'll let me drive home.

"Not really used to these mountain roads." He shrugs. "To answer your question, I've been writing for years. I don't tell this to many people, but I have a four hundred fifty page detective novel in my closet lying in its little boot-box coffin topped with a dozen or so rejection notices."

"That's a little sad."

The words are out of my mouth with no internal preview what-so-freaking-ever.

"That's a lot sad." His chuckle seems a little forced.

A blush heats my face. Again. Now he thinks I'm some kind of wiseass. With a peculiar skin condition. I have no clue how to talk to this guy. He is so far out of my league every swing feels like a miss.

"No, I meant... I just meant, it must be difficult. That's all."

There's that flash of white again.

"I know what you meant."

God, this is impossible. With Hawk, we finish each other's sentences. Or don't need to talk at all. Last month we drove to Fern Canyon, walked eight miles through the redwoods to Prairie Grove, had lunch and hiked back. We never said a word to each other the whole day. Never felt the need for words.

"So... you wrote a detective story and now you're writing a nonfiction book about Bigfoot? No journalism background? That's... um... different, isn't it?"

In the mirror I check out the current vehicle held up behind us. The shrunken driver looks to be approximately the same age as George Burns. He can barely see over the dash of the forty-foot motor home. Bet he's sitting on a couple of pillows back there. His hands are at the two and ten position, his mouth going a mile a minute. Which is a lot faster than the Infiniti is moving.

Oh good. Here's another wide spot to pull over.

"Well, yes. Going from fiction to nonfiction is a little different, but writing is writing."

"So why a book about Bigfoot? Must be lots of other things to write about out there."

"A publisher friend of my mother's actually suggested the idea. So, how far are we from Willow Creek?"

"About fifteen miles."

So, like, an hour.

Forty-five minutes later Mark pulls into the parking lot of the Flame restaurant in Willow Creek. We walk across the gravel to Jim McClarin's chainsaw-carved Bigfoot where we wait for a family of Japanese tourists to pose themselves around the statue. The top of the dad's head is just below the hairy looking knees.

The whole thing, the crude artwork in front of what's basically an old fashioned diner—it's so touristy tacky. I mean, people need to make a living. I get that. But, I know McClarin carved this image as a tribute to what he believes is a living, breathing entity. Some blend of human and animal, or maybe man's simpler, more spiritual brother.

So what's the statue doing here, so close to the highway Bigfoot could be thumbing a ride? All it needs is a waving arm to be the Pacific Northwest's answer to those little bobble-armed cat thingees the Japanese use to bring luck, draw customers into their restaurants and shops.

Mark circles the Bigfoot. Snaps pictures, the camera making a whirring sound that irritates the crap out of me.

"Stand over here at the base, Sam. Maybe, can you look like you're scared?"

"Nope. I can do pissed off really well though."

I walk around back. Patchy weeds edge a gravel picnic area. Little bursts of dandelions show dark green and fluffy yellow among the litter. A Mexican busboy sprawls across the top of a redwood table. Smoke from his cigarette layers his face like cloud cover. From here I can see the turn-off to Highway 199, official entrance to Bigfoot Country.

Mark's oxfords crunch in the gravel behind me. "How much farther is Bluff Creek from here?"

In driving hours or miles?

"We aren't going to get to Bluff Creek today."

Right now I just want to go home. Back to my little gray world where I know what everyone's going to say before they open their mouth. Where I don't have to pretend to be nice when I'm feeling bitchy. What was I thinking running off for the day with this outsider?

"Really? Why is that?" he asks. "I thought Bluff Creek was right around here."

Before I can answer, he takes a wind-mussed lock of my hair, slips it behind my ear and tells me, "You have beautiful hair. With the sun on it, it reminds me of fields of sunflowers in the French countryside."

If I have to blush, why can't it be a gentle pink-tinged tint instead of the impetigo red blotches I know are staining my face?

Did he ask me a question?

"What... um... what now?"

"I'm sorry. That sounded a lot less sappy in my head. I've been trying all day to define the color of your hair. Writer's curse, I suppose."

Curse of the horny is more like it. I should know. Still, French sunflowers. That's nice. Heat floods my chest, rushes upward to turn my face into a beet.

"I cannot remember the last time I saw a woman blush. It's lovely."

I walk away from him, head back to the parking lot where I pretend to study the statue. The Japanese family has gone inside. Probably ordering Sasquatch Sandwiches, Bigfoot Burgers.

Mark follows me back to the car.

"Samantha? I didn't mean to embarrass you. You're different from the women I'm used to. It's a nice change. That's all I meant."

"Bluff Creek," my voice breaks. "Fifty miles on a narrow two-lane paved road. Thirty miles on a gravel road on which you're not going to be able to take your sports car. Another twenty miles on a road that, at this time of the year, is either a deteriorated dirt one-lane or a stream bed, depending on how much rain they've had up here. Then, if you're looking for the spot where Patterson shot the film, it's another couple hours on the back of a horse."

He pushes the button on his remote to unlock his shiny little car, comes around to my side. I ignore him, open the door myself, and slide onto sun-warmed leather.

"I do something wrong?" he asks, settling himself into the driver's seat.

The busboy heaves himself up from the table, turns his head from side to side to work the kinks out of his neck before he goes back inside to finish his shift.

"I… it's just that… look. You and I have zero in common. And why are you so interested in some tacky tourist statue? What the hell kind of a book are you writing?"

He shifts sideways in his thirty-two adjustable positions, baby-calfskin covered seat, reaches across as though to touch my hand, changes his mind at the last moment.

"Look Samantha, I like you. I thought it would be fun to spend the day together. It's a great deal for me. I get a local tour guide who also happens to be a beautiful young woman. I was hoping you'd enjoy it too. No hidden agendas here. Just a first date. A nice day in the country with a woman I'm hoping to get to know."

I sit up straighter, cock my head at him. "This is a date?"

"Well. Yes. What did you think it was?"

I've never been on a date before. Gawd, how embarrassing is that? Hawk and I just hang out. We go places together. When we're on one of our periodic breaks, generally brought on by his falling off the wagon and making a damn fool of himself one way or another, I work and spend time with Lefty and Bubba. I don't date. Could that really be true? Twenty-eight years old and I've never been on an actual date?

I grin sheepishly at Mark. "I guess I don't get out much. Since we can't get to Bluff Creek today, you want to go out two ninety-nine a little farther to Grays Falls?"

"Is that a good place for a picnic?"

He really is nice to look at. I don't know why his enthusiasm over that stupid statue made me so mad. Give the guy a break, why don't I?

Both of us are quiet on the twelve-mile, thirty-minute drive. Mark, the leather-wrapped steering wheel clutched in his white-knuckled hands, insists on repeatedly peering down into the death drop on his side of the car, the winding Trinity River a jade green rope at its base. I amuse myself counting the number of cars backed up behind us before he turns into each and every turnout. The dashboard clock reads 11:38 when we pull into the parking lot above Grays Falls.

The Falls are rain deprived, an unimpressive tinkling instead of the mighty roar they'll be next month. The air smells of warm dirt. Tall pines look parched, the heavier oaks are dust filmed, their yellowing leaves droop in the heat. We have the picnic area to ourselves.

Mark shakes the folds from a red-and-white checkered cloth, lets it float gently over the initial-carved wood table. From a cooler he lifts little white cardboard boxes, the tops emblazoned with the Italian flag.

"You got all this at Enrico's?" I ask. "How'd you end up clear out in Cutten?"

"I asked the innkeeper to direct me to the best Italian deli in town. You are Italian, right?"

The innkeeper?

"How'd you know I'd say yes?"

The idea that he went to some trouble to try and please me makes me feel, I don't know, special. And uncomfortable. Why would he go to this much work for me?

A reddish-brown, white-striped chipmunk chatters in the oak above us, demands an invitation to our elegant picnic. The chipmunk is cute. The western jays that show up next are annoying.

"What the hell are those birds?" He waves his arms above the basket of rolls.

The jays bounce in anticipation, raining dirt and dead leaves down on us.

While I watch dumbfounded, he arranges the food around an honest-to-God vase of real flowers. Mums, I think or, maybe they could be daisies. I'm waiting for the photographers from *Town and Country* or *Martha Stewart Living*. The jays watch politely until Mark sits across from me on the picnic bench. Then the feathered thieves attack.

Mark leaps from the bench as though thrown from a catapult. He flaps his arms. Seems a bit panicky. The jays pay him no attention whatsoever. They light on the table like invited guests and begin their stiff-legged waddle across the red-and-white cotton.

"Shoo! Get! Oh my God!"

I lean across, lift a roll from its charming basket, throw it as far as I can from our table. The jays rise as one, descend on my offering and are immediately occupied squabbling among themselves.

"Eat fast," I tell him, "they'll be back."

After a quick lunch, we walk down the steep path to the river. I stop to watch an osprey float the air currents. Just ahead of me, Mark leaves the rocky riverbank and walks directly through a flaming red patch of poison oak before he disappears into the woods. Huh. Poison oak! I guess that rules out a kiss at the end of our first date.

I assume he wasn't impressed with the outhouse in the picnic area and is looking for a tree to christen. He reappears at a run, breaks through the manzanita and poison oak at the edge of the woods and stumbles over river rocks. He's fifty feet from me when I spot the problem. Close behind him, moving faster than something with legs that short should be able to travel, is the unmistakable black-and-white blur of a skunk.

The critter has got to be rabid. No way a normal, healthy polecat that encounters a big, clumsy human is going to do anything but spray and run. Seems like I did read where they're having a rabies problem up here, what with the rains being late and all.

Still in full panic, a basketball-sized river rock shifts under his weight and Mark goes down on one knee. He breaks his fall as best he can and continues his frantic scramble away from his attacker. The skunk closes the distance, fast.

I pull my .38. Harder to hit a small, erratically moving target than it is to drill a large man-shaped image sliding predictably toward you at the range. I squeeze the trigger. Slivers of granite are a miniature eruption a good six inches behind the waving black-and-white tail. My shot doesn't slow the creature, but Mark is now in full-fledged panic, caught, as it must seem to him, between an attack skunk and a deranged redneck. I take a slow deep breath, remember to squeeze, not pull, the trigger.

The good news is that I hit the damn thing. The bad news is that the animal keeps going for another ten feet before it dies, putting Mark downwind and less than six feet from a whole lot of stink.

seven

VD'S SPILLS CUSTOMERS onto the covered courtyard in back. We've even got six or seven hardcore dart players huddled under the porch overhang, though two of those are John and Oscar, our resident street people.

"So, like, what's your… you know, your best drink?" The speaker is as naively green as Los Angeles grass, fed with water stolen from our northern rivers.

I study the trio at my bar. College boys slumming, celebrating a first legal drunk. Two forest-green sweatshirts with HSU in bold, baby-puke yellow. The leader sports a fluorescent orange hoodie with a pot green marijuana leaf emblazoned on the front.

"I need to see your ID."

Lord, I do not need this tonight. These boys are already skating around the edge of Lake Over-Served. They fumble in pockets for ID, cut their eyes to make sure none of the scary locals are looking at where they've secreted their stash of drinking money. The kid on the end keeps adjusting his glasses, as though afraid the plastic frames might slide down his sweat-glazed nose. I glance at the ID, already know it's legitimate. No shifting eyes or shuffling feet, no tell that screams *liar*, just the sway and borderline belligerence of too much booze poured on too little common sense. And, yep, all three hail from southern California.

"Mr. Tommy Langley, happy birthday. You boys been drinking a bit already tonight, huh?" I draw three Coca-Colas, drop a cherry in each one, slide in a super-duper special flex straw.

"That's your best drink?"

"Tonight it is. On the house." If they were regulars, I'd serve them another drink. Maybe another couple of drinks. But this is a local red-neck hangout, not a college bar. These three LA transplants, in this crowd of indigenous rednecks, are dry grass waiting for that one small spark. Half the folks here have been drinking slowly, steadily, since before seven o'clock when the first dart was thrown. Nobody's drunk, but most are real happy, and a happy redneck loves very little more than thumping on some asshole from Los Angeles.

"Are you refusing to serve us?" Fluorescent boy is puffing himself up. Already he's drawn the attention of Bubba, who eases himself out of his chair. "Because that's illegal."

In an act born of a lifetime of privilege, coupled with insecurity at being out of his element, and stirred with a swizzle stick of far too much booze, the kid leans across the bar, his face inches from mine. I take an ever so gentle grip on the front of his sweatshirt, watch his eyes register that he may have just stuck his face in a hornet's nest.

Stacey bumps my hip.

"Hey boys," she sings, "you're too late to sign up for the tournament, but we've got a brilliant pickup game going on in the courtyard."

Her head is cocked to one side... just that fraction of an inch that, coupled with her smile and her boobs, is the equivalent of a neon sign flashing S-E-X.

"Come on now." She slips out from behind the bar, a wiggling finger pointing the way to the courtyard. "Don't forget your drinks. I just love a man who's partial to cherries."

The kid with the glasses leaves a ten on the bar and I grin at yet another demonstration of why Stacey is the best-earning bartender in the county. She's as capable as I am of throwing a drunk out on his ear. But when she does it, the guy comes back the next night with a sheepish grin and a big tip.

"Sam?" Lefty's grin is cheek-splitting wide. "This here is Caroline."

His poor bruised face looks worse than ever, yellowish brown spots now pocking the bluish bruise.

"Good to meet you." I extend my hand to a woman just shy of Lefty's five-foot-five-inch height. Shiny brown hair and dark eyes that don't appear to miss much, she's wearing a long paisley skirt with lace-up boots, topped by a thigh-touching, soft yellow sweater. She's cute. Wow. No wonder Lefty took care of her horse-sized dog.

"Funny smell in here. Kinda skunky," Lefty mutters. Before I can comment, he puts on his innocent face and asks, "Hawk around?"

"No, Hawk ain't around. He never works Thursdays. Like that's news to you."

The old timers in the corner are signaling for another round. I glare at Lefty, smile at Caroline. "Hope to talk to you later. It'll slow down here in a bit."

I'm policing empties, wiping down tabletops when Bubba finds me.

"You meet Care-o-line?"

"Ah, yeah. Pretty. Seems nice."

"How was your date?" His drawl is mighty close to a growl.

I carry the tray of empties back behind the bar, pour one last shot of Jack for Allen, a regular going through a bad breakup.

Bubba parks his ass on a stool, puts his meaty arm around Allen's shoulder, says something into his ear I don't catch. Allen laughs out loud. A first for tonight. I pour him a cup of coffee, remove the empty shot glass.

"Now Sam. Just so's we're clear here. Y'all can't go fishin' with me, but you got no problem tearin' around the countryside with some city boy what carries you a bunch a scraggly-ass flowers and returns you to us smellin' like a polecat?"

Huh? He's right. One look at green-eyed Mark with his armful of lilies and I forgot all about that salmon run. Didn't even occur to me that I ditched Bubba for Mark.

"It's just a hint of skunk." I reach across the bar, rub my palm over his rough knuckles. "Lord, Bubba. I'm sorry. Did you catch anything?"

"Didn't go. Waitin' on you. Soon as you get yo'self a day off, we're goin'. No excuses. Gonna let you make it up to me. Y'all carry the vittles."

Lord, I do love this giant horse's ass.

By 11:00 the Redneck Mothers have dethroned the Gnarly Nooners and things have quieted down some. Bobby Barellis has led the Swinging Dicks, a four-man team of hotshots from the District Attorney's office, to victory over the volunteer firemen. The volunteers all wear dark blue T-shirts, the silhouette of a suited-up fireman on the front, hose in hand. Across the back, orange flames flare around their oh-so-original name— The Hosers.

Letticia, tonight's high-scoring Mother, sips her beer. I refill the bowl of popcorn before coming around the bar to sit beside her.

She rubs my back. "Don't take this the wrong way, but what the hell are you doing buzzing around the county with some slick asshole from the city?"

"How could I take that the wrong way?" I take a handful of popcorn. "Who told you?"

"Don't matter. You know better."

"Hawk started it." As soon as I hear the words out loud I know I sound like a five-year-old, but goddamn it, Hawk did start it.

"Hawk jumped off a cliff, would you go right on over the edge after his Indian ass?" She grins to let me know she's making sport of me, stands up from the stool, slips her arm around my waist. "Come on. Stacey and Carrie have got this. Walk me to my car. Lucky for you my sinuses are so screwed up, I can't smell you."

The rain has turned to drizzle. The air, cold and heavy, settles over us, transforms Letticia's silver-streaked hair into a halo of curls. The streetlights are haze-ringed moons. A buoy marking the entrance to the bay moans into the dark. She unlocks her old Corolla and we slide into the smell of old french fry grease and wet poodle.

The car cranks easily. The heater rattles and sputters cold air onto my damp jeans.

"Wanna talk about it?" she asks.

The air inside the car is slightly warmer than outside, windows fogged, the heater's rattle a fluttery moan.

"I had a good time." I insist. "We…Mark and I… he said my hair was the color of French sunflowers."

Letticia's mouth twists sideways for an instant. If I hadn't turned to look directly into her face, I'd have missed it. She pats my hand, gives one of her Italian mother sighs.

"Well, Sam. Course a woman always likes to be complimented by a good-looking man."

"He'd been to Enrico's and bought picnic stuff. Salami and prosciutto. Marinated artichoke hearts. Smoked salmon and apples and grapes. Hard rolls, of course, and these crackers, made in, I think in Switzerland, they had pumpkin seeds…. anyway we went on through Willow Creek. Ate at Grays Falls."

The car's getting warmer. My breath no longer makes a little vapor cloud at each exhale.

"All right, Sammy, so this guy makes you feel special and maybe the men in your life don't always do such a great job in that department. But honey, just because they're not good at telling you how important you are to them, that don't mean they don't love you."

"Mark brought me flowers. Lilies. Really pretty. And… and Hawk fucked this co-ed bimbo tramp. The bitch was so freaking loud I could hear every goddamn thing the two of them did. Right below me. In the bed where Hawk and I…. Stupid, freaking, fucking cheating bastard."

Jagged cries, waves of racking pain force their way up from my chest. I wipe my nose on the sleeve of my sweatshirt.

"It's not just Ha… Hawk. I'm twenty-eight years old. Is this what my life is going to be? Bigfoot asses and beer and… and no babies or… maybe I might want to see the Eiffel freaking Tower or the Taj Mahal… or just something that isn't… here."

I wail, take the wadded, grease-smelling napkin Letticia offers, and blow my nose.

Steam rises in a fog off my jeans, the car as hot as a sauna by the time I have control of myself.

"I only knew your mom a few months. But, from the first night she worked at VD's, even though she was already sh…. Well, the thing is, every man in the bar was in love with her before the end of her first shift. She had a way of smiling at a man. Tall and handsome, ugly as sin, scrawny or fireman built. Didn't matter. Your mama convinced him he was God's gift.

One smile. Course it helped that she was drop-dead beautiful. Real curvy she was. Skin like porcelain."

Letticia has been holding my hand. She drops it now, pushes my damp scraggly hair off my cheek. "You look just like her, Sam."

I shrug, move away from her hand. "I don't want to look like that bitch."

"Don't matter. You do. You got the best of both, Sammy. Your mama's looks and your dad's good sense."

Dad is currently outfitting an old dairy delivery truck as a cage for Bigfoot, so good sense is stretching it a bit, but I take her point.

"Why'd my mom leave, Letticia? If I'm so goddamn precious, why'd she walk away from me and never look back?"

"Your mom was wounded, Sam. In truth, that was part of why she appealed so strongly to so many men. They couldn't help wanting to rescue her, save her from herself. Your dad took her in, gave her a job. She stayed as long as she needed. Then she was gone. I know it don't feel like it, but her leaving had nothing to do with you. Or your dad either. Your mom was the center of her own broken world. She couldn't love anyone else. Man or precious baby."

The windows have defrosted and I can see John and Oscar huddled under the awning at the entrance to Hurricane Kate's, a wrinkled brown paper sack being passed between them. What choices led them to urban camping in this night of cold fog and numbing rain?

Letticia puts on her seatbelt, turns on the headlights, throws one last dart.

"Talk to Hawk," she orders me, "before you two idiots muck up the whole damn deal. Now get outta my car and take another tomato juice bath. My eyes are beginning to water."

The crowd has thinned when I get back to VD's. I collect eight hot dog buns and a dozen weenies, layer them on top a couple of old margarine containers filled with leftover chili. Stepping back outside, the cold hits me all over again. The rain comes down harder, the night sky starless. I'm chilled to the bone by the time I walk the block to Hurricane Kate's. Stepping around a grocery cart gate, I hand over the food.

"Heard you had a run-in with a skunk?" John's jagged grin is just visible under the blue tarp where he and Oscar are huddled.

"Ah, yeah. I believe that skunk was rabid."

"I was talkin' about the owner a that fancy Infiniti."

Oscar's drunken laugh escapes from under the tarp, echoes out into the fog.

I'm already walking away, my head down, thinking about the warmth of VD's, when John's thanks catch me. I turn around, walk backwards a step or two. The rain already flows in rivulets down my neck. I call back to them to stay dry. In this weather they'd both be sleeping at The Mission if they hadn't passed that bottle earlier. There's consequences for all our actions. Some are just harder to live with than others.

Which gets me thinking about the consequences of my own choices today.

I'd left Mark at Grays Falls long enough to drive into Willow Creek and rent him a white Civic. Sweet-talked an unemployed logger into following me back out to the Falls in the rental. My First Date and I said our goodbyes from a goodly distance with me making sure to stay upwind when I tossed him the keys to the rental car.

I made it to Eureka in under fifty minutes, left the Infiniti for Mark to pick up in the parking lot of The Humboldt House where he's staying. Explaining the smell in the Civic to the rental company must have been an interesting experience for Mark. I was courteous enough to leave a note at the front desk with his keys telling him to scrub with lye soap in the hope of diminishing the effects of the poison oak before dousing himself with vinegar or tomato juice to dilute the skunk smell.

I do not remember asking for a sign from God about whether or not I should date strange men.

eight

THE INDIAN WAKES me from a fretful sleep. The bike's growl mixes with a dream of swirling fog and screeching jays. For an instant, I'm poised between one world and the next, neither making any sense.

6:38 a.m. by the red digital readout on my alarm clock.

On my back, staring up into the dark, I listen as the front door opens, know Hawk's pushing the bike through the bar and into his room. I roll over on my side, hang my arm off the side of the bed, press my hand flat to the floor. My bedroom floor, the ceiling over Hawk's bed.

I've almost fallen back to sleep when the third step from the top gives him away. I sit up, pull my fingers through my hair, blow into my cupped hands, and wish for a mint.

He steps inside.

"You awake?"

The street light gives just enough light to see his shape.

"I'm here."

"You armed?"

"Always."

Three long strides and he sits on the edge of the bed, lays his hand on the side of my face, rolls his thumb over my mouth. I want to draw him under the covers with me, pretend the last two days never happened. Instead,

58

I push his hand away, pull my legs up and wrap my arms around them, rest my head on blanketed knees. There now. Vulnerable parts all protected.

"I messed up," he says, "We, Leah and I, we... I had a drink. One drink at dinner."

Outside, a thin layer of lavender separates the deep navy blue of the bay from the darker purple-black of the morning sky.

Two years. Nearly 800 days sober.

I wait.

"Another couple of drinks at Roy's after dinner. We swung by Stop and Go. Bought a bottle. That's when we came here."

Pull back the covers, invite him inside? Or beat the holy hell out of him?

"I messed up, Sam. She didn't mean any—"

"Don't say that! Don't you fucking say it. The tramp meant something all right. You brought her here, Hawk! Here! To rub my nose in it. I get it."

My open palm against his cheek is as loud as a shot.

"I'm nothing to you but a convenient fuck."

I kneel on the bed, pound his chest with my fists. He makes no attempt to protect himself.

"You know that's not true, Sam."

Fighting my way out from under the tangled covers, I get out of bed, put some distance between us. At the window I stare out at the wet courtyard below. The morning light refracts through thick fog, creates a hundred shades of gray.

I snatch my old yellow robe from the back of the chair, turn toward him, wrap my arms around myself, and rub my hands on the soft frayed elbows.

His head is down, broad shoulders slumped, his voice almost inaudible. "I'm sorry I hurt you, Sam. When I left here Friday morning, I called John."

"Your sponsor?"

He nods, lifts his face toward me. "We spent the last two days talking. I thought I was past this self-destructive shit."

David fought for years to get Hawk away from his alcoholic mother. Whether out of twisted love, or the need for the extra money that came to her for having a child, Martha clung to her son. She'd spend the money David brought on whiskey instead of heat or food.

How many times did David wrap up a dirty, shivering child and carry him here, to this bar, to live in the downstairs room where Hawk still sleeps? Until, when Hawk was seven, in the middle of a court battle that might have finally given David custody, Martha fell asleep drunk with a lighted cigarette burning in her hand. Hawk escaped by crawling out his bedroom window, but he couldn't get back inside through the flames to rescue his mother. For this failure, he has never been able to forgive himself.

I walk back to the bed, cup his face in my hands. He wraps his arms around my hips, buries himself in the softness of my breasts. My need to lie down beside him and offer my body as shelter from his pain is a rip current rising up from my own depths.

Outside is a swirling impressionist study in black and white. The sun illuminates the darker charcoal of cloud cover and reflects off the tarnished silver of fog that floats over the surface of the bay. In this light, the pale yellow lilies on my dresser glow. I stroke Hawk's thick hair, breathe deeply of his woodsy, spicy scent, memorize this moment.

When I push him away, his face is tear-streaked, his eyes those of a pleading child.

I look over his head, make myself focus on the dresser, whisper into the morning air, "You broke my trust."

Stepping back from the feel and smell of his skin, I meet his eyes. My decision catches me off guard, strands me on a deep shoal of hard knowledge.

"I don't want to do this anymore." The words catch in my throat like ground glass.

This is how it must feel to cut off a trapped body part in order to save your life. An arm, a foot, a soul.

I walk back to the window facing the bay, the fog lifting now, the bay liquid mercury dimpled by a salt-laden wind. The bed moans as Hawk rises, the door a final, gentle click before the sound of his boots disappear down the stairs.

I lower myself into the chair, stare out at the bay, watch the cloud-muted light dance over the water's ragged surface. There are no tears in this emptiness. No anger. Nothing.

The clouds blacken. The door to Hawk's room opens and closes, then the front door does the same. Fog returns to the surface of the bay like a memory. The Indian is kicked into life. Its departing cry pulls a vibrating moan from deep in my center. The rain is a cold shimmering curtain obscuring the world outside my window when I get up, make myself get ready for the day.

An hour later Bubba sits across the table from me, two steaming paper cups of cappuccino between us.

"Coffee house froth, my secret vice," I tell him. "How'd you know I'd need it this morning?"

"Ain't none of your vices all that secret."

I'd bet a week's profit he already knows what happened between Hawk and me this morning.

"Ah, yeah. I suppose that's right. Are we going fishing tomorrow? Assuming the weather allows?" My plan is to pretend to be normal, to make believe this pain in the middle of my belly is nothing more than a virulent strain of flu that will pass, leaving me healthy again, whole.

"Supposed to rain purt near all week."

My cappuccino is a warm, sweet decadence. Each sip makes me love Bubba more.

"Lefty's Caroline is pretty, huh? Seems nice too."

He hands me a paper napkin. The tickling foam must have left its mark on my nose. "It ain't never a good plan to date a woman what has a dawg bigger'n you."

The phone's ring startles us both. I get to it just as the answering machine kicks in, talk over the recording while I fumble with the button to shut off the recorded message.

"Victor and David's. Hello? Sorry. This damn thing. Hello?"

"Samantha?"

"Ah, yeah. Mark?" He sounds good.

"The skunk smell isn't quite gone. I thought I'd call instead of dropping by just yet."

It feels good to laugh. Really good. "You end up with poison oak?"

"Not a spot. Maybe I'm not allergic."

"Lucky you. Find your car?"

Bubba's scowl burns the back of my neck. I try not to watch him in the mirror over the bar. One of his massive legs bounces against the underside of the table. He keeps looking over at the door to Hawk's room, so maybe he doesn't know what happened this morning.

"The Infiniti was precisely where you said it would be. Thank you for driving it back. The rental car agency added a hefty charge to de-skunk the Civic, but that was still better than stinking up my car."

"Made any progress on the book?"

No sense assuming he called to speak with me personally. After the disaster of our little date, could be he just wants to set up a meeting with Dad or David.

"Ahm, well, no, not much progress. I'm interviewing your dad a little later. That's all arranged. I just called to make sure you were okay, apologize for bumbling off into the woods and stirring up that skunk."

Bubba glares this way and I give him the one minute sign. Index finger straight up, eyebrows high, a reassuring nod of my head.

He does not seem appeased.

"Yeah. Well. It wasn't your fault. I'm sorry if it scared you when I shot the thing, but it had to have been rabid. No other way a skunk would have chased you. Maybe I should have just let it be but, at the time, I was thinking skunk stink was better than that series of injections you have to get to prevent rabies."

"Rabies? Really. Well, that's something. I never thought of that. So. The reason I called, I am convinced that if I spend the day scrubbing with mechanic's dry-clean degreaser, take a few more tomato juice baths, followed by a dip in rock salt and baking soda, all that ought to make me smell good as new."

My laughter isn't polite or ladylike. "Hell, by then you should be scrubbed pink as a shoat."

Across the room, Bubba's scowl has vanished. His grin is so wide that I know my conversation has crossed some line of propriety. Perhaps comparing a city boy to a piglet isn't acceptable flirting.

"Pink as a what?"

"Never mind. Did you want dad to call you back?"

"No. I was calling to ask you to dinner. What night would be good for you?"

I'm still laughing as we agree that he'll pick me up at seven Monday night. No way I can leave the bar tonight, Saturday, and, come hell or high water, Sunday I'm spending the day with Bubba.

nine

THE EYES OF Bigfoot follow me. Mahogany brown, rimmed in red, the pupils are crescents of yellow set in deepest blue-black. Not a friendly *Harry and the Hendersons* Sasquatch or a terrifying King Kong monster, but somewhere in the middle. I keep staring into those blood-rimmed eyes.

"That's some Bigfoot, Lefty."

I run my finger over the paint, walk backward toward the cab of the retired Challenge Dairy truck, try for a change in perspective. Nope. No way to escape those eyes. For two days Dad and David have been welding chains and giant handcuffs and leg irons on the inside while, on the outside of the truck, Lefty painted over the old Proud Elk Dairy emblem with this rendition of Bigfoot.

Lefty puts the finishing touches on the background. Blue creek and green trees are dwarfed by the hairy main character. Paintbrush in hand, he turns and looks at me for the first time since Dad called me out here to see their handiwork.

"Whoa, Sam. You clean up nice."

"Thanks. How'd they talk you into this art work?"

"Paying me. In a manner a speaking."

Ah well. It's not like he was ever going to pay that bar tab anyway. He pulls on his ear lobe, grins at me.

"I figured it was good advertisement. I'll sign 'er across the big foot. Maybe drum up some business. May not be good as Flatmoe but it ain't bad." He bends at the waist, dips the brush in a recycled gallon pickle jar of paint thinner. "How come you're all dressed up?"

"I'm going to The Humboldt House with Mark."

Second date. I've been trying on clothes all day. Finally called Stacey, who vetoed everything in my closet and lent me this blue dress that exposes more chest and leg than I've shown since I grew boobs in the seventh grade. The shoes, pumps is what Stacey called them, belong to Carrie and they pinch the hell out of my toes.

"Well, you look real fine and all, but why you going out with that slick bastard?"

Dad and David, perhaps drawn by the pheromone of Lefty's protective criticism, climb out the back of the converted van just in time to put in their two cents' worth.

Over yesterday morning's coffee and La Chalet smoked salmon omelets, these two old meddlers lectured me about the qualities of a good-hearted woman until I fled the restaurant, my hands firmly over my ears. Then, I spent all day yesterday letting Bubba explain to me why I needed to cut Hawk some slack.

I'm done listening.

David eyes my outfit, lifts one eyebrow so high it's a wonder his damn face doesn't cramp up.

"You sure you want to send that kind of message to this writer?"

I'm not sure of anything. My constant hunger is to hear Hawk's voice, touch his face, breathe in the woodsy smell of his skin. At the same time, a loop keeps playing in my head of all the times his need for self-destruction has pulled me over the edge right along with him. This is no longer about "loving him in spite of his wicked ways." This is about stepping outside the lyrics and writing a new goddamn song for myself. I arch my back, toss my sunflower yellow hair.

"Don't wait up," I call back over my shoulder.

Mark isn't picking me up for forty-five minutes, which gives me plenty of time to wrinkle my dress and think up another hundred ways this date can go wrong. I've gotten only as far as disaster one-hundred-and-sixteen—I drop my food in my lap, staining Stacey's dress and, when Mark tries to help me, we crack heads, giving us both concussions and ending our second date with a trip to the emergency room. The ringing phone breaks my train of thought before I can kill us both of a rare, hospital-born virus.

Caller ID gives her away. 6:25 on an evening when Marcelli's is open for business. Crap. Dad called in the big gun.

Two deep breaths and I answer, "Hey, Letticia."

"Honey? I want to talk at you before your date. Hang on, Sam. The damn dishwasher took a powder. Again. And the first batch of gnocchi is gooey and has to be remade."

"Ah, yeah." I wait for her to get to it. Another voice in my ear explaining why I shouldn't be dressed up tonight.

Outside, a layer of stratified clouds, black-bottomed with streaks of variegated gray roll in, obscuring the flame orange globe dropping into the ocean. There will be rain. And soon.

"Samantha, your dad says you're going out with that writer. Mark, is it?"

She knows his name. Probably has his social security number, credit score, and high school GPA.

"Yeah. Mark, it is."

Fog rises up from the white-capped bay, joins the low clouds in restoring the natural order of things in Humboldt County. Cold, wind, fog, and rain. Stacey knew what she was doing when she insisted on leaving me her deep blue ankle-length coat. It's heavy, soft, and closes with what I am almost sure she called frogs.

"Look, honey," Letticia says, and then in a louder voice to someone in the background, "table five needs soup."

I sit on the edge of my bed.

"Not you, Sam. Listen. I know your dad and David are pitching a fit about you throwing Hawk out."

"I did not throw him out! Is that what they told you? 'Cause that is not what happened...."

"I'm a little busy here, Sam. Shut up and listen."

I roll my eyes, tap my foot.

"And get that look off your face!" she orders.

I can't help glancing around.

"Now. You listening, Samantha Jean?"

"Yeah." I put both feet on the floor, sit up straight. "Yes."

"All right now. I love Hawk like a son. You know that's so. But he has his own demons. Not nobody can save that boy but his own self. 'Work out your own salvation in fear and trembling.' That's what the Bible says. Just be careful with this new fellow. You're not over Hawk yet. Trying to ride two horses at the same time, gonna get you thrown. You hear me?"

Which sounds pretty much like the way Bubba and I left it yesterday after our day of driving around with our fishing gear in the backseat looking out rain-speckled windows at dripping, fog-blanketed trees.

"Don't go jumpin' from the frying pan into the fire" is how the big guy put it.

That accent of his. I had an instant mental picture of an old black, cast-iron frying pan with red flames licking the bottom. I was just filling in the image with some bubbling red-eye gravy or maybe hot cakes, when he leaned across the bench seat of the F-150 and kissed me on the cheek before fleeing the truck.

The phone is dead in my hand, Letticia having said what she wanted to say and returned to work.

A knock at the door and a second later a breathless Stacey is in the room. She's holding a robin's egg blue wool hat with a tiny sprig of happy yellow buttercups at the brim.

"Forgot about the rain," she pants. "Your hair. Not good wet."

"Did you run here?" I ask.

There is no way in hell I'm wearing that hat. I don't care if I have to sit across a fancy restaurant table from Mark Neilsen looking like a drowned rat.

"Just from the car. Hold still. This hat is perfect for you. Same color as your eyes. And the flowers, see?" She pulls a lock of my hair so it's less than six inches from my nose. I'm cross-eyed trying to focus on the cutesy little flowers. "See? The hat matches your eyes and the flowers pick up your hair color."

She scoops my hair into a knot and stuffs it under the brim, pulls chunks of yellow strands loose as if she knows what she's doing.

"Perfect. A few tendrils to frame your face. You look great."

"Stacey, I'm not wearing this...."

"Mark's here. At the bar. Talking to your dad and David. I told him I'd tell you he was waiting."

Outside, the wind shifts, slams the first of the rain sideways into the bay-facing window. God telling me to wear this ridiculous hat? Telling me something? I never have been a good listener. Time to move forward, see where I end up.

"Dad and David?" I take the stairs two at a time with Stacey right behind me hissing for me to slow down, make an entrance. As if the dress, the freaking pumps, and the cartoon hat aren't enough to guarantee an entrance nobody in the bar is likely to let me live down before my eightieth birthday.

They sit at a middle table, the one with the name Tom Mix carved at an angle into the surface. Dad swears the old cowboy was a customer of Aunt Mandy's. I have my doubts. Another of those things in my life that can be argued until Kingdom Come but nobody's ever going to prove one way or another.

Mark gets up from his chair when I stumble into the bar. Seeing him there, looking like some modern day dressed-for-success Norse god, I come to an abrupt stop. Stacey nearly plows into my back.

She drapes the coat over my shoulders, whispers in my ear, "Breathe."

His smile is almost bright enough to make me blind to the scowls of the two old men still seated at Tom Mix's table. His sports jacket is tweed. I think it's tweed. About a dozen shades of gray with little speckles of pale blue. The cloth is soft as a dove's breast when my hand touches his arm for one electric moment as he helps me on with my coat.

He says his goodbyes to the two critics and leaves to bring his car around to pick me up in front of the bar. It would be a lot warmer if I waited inside VD's, but I follow him out and stand huddled under the small overhang at the front door while he struggles to open a large, black umbrella.

"The wind is going to peel that thing about two seconds after you get it open," I tell him.

My first words on this, our second, date. Well, I may be dressed up with a girly hat on my head, but as Dad says, "You can't make a silk purse out of a sow's ear."

Mark's smile is a magnet for one of my own. The rain pours over the edge of the porch, makes a small waterfall around us. A cold waterfall. He gives up on the umbrella, loops it over his arm like Mr. Tumnus, leans in the few inches it takes to brush his lips on mine. There is a moment when I must decide whether to retreat, or to move that teensy bit forward into his kiss. My brain stays put. My body leans in.

His mouth is soft, warm, just demanding enough. The kiss a perfect first.

When we break away, he takes off his possibly-tweed jacket, pulls it over his head and runs for the car. I wait under the waterfall, the borrowed pumps already wet, and ache for another kiss, a different kind of kiss altogether, a kiss from my first love.

ten

ENTERING THE HUMBOLDT House dining room is like walking into a sauna. If a sauna smelled of garlic and expensive perfume. When they take my soggy coat I expect it to steam as it's carried away. The tables are spaced for privacy, covered in snowy white linen. The floor tile is so dark red it's almost black. The windows hide behind wood shutters and are individually framed with what must be a hundred yards of heavy yellow fabric—draped, twisted, and contorted. The material itself seems a living sinuous creature.

At our table by the window facing The Ingomar Club, Mark holds my chair while I try to sit without wrinkling the dress or letting it ride up high enough to expose my underwear.

Hawk would call this place pretentious. Dad would name it a glaring example of conspicuous consumption. David would make a remark about rich people with more money than brains.

Candles flicker a warm golden glow on linen and silver. I decide to name this evening luxurious, elegant. I might even work my way to enjoyable.

Across the table, Mark seems to be drinking me in, his eyes dropping to what the Wunder Bra is displaying and then back up to my face.

"Tonight," he says, sotto voiced, "I promise. No skunks."

My demented brain imagines a skunk, striped tail held high, mincing across the dark tiles, peeking out from under the draped tables.

"Might be interesting," I tell him.

"Indeed. But tonight is a different species of date altogether."

At the word date, the blush rushes up my chest, covers my neck, and settles on my warm cheeks. This is my reward for hanging around with guys my whole life, doing the girly stuff for the first time at an age when most of my high-school classmates already have a baby on each hip. I redden like a fifteen-year-old.

The menu is gold-trimmed leather, big enough to hide behind. I peek over the top and ask, "How'd the interview go with Dad and David?"

This is my idea of flirting. God help me.

"Not well. I mentioned that I'd talked with Bob Hieronimus."

"The guy that Greg Long claims wore the monkey suit in the Patterson film? Why would you talk to him?"

Leaning across the table, my dress rides up my thighs. I jerk it down, feel like a clown in this outfit.

"There's some pretty good evidence that Hieronimus did have some kind of ape suit and he was certainly a member of Patterson's little band."

"Patterson was making a documentary in Washington State. About Bigfoot. There may well have been an ape costume, but that has nothing to do with the footage shot down here, at Bluff Creek."

I have no idea why I'm getting all Mary Magdalene at the Tomb of the Risen Lord about this. Hell, for all I know that picture above the bar really is Hieronimus in a monkey suit, though just allowing that blasphemous thought into my head makes me feel like rushing up to St. Bernard's and secreting myself in one of their ancient latticed confession booths.

Mark's back is pressed into his chair. He's looking at me like I've sprouted another head. So much for a second, skunk-free date.

"Ah, yeah. So." I know I should just shut up, close my mouth, enjoy the evening, but I am unable to follow my best instincts, "What do you really think about Bigfoot? Is this book you're writing going to be an honest look at what hundreds of people have seen, or are you another Greg Long, just looking to make a buck?"

The long burgundy skirt of the waitress sweeps over her booted insteps. She smiles a greeting, rattles off the specials in an orgasmic murmur. It's a lot more complicated to order a meal here than it is at Marcelli's. Evidently, Mark needs to know if I'm going to be having fish or meat before he can order the wine. Since The Humboldt House has its own wine cellar, this is a decision equivalent to negotiating a Middle East peace treaty.

Fifteen minutes later, with the help of the wine steward and the chef, who makes an appearance from the kitchen, and after much sniffing and swirling, we are left to sip a white wine with a name I cannot hope to pronounce.

Mark reaches his manicured hand across the table, runs his smooth finger along the back of my wrist. "How's your wine?"

I open my mouth to tell him it's different than Boone's Farm, swallow the smart-ass words at the last second, and simply nod.

"Samantha, to get back to your concerns about the book. I am in the early stages of research. At the very least, the sightings and foot casts, the Patterson film—these represent a phenomena. As to exactly what this book is going to turn out to be? I don't know yet. I'll be interviewing and investigating the story from a variety of angles. I'm looking for a hook, Samantha. A way to tell a new truth about an old story."

His smile is genuine, goes all the way up to his sparkling green eyes. Maybe I am a little paranoid. Haven't I always maintained that, short of sticking their fingers in the bullet holes of a dead Bigfoot, all the evidence in the world isn't going to convince a non-believer?

"I hope you know by now that I am also intrigued by the Bigfoot hunter's golden-haired daughter." He lifts his wine glass in a toast. "To getting to know one another better."

As we clink sparkling glasses of pale yellow gold, I cross my legs. My right toe accidentally brushes against his thigh. Having already slipped out of the uncomfortable shoes I had the bad sense to wear, my offending toe is quite naked. I jerk my foot back under my chair, look out the window, and study the three-story gray Victorian that is the prestigious Ingomar Club, as though I've never before seen the headquarters of Humboldt County's ruling class.

Ever so nonchalantly I bring my eyes back to Mark. His grin is wide and just as testosterone filled as any redneck who's ever eyed my ass at VD's.

"Your foot was fine right where it was."

I decide to ignore the comment.

"How long do you think it's going to take you to finish the research for this book?"

"Let's not talk about the book anymore. I want to know all about you. Your dad raised you, right? And you've always lived right there at the bar, Victor and David's?"

The waitress places our salads in front of us. Artfully tossed greens, slices of pear fanned in a half-circle along one side, sprinkles of glazed walnuts. The musky scent of sesame oil mingled with a bite of ginger tinge the air. Earl Putam, owner of The Humboldt House, strolls over to inquire if everything is satisfactory while I stare down into this work of art, reluctant to disturb the arrangement by actually eating it.

My Aunt Mandy worked for Earl's grandfather for a while before striking out on her own. The man in the thousand-dollar suit with the Stanford pretentions may fool some of the people most of the time, but to me he's always going to be the grandson of a pimp, just as I'm always going to be the grandniece of a whore.

"Is something wrong with your salad?" the Putam heir asks.

"Not a thing in the world, Earl. Thanks for asking."

I give my best fake smile, can't help thinking of Dad describing the grandfather as "so crooked he had to screw his socks on."

Mark watches this little exchange. "You two know each other?"

"In a manner of speaking."

I take a forkful of salad. Slightly bitter. A nice taste with the pears. Different from the chunk of iceberg lettuce drizzled with oil and vinegar I'm used to at Marcelli's.

Once Earl has slid away to bestow his presence on other guests, Mark asks, "You were a cheerleader in high school?"

I inhale a lettuce leaf, guzzle water to recover, narrowly miss having to have Mark administer the Heimlich to keep me from choking to death.

"I'm going to take that as a 'No'," he says when I can once again breathe normally.

"You can take that as a 'Hell, no'!"

"Hard to believe there were girls more beautiful, more appealing than you. Cheerleading just wasn't your thing?"

I don't answer until our salads are whisked away, replaced with some kind of creamy, tomato-based soup topped with Greek yogurt, tiny braised grape tomatoes arranged in a triangle pattern along the side.

"I waited tables at Marcelli's after school. Not a lot of time for extracurricular activities. Plus, I didn't hang with that crowd."

Not to mention that with Dad's weekly Bigfoot letters to *The Times-Standard*, coupled with the common knowledge that I lived at VD's, I wasn't exactly cheerleader material. In retrospect, I didn't help my high school experience any by insisting on wearing baggy jeans and boy's T-shirts, not one drop of makeup, and yanking my hair back in a straggly braid.

Anybody reckless enough to make a comment about my dad or, by association, Bigfoot, I immediately backed up against a locker and chewed on like a bulldog with a prize bone. I'm pretty sure that piece of behavior didn't improve my chances at acceptance into the popular crowd either. A disturbing image of my younger self stomping down the halls of Eureka High in combat boots and a man's Carhartt jacket insists on pushing its way into my memory.

Our waitress fills our water glasses, removes our soup bowls, and assures us our entrees are being prepared by Chef Michael at this very moment. I press my lips together, prevent the words *whoopty freaking do* from slipping from my tongue and flying out into this rarefied atmosphere.

"How about you, Mark? Letterman jacket? Debate team? Quarterback?"

"No," Mark says. "I kept to myself. If you saw my high school graduation picture, you wouldn't recognize me. I hope."

I raise my eyebrows, cock my head to the right.

"Okay. I'll come clean. Though I don't know why. I never tell this to anyone." He takes a deep breath. "I've basically reinvented myself since high school. Had my teeth straightened."

"And bleached."

God, but I cannot stop myself from being a wiseass.

He laughs.

"Yes, and bleached. On a regular basis. My hair, unlike yours, does not come by these streaks of color naturally."

"You dye your hair?"

This comes out louder than I anticipated, draws the eye of the diners to our left and to our right.

"I have a colorist." His laugh seems a teeny bit forced. "And, I've lost one hundred eighty-five pounds."

Here comes the waitress, our dinner held high on a silver serving tray. She displays the plates in front of us with a flourish, makes a minor adjustment here, there. Perfect. We assure her that we can actually feed ourselves and no longer need her assistance. There's such a thing as too much hovering service.

So he was fat. Somehow this changes the way I see him. Flips my image upside down and slams it against long-held prejudices and preconceptions.

Dinner turns out to be a two-hour event. By the time I've patted my mouth with the soft linen napkin for the last time and the waitress has cleared away the dishes, Mark no longer feels like a stranger. He knows my childhood dog was a mixed breed hound named Tricksy. I know his first dog was a schnauzer named Willey. He doesn't flinch when I drop casually into the conversation the fact that my mother left when I was six weeks old. He confides that his mother sells real estate and lives 3.8 miles from him. I confess to wanting to see more of the world than Humboldt County. He shares his dream to make enough money writing to be able to leave the city and live somewhere quieter, more beautiful—like Eureka.

So it seems only natural that I agree when he suggests ordering dessert delivered to his room where we can relax in front of the fireplace and continue getting to know one another.

eleven

SNUGGLED BACK AGAINST his length, I burrow into a pillow as soft as a butterfly's wing. The smell of fresh linen overlaid with citrus works its way through a fog of sleep and into my wine-addled brain.

I decide to chance opening my eyes.

A fireplace, gas fire logs throwing eerie shadows on corniced walls. A plush blood-red sofa arranged on a rectangle of soft carpet. In front of the couch, in the precise middle, squats a claw foot coffee table on which sits a translucent porcelain plate with the remains of chocolate-covered strawberries and two half-empty glasses of flat champagne.

Holy crap, what did I do?

The warm breath against my bare shoulders is slow and even.

He's sleeping.

That's good. Gives me time to think.

Oh God, oh God, oh God. Second date. Even if you count the hydrophobic skunk encounter as the first. Two glasses of wine with dinner, followed by a glass-and-a-half of champagne once we got to his room. I rush to blame my slutty behavior on the booze even as the realization forces its way into my consciousness that I simply loved being pampered, being treated as a girl and yes… if forced to admit it… touched by soft manicured hands. Plus there was that instant of hesitation when I could have said no. One quick moment before the point of no return. In that second, my anger at Hawk became a living thing, clawing its way up from my belly. A frenzy of hurt and rage drove my hands to the buttons of Mark's shirt, my mouth back to his.

Visions worm their way into my head.

The borrowed dress slipping to the floor, desperate kisses, skin against skin, push-up bra following the dress. Stumbling backwards to the bed, never breaking contact, touching, running my hands over a new body. Very soon after that, my feet, still wearing those ridiculous heels, framing his face. His pale lean body, heavier than I imagined, as he moves over me. The moment when he collapses onto me and I lie sobbing quietly, clinging to him, longing for Hawk.

What have I done?

My need to get out of here is a trapped rodent of panic in my chest. I want my own bed. Need to be gone before he wakes up. Inch by slow inch, I slide away from his warmth until I'm balanced on the very edge of the monstrously huge bed. The comforter comes away easily, but the sheets are wrapped and twisted around me like a cocoon.

The Egyptian cotton gives just enough so that I can force my right leg against it and create a tiny pocket of freedom.

Oh good. I'm a half-inch closer to escape.

Breathe. Exhale. There now. Inhale.

Raise my hip, edge the linen out from under me, gain another millimeter of freedom.

Something is happening to me. Something bad.

A heart attack probably. The air in this hermetically sealed room is being shut off.

In one pounding heartbeat, the tiny scrambling rodent of fear is a roaring, open- mouthed, saliva-dripping grizzly bear rising up from my belly and exploding into the room.

Legs kick, arms whirligig, my body produces a seizure that lifts me up off the bed and, thank you Jesus, Buddha, Allah, and Aunt Mandy, finally disentangles me from the shroud of linen.

I force myself to look at Mark. He's lying on his back, chicken-skinned now that I've flung the sheet to the floor. Miraculously his eyes are still closed, though there's a suspicion of a cat-with-the-canary smile on his face. He's shorter than Hawk by a few inches, blond hair sparse across a wider chest than I've grown to love. His soft penis lies along the right side of his groin. Hawk's always rests to the left.

Oh my God! Stop this. Now! No more comparisons. Get out of here before he and that particular appendage wakes up.

Stark naked in a darkened hotel room, I fish my cell phone from my purse.

No way in hell am I going to trot myself down Second Street from here to VD's wearing that damn dress and those disgraced heels.

"Hey, Sam." Stacey answers on the third ring. "How's it going?"

"Bring me some clothes. Some of *my* clothes. Jeans. A sweatshirt. Hell, grab my old Carhartt. I'm in room 3. A separate suite. At The Humboldt House."

"Uh-huh. We're just closing up here."

"Get someone else to close. Anybody. Just get up here."

"Lord, Sam. Calm down. You're not the first woman to wake up in a bed you never expected to fall into. I'll be there in ten minutes."

"Hurry!"

When I turn around, Mark's propped up on one elbow, a sleepy smile on his face, caught running his eyes over my naked backside.

Patting the bed beside him, he cajoles, "Come back to bed. No reason for you to run off. Stay the night. We'll have breakfast in bed. After we've worked up a little appetite."

Honest to god, I'd rather face an attacking cougar, a growling wolf, a hydrophobic skunk. Anything but this man, in this hotel room, at this moment. Feeling more exposed than I've ever felt in my life, I lean down, grab the twisted top sheet from the Italian-tiled floor, and drape it around me. My reflection looks back at me from the gold, gilt-framed mirror across the room. The mascara Stacey insisted on brushing on my lashes is now smeared around my eyes. My hair is a ratted mess. I look like a demented raccoon. In a fright wig.

Where the hell is Stacey?

"I… um… I need to get back. The bar. Closing time." I thread my fingers through my hair, do my best to fluff it out. "Really. I had a… it was nice. Dinner. And, you know, everything."

"Yes. It was nice. Dinner. And everything was spectacular." He grins at me. "You either have to get dressed, or you have to come back to bed. You can't stand there in the firelight, looking like that, and expect me to just let you leave."

His eyes look directly at my left breast. Nipple and all peek out at him. I jerk the sheet up where it's slipped, turn my back on him, and, as best I can in the wadded linen, flounce to the window and stare out onto the wet street. His voice whispers my name a time or two, but I do like my old dog Tricksy—stare into nothingness and pretend not to hear.

A knock at the door is my clarion call to freedom. I drag the sheet behind me to the door, jerk it open, and take a paper bag from Stacey.

"Wait for me," I whisper. "It'll just be a minute."

"Can't do it. Gotta get back. I left Bubba in charge."

The bitch walks away laughing.

I clutch the paper bag to my chest, slide my way to the bathroom. The sheet trails behind like a wedding dress. Probably this is as close as I'll ever get to being a bride. This elegant room damn sure feels as long as a church aisle right now. He sits up in bed, watches me shuffle along, doing my best not to get my feet tangled.

"Samantha?"

I keep moving. Refuse to look at him.

His sigh is epic.

"I'll put some clothes on and drive you home."

A nod is all I can manage. I keep inching my way to the bathroom.

Finally sequestered behind the locked door, I realize my underwear is still on the floor somewhere between the couch and the bed. Damn! I'll have to do without.

In seconds, I'm back in my jeans and T-shirt.

This is much better.

One baby bunny soft white hotel washcloth ends up smeared with mascara, but I manage to get my face washed. My hair still looks like I rolled around in wild abandon with some stranger in a hotel room, but with no comb or brush, there's not much I can do about that.

Mark is barefoot, dressed in khakis and an open-necked white shirt when

I step out of the bathroom. As nonchalantly as possible, I gather my bor-rowed clothes. The dress is tucked half under a couch cushion. The lacey bra must have ended up twisted in the sheets. I find it in front of the window, flung there, no doubt, by my little panic attack. Stuffing everything in the paper bag, I realize Stacey didn't bring me any shoes. No way I'm putting those fuck-me pumps back on my feet. I'd rather get frostbite.

"Feeling better?" he asks.

Why does he always have to look so calm, so damn sophisticated and at ease?

"Much better." I run my hands down the front of my jeans. "This is the real me, I'm afraid."

His eyes play over me, mascara-naked eyes to bare feet.

"You're lovely," he says. "Please. Sit with me. Room service is closed. But they're bringing us a pot of coffee. Don't run off without talking to me."

My courage has returned with my own clothes. I plop myself onto the soft upholstery of the couch, drop from a foot above the cushions like a lumberjack. In my graceless descent, my left foot collides with the edge of the coffee table. The elegant plate with the remains of the chocolate-coated strawberries flies an inch or two into the air, rests precariously a moment before sliding onto Aladdin's carpet.

Honestly, I know how to behave like a girl. I do. Something just comes over me when I know it's expected.

"Sorry. I get a little carried away sometimes," I try to explain as, once again, a blush overtakes me.

A soft knock at the door and the guy delivering the coffee is inside.

Oh, hell.

It's Morgan, one of the dart players. Must be some Humboldt House rule about pretending not to recognize locals when they're caught in rooms with rich guys. Morgan flashes me a sly wink as he lays out the silver urn of coffee, a sugar bowl, cutesy little pitcher of milk, two baroque silver spoons, and dainty coffee cups. Mark slips him what looks to me like a twenty and we're alone again.

I pretend deep involvement in spooning sugar, dumping half the con-tents of the cream pitcher into the coffee Mark pours into my tiny cup. Prob-ably should be crooking my pinkie finger as I sip.

When I finally look up, he smiles into my eyes.

"So," he says in that pronounce-all-the-consonants voice of his, "You don't do this kind of thing often."

"Jump into bed with a man I've just met? Eat…*dine* in the only five-star restaurant in the county? Drink half a bottle of wine that costs as much as I make in month? No. I don't do this kind of thing much."

I sound angry. But I'm not angry.

Am I?

He sips his coffee. No curled pinkie.

I lift my cup with both hands, cradle the warmth in the eggshell-thin porcelain.

"Sorry. Honestly, half the time lately, I don't know what I'm doing. Or why,"

"Stop being hard on yourself. So you're not a sophisticate. You're take-a-guy's-breath-away beautiful. You do know that?"

My toenails are Pink Paradise. Stacey insisted I get a pedicure. I wiggle each little piggy, starting with the one that went to market and ending, one slow breath later, with the little porker that stayed home. Only then do I force my eyes up to meet his.

He cups my cheek in his hand for one teasing instant, his smile a warm caress. "Has it occurred to you that your naivety is one of things I find so appealing?"

He really is irresistible. And when's the last time Hawk told me he found me appealing. Or beautiful?

Hell, between Morgan and Stacey, everyone on Second Street, including the homeless John and Oscar, are going to know I slept with this city man. What's the harm in enjoying the reputation I've already earned?

My cup tilts in its fancy saucer, the cream-lightened contents spill onto the waxed shine of the mahogany table. His mouth tastes of warm coffee. When his hands slip under my T-shirt I have one sharp ache of longing for Hawk.

I throw the image away, like a woman tossing cold coffee from a perfectly beautiful cup.

twelve

IT'S THE SMELL of spiced rum in the cold, morning-empty bar that tips me off. Huddled in the shadow of the black bear's head, he twirls the dark liquid in one of the heavy squared glasses we keep reserved for Dad and him behind the bar. Hidden by his wide hands, I can't see the etching, but I know it says *World's Best Dad*. An empty, matching glass rests across from him, its bottom already stuck to the Formica table top.

I was eight, Hawk nine. Father's Day. Our choice of matching highball glasses caused a snort of disapproval from the owner's wife when we bought them at Ten Window Williams. But she took our allowance money easily enough, left us to peer at gold watches and glittering rings while she carried the heavy bottomed glasses behind the counter to have them etched.

Yesterday morning, it seems like that was. Funny how time overlaps, folds in on itself. At moments like this one, I am convinced that our belief that our days march in linear formation is the cosmic joke of a comedic God.

The coffee is thick and smells burned, but it's still caffeine. I pour half a cup, retrieve a carton of half-and-half from the bar fridge, and top off the sludge.

"Morning, David."

Uninvited, I sit myself across from him. My index finger traces the image of Captain Morgan on the squat bottle of Private Stock on the table between us.

"Where's Dad?"

"Went to bed about an hour ago."

The image of these two sitting in a cold, pre-dawn bar sipping rum and making plans does not give me a feeling of security.

"Awful early, or else awful late, for sipping."

His eyes are red-rimmed, his usually clean-shaven face scraggly with salt-and-pepper whiskers. He ignores my comment, goes on the offensive.

"Where's your Jody man?"

This is an old guy reference. I've heard it all my life and still have no idea of its origin. But I'm real clear on the meaning. Jody is the SOB who sneaks in the back door as the rightful lover walks out the front.

"Left Sunday. He's back in The City. A meeting with his publisher."

Here's what I know about dealing with drinkers—they will always blame you for their injuries. Never, ever, accept this load of crap. Hell, I was trained by masters. One of whom sits across from me.

"Not like you to be hitting the Captain Morgan this hard."

He turns the glass in his hand, runs his thumb over the groove of the etching. When he meets my eyes again, the anger has been replaced with something I read as self-recrimination.

"Life doesn't always turn out the way you planned."

Filtered through dense fog, the squared patch of silvery light at the window sparkles on the tears in his eyes. I drop my shoulders, push back in my chair. David isn't the maudlin kind. What is going on here?

A tear overflows his left eye, tracks through his scrubby day-old beard.

"You get old, you think about your own mortality, the death of youthful plans and schemes. But you don't give much thought to losing the people around you."

My chair tilts sideways, falls backward onto the deeply scarred wood floor. I'm on my feet, heart hammering in my chest.

"What are you saying? Is something wrong with Dad? Or Hawk?"

"Sit down, Sammy. Your dad's seventy-eight. I'm two years ahead of him. That's all I'm saying. He and I are all set for one last hoo-rah. Van's ready. Getting more and more sightings up near Redwood Creek. Maybe we'll get lucky. Neither of us is going to live to see many more hunts."

"Jesus." I pick up my chair, collapse onto it. "You scared me. Dad said something the other night about how I wasn't going to have him around forever. What's going on with you two?"

"We're old men. The both of us. A couple of tired old fools who hoped for better for our kids. Night's falling on our lives. And Hawk? Hell, Hawk's still fighting the same struggle he's been locked into since his mama died." He stares out the dirty window at a wall of pearly gray fog. "I should have done more for that boy."

"You're not responsible for Hawk's drinking."

He turns his face away. A drop of pain gathers at his chin line, hangs suspended, before momentum drops it onto his plaid shirtfront.

"It ain't just Hawk." His voice is a low, whispery growl.

When he turns back to me, I meet his eyes, refuse to look away.

"Hawk and I aren't kids anymore. You gotta let us find our own way."

"This… it's not… what I wanted for you two. Always thought I'd live to bounce grandkids on my knee."

He swallows the remaining half-inch of dark rum. Dust-speckled light brushes the inside of the glass with swirling streaks of dark amber.

"Your dad ever tell you about our first day in Korea?"

I shake my head.

"Ever hear that expression a cold day in hell?"

"Ah, yeah. Dad got frostbite over there. Right?"

"That was later. We got there two days into a cease-fire. Dug down through the snow and into the hard dirt. Made our two-man foxhole. Your dad and I, brand new, and green as grass. Chinese firing fragmentation rounds over our heads. Shrapnel raining down. Hot, flesh ripping, metal shards. I remember steam rising up from the indentations it made in the snow all around us. Welcome to hell."

"Marines, right?" I lift my coffee to my mouth, set it down hard when the sludge smell roils my stomach.

"Young and dumb and full of co…."

He coughs, looks down into his glass, eyes the bottle I'm holding firmly in my left hand.

"Anyway. We joined up together on the buddy system. Recruiter's office was across from the old Eureka Theater in those days. Went through boot together. Shipped over."

I empty the bottle into his glass. He swirls the rum, creates a tiny whirlpool, leaves the drink on the table.

"First day in that hellhole. Colder than we've ever been in our lives. Sergeant has everyone building platforms over the foxholes. Protection against the raining shrapnel. Between barrages, we're up there putting sandbags on the roof. About the time we think we can hunker down under our make-shift shelter, the Lieutenant decides he needs to know what the profile of all this construction looks like from the Chinese side. Make sure the extra height hasn't turned our foxholes into bull's eyes."

He rolls his glass between his palms, taps a cadence with the bottom against the scarred wood of the table top. Red-veined and glazed, his eyes are seeing a different reality than this old bar.

"The two of us stumble around in the snow. Know we're exposed. It hits us, for the first time, that maybe we're not going to make it out of this frozen mess. In the corner of my eye, I catch movement, a strip of dirty white cloth fluttering against all that snow. Your dad, twenty feet or so behind me, sees our mistake at the same time it dawns on me.

"We've wandered inside the perimeter of our own mine field."

I widen my eyes but keep my mouth shut. David isn't talking to me. He's reliving a nightmare. His voice drops so low, I have to lean in to hear him.

"Panic grabbed me by the balls. Shook me like a ratty old bar towel. Heart was so loud in my ears I had a thought it was mortar rounds coming at us. Right then. That moment. I was no good for anything but the rag heap."

Dad and David were in their fifties when Hawk and I were born. I've never thought of them as young soldiers. Hell, I've never thought of them as young. Period. If I looked back on their lives at all, in my youthful narcissism, their story didn't begin until I came into this world. My earlier disorientation returns—time layers, overlaps, compresses into one vaporous entity we walk through, and around, and in, rarely bumping against anything but our own vain preconceptions.

David's knuckles are rough against my palm when I reach across the table.

"Frozen there in that wasted land. It was your dad's voice coming from behind me that snapped the panic like a twig and forced the breath back into my lungs.

"'Well, Ollie. This is another fine mess.'"

My laughter bubbles up, prances lightly across the bar. "Same thing he told me when I wrecked the F one fifty."

He pushes his glass away, lays his hand over mine and squeezes. "Which time?"

"Same old line all four times. Don't keep me in suspense. How'd you get out of the minefield?"

The crinkles at the corner of his dark eyes are deeper than I remember, his olive skin more weathered.

"Once your dad vanquished the panic, it was easy. We just stepped backward into our tracks in the snow. Very carefully."

"How come you thought about that this morning?"

He pushes himself up from his chair, slides it back with his foot, and heads for Hawk's room. It takes him a full minute to fumble in his front pocket for the key. Then he unlocks the door and steps inside.

I've decided he's not going to answer my question when he turns, wipes at his swelling tears, and looks me full in the face.

"I keep seeing those strips of torn white cloth. Those markers delineating the minefield. A cold wind waving them against mud-smeared snow."

He sways slightly, balances himself on the door jam.

"It's a crying shame, Sam, but we don't know what gifts we're given until destiny, or death, swoops down and snatches them out of our hands."

I wash and dry the etched glasses, place them back behind the bar where the Private Stock will go once I carry a new bottle in from the storeroom. Despite his reassurance that nothing is wrong, the conversation has me jumpy, suspicious that I'm standing in the dark here, the knowledge of something bad gathering just beyond my understanding.

The thick viscous coffee is washing down the drain when a shave-and-a-haircut-two-bits knock announces Bubba's arrival.

When I throw the lock and open the door, he's holding two venti grande paper cups with the Starbucks logo.

"Something smells suspiciously like macadamia," I grouse after he's inside, the door locked once again to the fog and the homeless seeking shelter on our doorstep.

"That there one is mine. Not wantin' to spend my mornin' at the emergency room, I did not co-mingle the con-tents."

Three sips in, I notice Bubba is wearing freshly pressed khaki pants and a button-down rust brown shirt with mahogany stripes, his feet encased in Doc Martins instead of his usual Wolverines.

"You clean up good." I give him the once over, wiggle my eyebrows, and cock my head. His blush only spurs me onward. "You even got a haircut. What's all this about?"

"I'm interviewin' this mornin'. With the city. Heavy equipment operator."

"I thought your farming skills were keeping you in cash?"

Between Hawk's disappearance, David's odd behavior, and now this with Bubba, I feel like someone has taken my world, held it up by the ear, and shook it. What the hell else is going to fall out?

"Might be some day I want more than just an old rental house and a flatulent bulldog."

I am speechless. Almost.

"Flatulent?"

"It's a real word. My granny told me a story the other day about how the preacher come to dinner. She used that word—flatulent. Had to look it up. But I do like the sound of it."

Coffee snorts out my nose, clears my sinuses for the next month.

"So who had the farts? Your granny, or the preacher?"

"That was the point of the story. Granny mentioned how seems like, when a preacher farts, there's generally a large dawg nearby to take the fall."

thirteen

BIGFOOT ROCKS TO the music of an iPod. The white cords fall from his ears into a deep V across his dark, massive chest, the tiny white rectangle of the iPod cupped in one giant hairy hand. On the next stool is the charming depiction of two Bigfoots humping face-to-furry-face. I've seen this one before. No need to walk around back to check out the preferred position on that side of the T-shirt.

"So, what d'ya think?" the Humper asks the guy next to him. He slides off the stool, holds his arms out to the side and turns in a full circle. "Bigfoot do it face-to-face or doggie style?"

His buddy grins. "You asking if he's human or if he's animal? Or you just like wearing a shirt illustrating something you're not getting either way?"

Five of these nincompoops. In their thirties. Never seen them in here before tonight.

Stacey's got the bar. I'm struggling with this week's schedule.

"I'll be right back," I tell her on my way past. "I left Amy's number upstairs and I'm going to need her to work backup if I'm getting out of here this week."

She waves me away as she sets a pitcher in front of our charming new patrons. These five are looking for trouble. I turn at the stairs and look back, make sure she's got this covered.

It's probably just overgrown adolescents making crank calls, but twice today I've answered the phone to have bile poured in my ear. Both calls were eerie, creepy voices, spouting what sounded, what felt, like real hatred against Dad and David.

"Tell the old guys they thought they got away with killing that family. Those Bigfoots. But now, I'm coming for them."

Too stunned to respond to a death threat from the love child of Darth Vader and Sylvester Stallone, I tried to sort through what I thought I'd heard. The caller hung up while I was still staring across VD's, blinking my eyes like a baby seal studying an approaching, club-wielding, Eskimo.

Three hours later, when the phone rang again, I made sure I answered it.

Same mechanical voice created, no doubt, with a computerized voice distorter. Terrific. A homicidal nerd Bigfoot-fanatic stalker. Honest to God, no way anyone could make up the crap that goes on in this bar.

Freaky voice gave me the creeps. "I am the avenger. I speak for Bigfoot."

What is this guy, some perverted Lorax? Prepared this time, I interrupted the Bigfoot killer tirade. Did my best to put a stop to the ramblings of a lunatic. I lied.

"Look, Buddy. I've got no idea what your problem is. But this is not our first go-round with fanatics. We record each and every call that comes in here. You want cops knocking on your door? Great. Keep calling. If not, I suggest you find another way to amuse yourself."

I hung up before the voice could pour fear into my head again. I knew it was just kids, but something about that voice gave me the shivers.

So, now, headed upstairs with five unknown troublemakers lined up at my bar, I hesitate before abandoning Stacey. It's stupid, really. Prank calls come in all the time. The name of the damn bar is VD's! Half the kids in the county phone at least once to giggle some perceived original query. So, there's no reason why these two calls have me looking over my shoulder, the hair on the back of my neck electrified.

Still, I'm relieved when the front door swings in to admit Bubba and Lefty. I wave and nod my head toward the brewing trouble at the bar, watch Lefty slide in next to the guy on the end before I head upstairs.

It's been two weeks since Mark went back to San Francisco for meetings with his publisher and some family matters to take care of with his mom. He'll be here tomorrow, and then he and I are headed for Bluff Creek. He wants to experience Bigfoot country firsthand.

I'm not sure how I feel about seeing him again. Last Wednesday between shifts, I curled up in bed, phone in hand, watched the fog disappear like magic from the bay. With Mark's voice in my ear, I reveled in the sun's daily fifteen-minute appearance. Maybe it was the joy of sunlight. It made me giddy. I chattered to him long distance like a schoolgirl, until the fiery orb bedded down into the dark blue Pacific.

I've not talked with him since, refuse to pick up the phone when his number lights up my little screen. I love that he calls me beautiful. Hate that he's not Hawk. I know for sure I'm worried about backpacking tomorrow. Coastal Humboldt County has been hammered for four days straight with rain and wind. Our usual early fall weather. But the storm due tomorrow is predicted to make its way over the mountain and pour an abundantly wet blessing on drought-afflicted Trinity. Bluff Creek runs through the heart of that inland county. Hiking in the first big storm of the season is never a good idea. Plus, I think I'm coming down with something. Rarely sick, for a week I've been exhausted.

Of my old love, I haven't seen hide nor hair. Phone service on the reservation is patchy. I get that. But if the man truly had feelings for me, wouldn't he be willing to climb a mountain, hold one hand up over his glorious head, and walk in circles until he had a signal?

He has sent gifts. Hawk-style treasures.

A week ago Monday night, one of the Riesling boys came by VD's. Walked inside, straight to the bar, reached across, and handed me a paper bag. Turned and walked back out.

"Nice talking to you," I called to his back as I opened the wrinkled sack to find a cream-flecked gray rock in the natural shape of a heart. No note. None needed.

Thursday morning, same week, Nancy Ryerson called and had me meet her out front. She hugged me quick before fleeing the rain-blackened streets, leaving a yellowed pillowslip of bear jerky in my arms.

Riesling and Ryerson are both in Hawk's AA group, which I took as a good sign until Sunday morning, when Dickie Brook disturbed me from inhaling my drug of choice—Starbucks Kona Peaberry. Dickie's the Assembly of God minister up in Hoopa as well as a sheriff's deputy. So when he kissed my cheek, helped himself to a slurp of my coffee, and slid a sealed envelope across the table, I wasn't surprised to find an impound slip for a powder blue '52 Indian inside.

"Damn! Is he okay?"

"Banged up. Nothing more. The man must have Saint Michael himself looking after him."

Since then I haven't heard a word.

Upstairs in my room, I ignore the need to produce this week's work schedule, forget about finding Amy's number.

The heart-shaped rock is a dull weight in my palm. A comfort and a burden.

I sit and stare out the window at a scrim of ragged black clouds over a round, yellow moon. The remnants of last week's storm are leaving, just as this week's rain blows in off the Pacific, generously frosting Humboldt Bay's dark surface with swirls of whitecaps. Fingers of cold, wet air push their way around the rattling window frame as I stare out.

No rain yet. But soon.

Twenty-six days since I laid eyes on Hawk. Feasted my eyes, that's what I'm really thinking. I hope now, finally, he's sweating out the toxins and communing with his higher power. The possibility that he may, instead, be holed up with his latest dalliance makes me queasy.

It's not like this is my first rodeo with his cheating. We've had our bad times over the years. To be accurate, we've had the same bad time over and over. He falls off the wagon, gets drunk, and has sex with grossly inappropriate women. Younger women, like Little Miss Fuck-Me-Harder, or his third cousin Janet or, two years ago January, his psychologist.

It's not just sex, either. For Hawk, alcohol conjures up a dark, brooding pain. At nineteen, in the maw of the beast, he slid around the gravel-strewn shoulder of a reservation road on a Harley Sportster, coming within a prayer of losing his right leg. Four years ago May, he threw himself from a granite overhang on the Klamath into a river running drought low and broke both ankles. Somewhere along the way, the jumble of sadness and anger I feel at these betrayals of both himself and of me has jelled into a bone-weary grief.

And yet....

I don't feel whole without him.

Dull rain strings pearls of gray against the window. A fairy wind carries the moisture inland off the bay, the beaded window flooding to mesmerizing rivulets of running water between one breath and the next. I pull the quilt off the bed and tuck it around me in the chair, let myself fall under the spell of the quicksilver rain as it finds its own path along the surface of the glass. Past miniscule particles of dust, around remains of a spider's web, the water creates its own trail, sheer persistence removing obstacles known, mostly, only to itself.

Through the glimmer of rain I see him walk back to me. In his right hand is cradled an exquisitely wrapped gift, the small bundle glowing incandescent through the veil of water. I ache to touch him, to push my body so close to his that we are one person, one breath. Distorted by the pouring water, his image is a wavy, indistinct longing with no hard lines of definition. If I touch him, my hand will feel, not flesh and bone, but luminous hope, phantom ideal. He continues to stride slowly toward me, the glowing gift held now in both hands, tight against his chest. He smiles and, at that moment, I see another man, a man just visible through the mercurial gauze of water. Both men waver in the mist. One recognizable. One indistinct, moving toward me, almost in view. Both stand in the silvery rain extending their arms to me offering a precious gift, a shimmering surprise.

"Hey, up there! We could use some help," Stacey's voice calls up the stairs, startles me out of the dream.

My heart jackhammers in my chest.

Jesus. What the hell was that?

Now I'm falling asleep in the middle of a shift? As for the dream or vision or whatever the hell it was, I'm not going to think about it right now.

Maybe not ever.

I get downstairs just in time to see the first punch thrown.

iPod Bigfoot Guy is already bringing his fist forward for a roundhouse punch to Dad's jaw when Lefty hits him with a behind-the-knees tackle that sends both of them tumbling to the floor.

"Get on out of here, Son." Dad's voice is even and low, but little spots of color on his cheeks give away his anger.

Lefty, having fallen on top, is up first and, with Bubba's enthusiastic help, they have the offender on his feet and standing between them. Though *standing* is a stretch, since his feet dangle about six inches off the floor on Bubba's side of the arrangement.

"I ain't afraid of any of you! I seen the pictures. You guys, you old timers, you killed that whole family of 'em."

"What is going on?" I'm wedged between Dad and The Ranter, but my brain is fuzzy, still caught somewhere between the dream and this damn fistfight in my bar.

"Look, Son." Dad lowers himself into a chair. "I appreciate your passion. I do. But you've got it all wrong. If we can sit and talk, reasonable men listening to each other and learning, I can straighten this misconception out for you."

"No deal, old man. You been found out. When that book comes out, you're gonna be shown up as the fuckin' murdering savage you really are."

Bubba and Lefty lower him to the floor. The kid shakes off their grip and saunters out of the bar. His buddies stagger out after him. The guy in the Humping Bigfoot shirt looks disappointed that he's missed out on a brawl, while the other three seem relieved to have gotten away unscathed.

"Holy Jesus!" I rant, "I leave for two minutes and this is what happens, a freaking fistfight!"

"First off," declares Bubba, "it weren't two minutes. More like an hour you were gone. And second off, this here whole entire mess has got itself stirred up by your fancy man."

"What?"

The clock over the bar shows 10:27. I *was* asleep for almost an hour. How can that be? I never fall asleep this early. Never.

And what does any of this nonsense have to do with Mark?

fourteen

STACEY SLIPS HER arm through mine, leads me to a table in the back, the one under the forlorn, one-eyed elk.

"Sit," she commands gently. "I'll bring you a cup of coffee."

Dad, Bubba, and Lefty shuffle across the wood-planked floor, take a few minutes to adjust their hardback chairs. The only one who will look at me is Dad, and he sits close enough to squeeze my knee before he clears his throat and gets on with the story.

"Tell me what you remember about how Patterson and Gimlin shot that film of Bigfoot, of Patty, back in 'sixty-seven."

Oh Lord. I am sick of this. I swear if I ever do actually see a Bigfoot, I'm going to prance right up and punch him in his big fat furry nose. Show yourself, goddamn it, or slink back into whatever cave or dimension you come from.

A sigh of disgust forces its way up from my true feelings and lingers in the air.

"Patterson was up in Washington. Obsessed with Bigfoot. And, just for the record, this was all, like, decades before I was even born."

Dad raises an eyebrow. I ignore him and drone on.

"Roger Patterson writes a book about Sasquatch, is working on a documentary up there in Washington, when somebody, maybe Hodgson, calls him and reports that a lot of giant footprints have been found in Trinity County, on a remote section of Bluff Creek."

Stacey puts coffee in front of me. I warm my hands around the mug, take a sip, still trying to shake off that weird dream.

Dad, not happy with my lackluster recital of the sacred chronicle, goes on with the narrative.

"Ah, yeah. Patterson and Gimlin load the horses in the truck and tear down to Trinity County. They leave the truck at Indian Rock campground and take the horses back into the woods in the general direction of where these new prints have been seen."

"Can we, for the love of God, skip ahead?" I interrupt. "The two of them are a few hours in, on horseback, when Patterson sees the Bigfoot."

"Patty," Dad insists and points his chin toward the dusty photo of the female Bigfoot hung over the boozy colors and myriad shapes of the bottles behind the bar.

"Ah, yeah. Patty," I acknowledge. "Let's see. They catch a whiff of something strong enough to make their eyes water. Garbage or body odor. Something like that. The horses rear, Patterson is either thrown from his horse or he slips off. Some debate on that as I remember."

Dad nods his head. I take another sip of coffee. Maybe it's the flu, that might be the problem with me. The coffee sits on my stomach like acid. Feels like it might come back up.

"The point is," Dad jumps in again, "Patterson is running through the woods, stumbling across Bluff Creek. All the time holding that camera, doing his best to get footage. The whole film, start to finish, is less than two minutes long."

"I've seen it," I say. "Probably closer to a minute of actual frames with Patty in them. Half the tape is the camera going at crazy angles as Patterson runs along. So?"

Bubba, sitting across from me, leans forward, taps his fist on the table.

"You're lookin' a mite peckish, Sam. When's the last time you ate? Want I should run up to Marcelli's and carry you back some raviolis?"

My stomach roils, nausea requires me to grip the edge of the table, concentrate on breathing slowly.

"No food," I whisper to Bubba.

Dad studies me a few seconds, then gets to the point.

"So. Patterson promoted that tape. Sixteen thousand people saw it in Salt Lake City alone. He peddled it around, showed it in auditoriums and such all over the country. Well, those people wanted to see more for their hard-earned money than a forty-five-second film with no sound, no nothing. Just a few seconds of Patty walking through the woods."

My stomach settles some. Maybe the fight bothered me more than I thought. Seeing that fist swing at Dad's face. I must be getting old. It's not as though, over the years, we haven't had our share of good ole boys in here causing a ruckus over one damn Bigfoot controversy or another.

"Remind me again," I ask Dad. "You were involved in the Patterson film somehow, right?"

"That's what I'm getting to here. Me and David and a couple others went up along Blue Mountain Road and shot more footage. Scenery. The creek. Mountains. Since we were up there, I brought Tricksy and David brought that wolf dog of his. When you were little we had Tricksy the Third. Maybe the Fourth." He scratches his head. "It doesn't matter. Back then, we had the original Tricksy."

"Blue Tick wasn't she?" I ask while suppressing a grin at the thought of David's wolf dog.

Every other redneck in the county has a shepherd mix that they swear is half-wolf, pronounced "Woof." As in, "Hell yeah. I got me a Woof Dawg." Which is mighty peculiar as there hasn't been a wild wolf in these parts in well over a hundred years.

"Ah, yeah," Dad says, "The Tricksies were Blue Tick and Red Bone mixed. All three of them. Good trackers every one."

"The one we had when I was little had the softest ears. That's what I remember. And she'd run off. Seems like every time we took her camping, she'd disappear and we'd spend the next three days looking for her."

Dad's smile puts me right back in those woods. Him and me and Tricksy. It seems like it was always raining, and muddy, and cold. In my memory we spent as much time huddled under dripping canvas, Dad weaving Bigfoot stories, as we spent slipping our way through drenched underbrush hunting the dog.

Bubba stands, rolls his shoulders. For a split second I catch a look in his eyes that makes me touch my hand to my hair. Some small spot in my center softens as I look into the flecks of green and gold in his light brown eyes. I blink. The moment vaporizes.

"Be back," he says, and then his wide frame moves for the front door.

Dad pays him no mind.

"Every one of them dogs was like that. Run off into the woods after one damn thing or another ever' chance they got. Which is why, the day we were taping footage of scenery to edit into the Patterson tape, I had the original Tricksy on a lead. See, this here promoter, he took the footage we shot and he spliced, and edited, and made a longer film. About twelve minutes of our footage, as I recall, culminating in The Beautiful Patty hightailing it through the brush. That way, with the longer film, there was some suspense built up, and the paying public felt like they were getting their money's worth."

"So?" I need to finish the schedule, and this Bigfoot miasma has been an undercurrent running below the surface of my entire life. I'm about sick of the story and every stinking new twist and turn that goes along with it.

For Dad, however, this is still the blood of life.

"So, a couple of frames of the added footage, the frames we took, had a shot of me and David and Tricksy in that harness we had, you remember?"

"So the dog wouldn't run off on her own, tracking every deer and bear in the woods. A red harness. I remember."

"Well, see, there's a frame in that film that shows a few of us standing on Blue Mountain Road. A few minutes before that particular sequence of film was shot, that wolf dog of David's lit into Tricksy. Tore a half-dollar sized chunk out of her ear before we could get them separated. When I pulled the wolf off Tricksy, she lunged for the other dog's throat and got my hand instead. So, in that particular frame, I was bleeding some."

I want to put my hands over my ears, make nonsense noises to blot out the sound of this never-ending history. Instead I scoot my chair over, lay my head on Dad's shoulder and close my eyes. *Please, please, make it end,* I pray to Saint Jude, patron of lost causes, for surely I am going to lose my mind or, at the very least, the contents of my stomach, if Dad doesn't get to the point soon.

"That area we were in that day, up on Blue Mountain Road, Ryerson and Brockmueller had logged all through there. In a couple of frames of the film, there's a pile of slag behind us. Shoulder-high piles of trimmed limbs and logging trash. In that old black-and-white film it just looks like a darker, blurry, mound."

The front door swings open and a three-foot-high stack of white Styrofoam with denim legs comes directly to our table.

"Chicken soup with homemade noodles for you." Letticia deals the garlicky containers onto the table. "Bubba called. Said you needed Italian soul food."

I pop the plastic top from the giant cup she hands me, release the smell of comfort into the air. Ignoring her offer of a plastic spoon, I scarf directly from the Styrofoam cup. God, are those Portobello raviolis she's unwrapping? Whatever was wrong with my stomach seems to have passed.

I am starving.

Bubba is back, his laptop tucked under one massive arm. He scoots the cartons around, clears a spot just big enough to set the computer.

"Look here," he orders me as he helps himself to veal parmesan.

The container of God's sweet manna still clutched in my hand, I walk around so I'm looking over his shoulder. On the screen is a fuzzy black-and-white picture of a much younger Dad and David. Tricksy the First strains out to the end of her leash. Her nose up, the dog looks to have picked up a scent she wants to tear after through the woods like a striped-assed ape. Dad's right hand is clearly wrapped in something and, even with the grainy texture of the film, it's not hard to imagine that the dark stain spreading across the make-shift bandage is blood.

Dad comes around to stand beside me. Tapping the monitor, he points out the dog's harness. "See how that red harness picks up the light somehow and is the darkest spot in the frame? We figure that's what he spotted first. Seemed out of place."

"Who spotted?" I ask around a mouthful of noodles.

Lefty, who's been silent since we sat down, pushes his way in to look over my shoulder. His face inches from mine, he puts his hand on my shoulder.

"Your city slicker. That's who."

fifteen

STACEY AND CARRIE cover the bar on this now quiet Wednesday night. We have four regulars on stools, two men and two women. The men nurse beers while the women throw back shots at the relaxed pace of confirmed alcoholics. Two tables along the wall are occupied, one under the head of the black bear and the other directly below the mangy deer head we always decorate as Rudolph for Christmas. All regular customers, most are eavesdropping on our conversation. A few wander over from time to time to help themselves to the bounty of Italian-love leaking Rorschach blots of garlicky red onto the scarred surface of our table.

I've finished the chicken soup and am elbow deep in Portobello mushroom raviolis. Bubba flips through internet sites, playing talk radio excerpts and flashing onto Bigfoot blogs, returning again and again to that one frame. Dad and David, young, handsome, back in their glory days, with a blurry heap behind them in the left corner of the picture. The original Tricksy's harness the blackest image, drawing the eye to Dad's bandaged hand, which leaks a dark stain onto the forest floor.

Bubba finds what he's looking for on the laptop in front of him. He pushes the arrow on the speaker icon all the way up.

"Those old guys. They killed a whole family of Bigfoots. Look at the film! That pile of bodies has gotta be five feet high. The one guy, Foster, he's got blood, like, dripping from his hands!"

"*Damn straight! That huge furry heap behind 'em, you know they didn't mean to get that stack of bodies in the picture. The bastards killed 'em—that female, Patty, and a mess of little ones, all of 'em. Buried the whole mess in the woods up there where they'll never be found.*"

"*This is George Noory with* Coast to Coast AM *Radio. Have you seen this newly discovered footage? Check it out on our website, take a look. Call us here and speak your mind. Join Dan from Arcata, California, and Joe from Farmington, Arkansas. Let us know what you make of this newest development in the hunt for the illusive creature of the Northwoods.*"

"Could someone please just tell me what the hell all this is about and what it has to do with Mark?"

Lefty, with the smallest appetite of the group, has consumed as much food as he can hold. He leans back, pats his tight, round stomach, and does his best to clear the mental fog for me.

"Your friend Mark Neilsen dug up a copy of the longer version of the Patterson film. The one with the footage taken by your dad and David that was spliced into the original. When he cleaned up that one frame he got the photo you saw. Posted it on the net.

"The picture's on a dozen Bigfooter sites now. Tricksy in the center. Your dad on the other end of the leash, his hand bloodied. David to the right and, in the far left corner—a heap of logging scrap that Mark Neilsen is telling the world is a pile of Bigfoot bodies."

A black pit opens at my feet. I sway. Vertigo whispers my name, entices me to pitch myself forward, lie face first in a heap of shame. Why did I let myself believe that a man like Mark, an outsider, wanted anything from me other than information about my dad? He told me I was beautiful and I fell for it. Hook, line, and open legs.

My denial a thin, frayed thread, I stammer a protest, "Ah, yeah. I see that some idiot has found this one frame in a film taken over forty years ago. A frame that doesn't seem to belong in the series. I see how a blurry heap of limbs and logging trash could look like a furry pile of bodies. *To a lunatic.* I see that. But how does this have anything to do with Mark?"

That's what I say. But I'm remembering Mark's face splashed with candlelight, his thumb stroking my wrist, river-green eyes looking directly into mine from across a snowy white, linen-draped table.

"I need a hook, Samantha. A way to tell a new truth about an old story."

Letticia's brown arm a solid brace around my waist, she guides me into the gold-flecked Naugahyde chair that Lefty has scooted across the wood floor and parked next to Bubba at his laptop. Thick fingers peck the keyboard. Bubba locks in on his target, and I look at Patterson's image of Patty. The same image that hangs over the bar.

Female Bigfoot looking back over her shoulder at the shooter. Behind her are superimposed a young and virile Dad and David, cartoon rifles rising to their shoulders in an endless loop, taking aim at a creature whose come-hither look now seems less like a flirt, and more like fear as she runs for her life. Upper right corner of the screen, impersonating an honest man, is a studio portrait of the only lover besides Hawk I've ever had.

"Son of a bitch!"

Unbidden and unwanted, an image of those damn fuck-me-pumps framing Mark's lying face transposes itself over the image on the monitor.

I run for the customer bathroom. From the corner of my eye I see Stacey come around the bar. Letticia's hand stays around my waist, her short legs do double-time to keep up with me. I almost don't make it to the sink before all that lovely comfort food purges itself from my unworthy belly. Letticia gathers my hair into a tail at the base of my neck, coos softly while she rubs my back. Stacey offers a folded wad of cold, wet paper towels.

Sweat is slick on my ghostly face when I lift my head and confront my reflection in the mirror. My only color is the two smudges of black under my eyes. A zombie football player, that's what I look like. Cold water revives me enough that I can rinse my mouth, clean the sink with wet paper towels.

Letticia clucks like a hen with a sick chick. It's beginning to get on my last nerve. Her hand hasn't stopped with the slow circles on my back since I bolted for the bathroom. And Stacey's no better. If she tells me to breathe one more time I'm going to come completely unglued.

Do they not understand what I've done? Ratted out my own father, slept with a liar who never wanted me at all. No wonder Mark drank so much wine with dinner. Probably had to be half-drunk to stomach taking me to bed. I want these two interfering women to leave me alone in my disgrace.

Pray that neither of them will abandon me.

What have I done?

"Come on," Letticia orders, "you're going upstairs. You need a shower and bed."

She leads me from the bathroom, my hair stringy and vomit-tainted, my face bloodless, beaded with clammy repentance.

It's Hawk's pointy boots I see first. Hand-tooled alligator, the spread wings of his namesake disappearing up under his soft blue jeans. Letticia doesn't miss a step, hands me over like a doggie bag. She's all yours now, her attitude says. Her warm mouth kisses my forehead while Dad, Bubba, and Lefty sit like a posse at a hanging and watch Hawk lead me upstairs.

My throat is raw, I ache all over and, for some reason, my eyes pour tears like a little girl. I should push Hawk away, climb the stairs alone, and think through what I've done and how to fix it. But Hawk smells like the woods of home, his strong arm circles my waist, pulls me into his long lean frame. Just for a little while, a moment in the great long trail of life, I decide to surrender to my need to be sheltered, to allow this complicated man to care for me.

sixteen

STEAM, LIKE LIVING lattice on the glass door, creates the illusion of sanctuary. Leaning heavily against the molded plastic of the shower stall, my skin as red as a newborn's, I imagine the hot water cleansing me of my sins. Light from votive candles flicker, throw wavering shadows against the wall.

On the other side of the glass, Hawk's blurred image waits, an old white bath towel draped over his arm. The smell of the lavender soap Stacey gave me for my birthday mixes with the tar of my dandruff shampoo. A significant improvement over the previous odor of vomit. The lingering scent of shame, however, still hangs, pervasive, in the thick, sultry air.

Fifty gallons of hot water fail to cleanse me of my iniquities.

I turn off the cooling water. My voice is oddly supplicate.

"Wait in the other room. Please."

"You going to be okay in here?"

"I'm fine," I lie.

The bathroom door opens to expose a quick rectangle of darkness. Footfalls tap out a short rhythm, then light streams in along the door's open edge.

"I'm right here if you need me." His voice is a luxury to me. A sound I've ached to hear, soft tones and warm rhythms for which I've grieved.

I dry off, slip on my old yellow bathrobe, tie the frayed belt with a knot. In the five minutes it takes to brush and blow dry my hair, the shaking returns.

The oxidized mirror over the sink taunts me with a brief picture of a hollow-eyed, needy child. I blow out the candles and flee the image.

He sits in the wingback chair by the window, right foot propped over his left knee, looking so comfortable I wonder for a flash if he's been there all along. The month of his disappearance an illusion.

An inviting triangle of sheet is exposed where he's turned down the bed. Robe cinched tight, I slither under the covers, the sheets cold on my bare feet and legs.

"Can you turn out the light?"

The streetlight, haloed in fog, silhouettes him as he walks back across the room, sits on the edge of the bed. His hand on my cheek as he brushes back a loose strand of hair catches my breath in my throat, transmits an electric shimmer into my belly.

"I've missed you." His husky whisper a balm.

"Me too."

"So." Heavy sigh in the dark, deep breath drawn past soft lips. "While I was occupied being a fool and a drunken jackass, you went out with the writer?"

"What's going on with you and your newest little playmate?" It's a good counteroffensive, but it doesn't prevent my heart from chanting a hard rhythm of panic.

The bed grumbles as he shifts his weight away from me.

"I'd take that escapade back if I could, Sam. There's nothing I can do about it now. You have to decide if you can forgive me and go on."

I really hate this AA crap. All reasonable, psychologically sound blather which, as usual, puts the fate of the relationship squarely on my shoulders. I've missed this man so much and right now I just want to sucker punch him.

Wind off the dark bay shifts, rattles the window, cold tendrils seep around the sill. I shiver under the covers.

It would be so easy to flip open the blankets, invite him inside. We could warm each other, give temporary healing the way we've done since the night of my sixteenth birthday.

"I'm scared, Hawk. I can't keep taking you back. It's too hard. But when you're gone it's like a part of me is dead. I go on day to day, night after night. But it's not really me doing any of the things I do to get through the time until you're back."

"I'm here now, Baby."

He doesn't move, and yet the tension of his restraint shifts the atmosphere in the room. His struggle not to slip under the covers and lie beside me, to keep his hands resting on his knees and his feet planted firmly on the plank floor, is palpable.

"I messed up with Mark. Bad. I keep replaying what I said while I was with him. Trying to figure out if I told him anything he'll be able to use against our dads."

"Weird, huh?" He shakes his head. "A pile of logging slash purported to be bodies? The story of massacring a whole family of Bigfoots? Hard to believe anyone would believe either of our dads would have done such a thing."

Hard to believe anyone would get this excited about the imagined deaths of creatures of whose existence there is no proof.

"Please, let's not bring Bigfoot into bed with us."

An explosion of thunder seems to sway the loft on its foundations. Icy air insinuates itself along the trembling windows. The storm is moving in off the ocean. Bare under the robe, a shiver goose bumps my skin. I instinctively slide closer to where Hawk is sitting. The edge of the mattress, indented with his weight, rolls me further toward him. I have an image of water bubbling up from a mountain spring flowing naturally to its salty, fated destination.

Slow and smooth, with no hesitation, he stretches his long body on top the covers, gathers me against him. His woodsy, spicy scent puts into my head a moment in that giant hotel bed with the soft sheets when, in desperation to end the by then nearly boring process, I conjured up this very smell. Made one man disappear and this man take his place.

"I am so stupid! Believing him. Thinking he thought I was beautiful. I feel like an idiot."

"Whoa now." His voice rumbles in his chest, his breath tickles my ear. "The way I heard the story you, literally, skunked the guy but good." His fingers slip under the bulky sleeve of my robe, caress my wrist. "It's not like you slept with him."

He misunderstands the stiffening of my body, the way my hand stops its movement along his side.

"I'm not saying he didn't have that in mind. Sleeping with you. If you were that kind of woman, I'm sure he'd have been delighted."

An hour creeps past between one pulse beat and the next. Then my heart is hammering in my chest, desperate to feed my brain, help me sort out this mess.

"Who told you I went out with Mark?"

"Bubba."

"When did you talk to Bubba?"

Thunder rumbles in from off the bay. This may not be the best omen.

"He found me the day after you played bad tour guide at Grays Falls." Hawk's soft chuckle is a minor echo of the storm's voice. "The big guy was waiting for me after my Tuesday class and threatened to kick the shit out of me. Said I was the dumbest college-educated Indian on the face of the planet."

Hawk doesn't know I spent the night with Mark!

I don't have to tell him. It's none of his business really. I'd have never gone out with Mark in the first place if Hawk hadn't been off on one of his tears. He's the one who started the whole situation when he brought that rhinestone-assed skank here.

Just like that, the memory of his voice mingling with hers, the sound of the headboard hitting the wall, and I am flooded with pain and rage. In less than a second I go from feeling warm and protected, safe and happy, to angry enough to pound the living shit out of this man.

Pushing his hand away from my wrist, I twist sideways, scootch back to see his face.

"There was another date. After the skunk fiasco."

This man knows all my secrets. To keep this from him would alter our entire relationship, make me someone he doesn't really know. That's why I'm telling him. Mostly. If a tiny spark of jealous fury also ignites shavings of resentment, fans them with confession into a roaring fire of revenge, well so be it. Maybe I'm good and sick of being the virtuous one in this relationship.

seventeen

THE FLAT, BITING smell of stale beer mingles with the astringent odor of gin, both blending with the smoky scent of the Jack that is the preferred whisky at VD's. Two minutes after closing time and Stacey's already locked the doors.

"Slow night?" I pour myself a glass of orange juice and slip onto the barstool next to Bubba.

Stacey shrugs, doesn't stop her rough polishing of a beer glass.

At the other end of the bar, Lefty and Caroline are bent toward each other, foreheads almost touching, busy with the whisperings of early love.

Two hours ago Stacey ventured upstairs, knocked on my bedroom door, and asked if she could help. When I sent her away, Bubba's heavy steps soon pounded up the stairway.

He didn't bother with knocking, just stuck his shaggy head in.

"You want I should carry Hawk back here. Or... I'd be de-damn-lighted to thump on him till he comes to his senses."

After sending Bubba away, I was left to my misery.

Thirst has driven me downstairs. I sip my orange juice, lean my head on Bubba's solid shoulder.

"Dad already in bed?"

"Yup. Ain't nobody here but us chickens."

"Bye now," Caroline calls as Lefty walks her to the door. "I hope things work out for you, Samantha."

So, Lefty's filled her in on the gory details of my current mess. Hawk's fall from grace. My slut imitation with Mark, the man who, it turns out, is slandering my father. Tonight's charming scene that began with me throwing up and ended with Hawk disappearing into a cold rain. Again.

I don't want to think about how this all looks to an outsider. How on earth to explain the devastation to Dad's reputation of being accused of killing an entire family of the creature he's revered and sought his whole adult life. It's like claiming King Arthur found the Holy Grail, beat it into a hunk of gold, and sold it to the highest bidder.

I wave weakly to Caroline, grin a little as she and Lefty kiss goodnight, do my best not to look in the mirror over the bar. I did change into clean jeans and a soft sweatshirt before I came downstairs, but made the mistake of looking in the bathroom mirror when I brushed my hair.

"I'm out of here," Stacey informs me. She hands me a wet, relatively clean, bar towel stuffed with crushed ice. "Put that on your eyes. It'll take down the swelling from the crying."

My head against Bubba, the cold towel is already over my eyes when I hear the front door open, close, and then open again.

"And for the love of God, try and remember next time," Stacey's voice yells. "There's not a man in this world worth ruining yourself, swelling your damn eyes shut crying over."

The door slams shut. Two breaths later, it opens again. "And another thing," the same voice preaches, "you tell Hawk for me that he needs to have himself a little reality check. What's good for the gander is good for the goose is what my old Portuguese Meemaw always said."

I'm smiling when the door shuts and stays shut. It's pleasant here in the dark. Cool ministrations on my puffy eyes, Bubba's earthy, marijuana-tinged scent mixing with the boozy bar smells. I decide to just stay right here.

Crying for hours has left me drained, empty of sadness or hope or any emotion really. It occurs to me that this hollowed out sensation is a flipside of the way I feel after really good sex with Hawk. Both experiences render me completely relaxed. Except, instead of filled with contentment, this one has left me gutted.

Which is still better than the earlier pain.

A scratchy kiss on the forehead and Bubba's thick hand lifts the wet towel from my eyes. "Enough beatin' yourself up. Hawk's his own worst enemy. The man don't deserve you. I got me three baby sisters. Anybody treated any one of 'em like the way Hawk has done you? The law'd never find the body. I guaran-damn-tee that. As for Mark. Ain't nobody ever told you revenge is sweet?"

Lefty slips onto the stool next to mine. "Yeah. We got us a plan."

DAWN IS A shivering promise of steel gray behind the Kneeland Hills, the bay not yet touched by the sun's meager warmth, the bed sheets cold as I crawl between them. My body craves sleep but my mind insists on racing in ever-tightening circles, searching out flaws in our trap for Mark. It's a good plan. Yet a niggling worm of doubt insists on warning me we are forgetting something, some unseen variable that is going to take this payback to a level we are not anticipating.

My part in the plan is the simplest and the most difficult. I have only to greet Mark as though we pack of rednecks are so out of touch that not a one of us has laid a finger to a keyboard and googled him. I have to pretend to feel about him today the exact way I felt about him yesterday.

My goal is to mimic the way I thought about the world eight hours ago, when I was beginning to believe that I was pretty or funny or smart enough to be attractive to a man like him. My mission is to duplicate my response when I had almost forgotten that lost little girl too ugly or stupid or ungainly for her mama to love, back when I trusted, if not my heart, well then at least my body, to a man who moves in sophisticated circles with people who eat in restaurants with linen-covered tables, heavy silverware, and grossly expensive wines. A man who thinks nothing of lying to a woman in order to get her into bed or to extract information from her. A man who has more in common with the whoremonger than with the whore.

The timer-controlled streetlight on the corner shuts off. My world instantly drops into the luminous pearly gray that is late summer's dawn in Humboldt County. I pull a second pillow under my head, prop myself high enough to watch as the weak light of dawn turns the fog-obscured bay into a wonderland. Like spirits rising from the water's surface, the fog lifts, dissipates, becomes a part of the clear morning air. Local weather patterns demand that this clarity will last less than fifteen minutes. Then the low-hanging clouds will block the path of the sun's warmth. The thick mist will settle, once again, hover over the dark surface of the bay until sunset, when the phantoms will vanish to allow another few minutes of startling brightness.

I close my eyes to a kaleidoscopic maze of light on shimmering, bottle green water.

Open them to a silvery veil of rain pouring from the eaves, dense fog pressing at the windows. I'm lying in the same position in which I fell asleep. My hand still wedged between the pillows, facing the now invisible bay. I closed my eyes with angry thoughts of Mark romping through my brain. But my first thought at waking is of Hawk.

There is that moment of blissful ignorance, when my sleep-fogged mind has forgotten what happened here, his body stretched the length of mine in this bed, when I told him I had slept with Mark. At each waking breath, the memory of Hawk's words, like embedded shards of glass, work their way, ever more deeply, into my core.

"You were the only person in the world I really trusted." he said. "I can't believe you ruined that."

Even as the pain swells, crescendos into hot tears, I clothe my feelings in anger. Stacey's right. Who does he think he is? He's allowed to break trust with me again and again over the years? It's permissible for him to panic and to pull back, strike out every single time we get to a comfortable intimacy? But I'm supposed to be the good-hearted, all-suffering woman?

Fuck that!

I throw off the covers, stumble to the space heater, and crank it up.

"Do *not* think about Hawk!" I order myself, speaking aloud in the hope the thought will penetrate through my ears and into my dulled brain.

Today is about Mark.

Tonight is about revenge.

In the bathroom, I push the High switch on the wall heater and turn on the shower so it can warm while I pee.

The room already steamy, I step into the shower stall and flash right back to last night, when Hawk was a misty presence on the other side of the glass door. *No!* No thinking about him. Ignoring Stacey's fancy liquid lavender soap, I scrub myself with an old washcloth and a chipped bar of Dial, scratch at my scalp with industrial-strength dandruff shampoo until I half expect to come away with blood under my nails.

Mark will be here in less than an hour. Enclosed in steam, scrubbed raw, I do my best to channel the spirit of my Aunt Mandy.

Oh legendary family whore, help me now in my hour of need, instruct me on how to hide my anger and convincingly fake happiness when I next see Mark—that lying cheat of a man.

eighteen

THE HOME TEAM is all here. Waiting on the visitor. Dad and David are at their usual table in the back, Bubba and Lefty are snugged up to the bar. Stacey, who isn't even scheduled to work this morning, has come in to polish spotless glasses, refold bar towels, and rearrange bottles.

I've unlocked the front door. The guys and I have reviewed the plan. We're as ready for Mark as we're ever going to be. I hope to God this knot in my stomach is just anxiety about being able to play my part, coupled with lack of sleep. It feels more like that black shadow I occasionally feel rushing toward me on a hike deep in the forest. A premonition of impending danger I've always before heeded, veering from my desired trail and allowing intuition to guide me on a path different from the one I first chose.

Mark's entrance brings a chill to the room that isn't entirely attributable to the wet, cold wind and morning mist that gusts in from the street.

Flowers, lilies again, in shades from cream to pale orange, deep yellow rosebuds, everything surrounded by a nebula of baby's breath. He holds the offering close to his chest. To accept this token of treachery I'm forced to step close, lean in, pretend to welcome a kiss.

Citrus mixes with the smell of flowers. His mouth is soft and warm, his whisper tickles my ear just before I draw away.

"All the way here I cautioned myself that you could not be as beautiful as I remembered."

I have secured possession of the bouquet, but doing so frees both his hands, which he uses to gently grip my forearms, pulling me into his embrace and mushing the flowers between us. Breath intimate on my neck, his voice warm in my ear.

"Now I'm standing here and you're even lovelier."

My stomach roils. I suppose throwing up on his shoes would blow my cover.

"Let me put these in water." My smile is stiff, but it's in place.

I step away from him, hope he'll attribute my uneasiness to our audience.

"How was your drive up?" Dad asks. "That slide there at Confusion Hill cleared yet?"

Mark shifts from foot to foot, clears his throat daintily, finds his voice to answer. "Highway 101 was reduced to one lane with traffic congested nearly to Willits."

The city boy can't seem to make up his mind where to light. He starts back toward Dad and David, seems pushed backward by the force field of anger coming from that direction, looks toward Bubba's broad back, Lefty's skinny butt on their bar stools. He removes a handkerchief from his pressed cargo pants, wipes his hands, shuffles his loafers, finally widens his stance, settles manicured hands deep in his pockets. To me he looks like a guilty man bracing for a blow.

My team are horrible actors.

"Thank you for the flowers," I trill, plop the romantic bouquet into an empty five-gallon dill pickle jar.

"Won't be nothing left but dead blooms by the time you get yourselves back from the mountains," Bubba rumbles.

I'd kick the big galoot if I could reach him. This is his idea of pretending we're delighted to see the man before we wreak havoc on his traitorous soul?

Catching my glare, Bubba licks his lips, directs his question to Mark.

"So, y'all set for this here gallivant into the great Pacific Northwest?"

Mark rocks back on his heels, catches Bubba's eye in the mirror.

"I purchased hiking boots for the adventure. Samantha warned me that we'd be doing some walking. 'Mud crawling' I believe were her actual words."

New boots! He'll be hobbling on wet blisters before nightfall.

Lefty swivels on the stool, plasters a stiff, lopsided grin on his face.

"How's the book going?"

Mark evidently takes this obvious sarcasm as honest inquiry.

"My publisher is pleased. I believe we've found a way to update the story, add a touch of the absurd, open its appeal to a wider audience."

Is this guy for real? Every molecule in my body aches to throw myself at this lying intruder and kick some respect into the clueless bastard. Eye contact with Bubba makes me hesitate. His subtle head shake slows me further. But it's his firm hold on my wrist that actually arrests my attack.

"You'll have to tell me all about it on the drive inland," I say, hoping he takes my growl for a purr. I keep my head down, know if he sees my eyes, the gig's up. "We're going in the F-150. It's all rigged for hauling our gear. Dad and David are heading out this afternoon, too. But, like always, those two are heading into undisclosed areas."

"Ah, yeah," Dad says. "You need to get on the road real soon here if you're planning on making Bluff Creek by nightfall. And Sam, I need a word with you before you leave."

"Mark." My mouth is stuck in that grimace I hope passes for a smile. "You want to run upstairs and change into your hiking clothes while I talk a minute with Dad?"

My voice remains an octave above normal, but hopefully the man's ego will translate this as uncontrollable glee at his return.

"I'm ready to go." Mark shrugs. "With the exception of my new boots. I'll just wait to put them on until we get there." He grins, blinds us with those whitened teeth. "They're a little tight, haven't stretched to conform to my feet just yet. No sense wearing them any longer than necessary."

"Holy crap!" Stacey says, eyeing his flawlessly pressed cargo pants and button-down shirt. "You done a good bit of camping? Hiking in the woods? Stepping off the pavement?"

Mark smiles good-naturedly.

"Well. No. But I run marathons, play racquetball at the club four days a week, and I'm an avid swimmer."

"Damn," says Stacey, "I am getting more and more disappointed I won't be going on this hiking trip."

I open my mouth to explain to Mark that he's going to need layers of clothing. Long underwear, sweatshirts over T-shirts, extra socks, and a water-repellent jacket, hat, gloves. Moleskin would be a nice addition to his pack also.

Bubba cuts me off. "Sounds like you're good to go." He smiles wickedly at Mark. "Your pack in your car?"

"It is, yes. A friend of mine knows an engineer who designs backpacks. I had him custom-make this one. He modeled it after the Marmot Eiger sixty-five, though this one would be more like a one twenty-five. This beauty is fully stocked with all the necessities. Folding propane stove with extra tanks. Cookware which fits inside itself—like a utilitarian Russian doll. Globalstar satellite phone. There's even a battery-operated coffee grinder and a pound of Starbucks."

While he's reciting this ridiculous list that falls under the category of "unnecessary things that weigh you down when you have to strap them to your back and carry them up and down mountains and through stream beds," I motion for Dad to step out back with me.

Oscar and John are across Second Street, hunkered down in the overhang of the Salvation Army drop-off. I flip up the hood of my sweatshirt and wave. John's awake, steaming coffee from a Styrofoam Ramone's cup fogging his face. He snaps off a smart military salute. I assume the lumpy heap in a ratty blue sleeping bag behind him is Oscar, still asleep.

Morning drizzle has wet my hoodie when Dad comes through the back door.

"You sure you don't want to wait a day or two for this to clear before you head into the woods?" I take my hands from the front pouch of the sweatshirt, wave them through the wet air.

"This here?" Dad slips his arm around my waist. "This is Humboldt sunshine, that's what this is. 'Sides, it's not me you should be nervous about."

"I'm going into the woods with a city slicker who'll be crippled before we've hiked two miles. I've got my thirty-eight, Bubba and Lefty will be right behind us and, most important, we got us a plan."

"That last part is what concerns me. You sure you won't change your mind and tell me what you three are up to?"

The smell of coffee seems to have roused Oscar. He's sitting up, still inside the patchy warmth of the sleeping bag. It looks like he's doing his best to persuade John to share the Ramone's bounty.

"I tell you what," I say, "you let me know where you're going. Not this within-a-hundred-mile-radius crap, but exactly where you intend to be camping. You do that and I'll fill you in on all the dirty details of the great plot for revenge."

Dad kisses the top of my head. "I got no idea where you got your stubborn streak."

"Ah, yeah. Big mystery. At least promise me that if this storm makes it over the mountains, you'll hole up somewhere. Stay dry until this passes."

"I'm not a child, Samantha Jean. Been doing this since long before you were born, remember?"

"But this time there's some lunatic out there who thinks you killed a family of Bigfoots. You give that letter to Bobby Barellis?"

"Spoke with your pal at the District Attorney's office yesterday. Not much they can do."

"I talked to Bobby yesterday, Dad. He said he advised you to stay put until they find out who this nut case is."

"He also mention there's not a snowball's chance in hell of ever finding the guy?"

His cheek is scratchy when I kiss him good-bye. The cold brass of the doorknob is in my hand when I hear him call over his shoulder, like an incantation thrown into the mist, "I love you Sam. You don't ever want to forget that."

I let the door swing shut, turn toward him.

"I never do," I say to the gray outline of his back before squaring my shoulders and walking inside like my fate is in my own hands.

My pack is ready. It's always ready. The same way I clean my Colt after each and every firing, the small pack I have carried since I was twelve is cleaned and repacked within hours of returning from each and every hiking trip. I pick it up, sling it over my shoulder.

"No kidding? Even got you a GPS?" David asks when I link my arm through Mark's and lead him out the door and into the first stage of his comeuppance.

The F-150 is parked in the side lot. Mark drives his Infiniti next to the truck and we off-load the biggest damn pack I've ever seen in my life. Got to be well over a hundred pounds of expensive and high-tech trash tucked into dozens of side pockets and inner hidden slots. He hefts the monstrosity into the top-loading freezer I have bolted into the bed of the truck.

"A freezer?" Mark asks, "You use an old rusty freezer as a lockbox?"

Sure. That's what's wrong with this picture. The inventive recycling of a defunct freezer, not a pack as big as a bear he thinks he's going to be able to schlep up one side of a mountain and down another.

My jaw hurts with the grinding of my teeth.

"We need to lighten this pack a little. No way you're going to be able to carry this much weight over the ground we're going to be covering."

"You're okay with your girl-pack there," he says, cutting his eyes to my twenty-eight pound, faded yellow Northface. "But Samantha, we're going to need more gear than that. Honey, I work out, bench press two twenty-five. Three mornings a week. I don't think it's going to be a struggle for me to carry this lesser weight a few miles in a special ergonomically-correct backpack."

The first genuine smile of the day spreads across my face.

"Okey dokey, then. Let's head out."

nineteen

BETWEEN EUREKA AND Arcata, where Highway 101 skirts the edge of Humboldt Bay, thick, pewter-tinted mist becomes heavy drizzle. Wind slams in off the choppy water buffeting the F-150. In less than a minute, rain limits my visibility to under ten feet.

"Reach under your seat," I instruct Mark. "Grab that piece of oil cloth. See those screw heads along the top of your door over there? There's holes in the cloth they fit into."

The windows in his Infiniti go all the way up to hermetically seal him inside the wood and leather interior. He stares at me as though I've created this storm for the sole purpose of annoying him.

"Maybe it would be prudent to return to the bar, leave this… vehicle… and make this trip in my car."

His voice seems a little tight. Could be he's already grown tired of the loose spring on the passenger seat. That lime-green Gore-Tex jacket of his is getting a good test. I assume it's wicking away the rain blowing in through the slice of passenger window open to the good clean air.

"That luxury car of yours isn't any good to us once we get off the highway. Jeez, don't be such a baby. I'm the one on the bay side of the truck. All you're getting is a teensy bit of runoff."

He unzips the collar of his jacket, extracts the folded hood and pulls it up around his face. The oilcloth he drapes over his right shoulder. "If I cover the window, you'll be unable to see out of your side mirror."

I roll my eyes but keep my mouth shut.

Apparently I'm not very good at this pretending to be happy to spend time with a man I'd really prefer to toss in the bay.

Aunt Mandy, Queen of Faking It, pray for me.

Across the highway, under the leaning barn that at one time housed the contented cows of Humboldt Creamery, there are now llamas. Owned by old hippies who wandered up this way in the sixties and never left, these wooly critters are dyed the colors of Easter eggs and clipped like poodles. On the rare sunny day, the little pastel flock can be seen grazing happily while tourists slam on their brakes, endangering the lives of anyone on the highway behind them.

This morning, buffeted by wind, encased in thick fog, I can't even see the dilapidated barn. I'm imagining the entire peculiar little group of split-hoofed animals happily chewing their cud under the shelter of the ancient building when a gust of wind, like a solid object, crashes against the truck. The Ford skitters sideways, crosses the white line into the passing lane before I can correct and bring it back into the left lane.

"Are you angry with me?" Mark demands from his soggy side of the truck.

Uh-oh.

"Course not. Why would you think that?"

"For openers, you appear to be doing your best to kill us. What would I have to do to get you slow down?"

"You think I'm driving too fast?"

"I believe, given the condition of our means of conveyance, coupled with the fact that we're in the midst of gale-force winds. Yes. You are driving at an excessive rate of speed."

I look across the truck at his pale face, can't keep an evil grin from spreading across mine. It could be I am a bit heavy-footed. The speedometer hasn't worked since two summers ago when I tore the cable crossing Bear Creek. In my defense, the undercarriage-busting attack-rock was completely hidden by the rising water. So while I can't say for sure how fast I'm going, the truck is merely doing a good shimmy, not yet shaking the fillings from my molars.

Still, I am supposed to be feigning adoration for this man, not acting as though I'd like nothing better than to smear him all over the wet asphalt. I ease off the accelerator, allow a Toyota Prius to pass me. What more can I do to fake a show of concern for his feelings?

It's hard to concentrate on making nice when I know Dad's going to be driving through this same coastal storm in just a few hours. In a broadsided 1983 Ford L series delivery truck with over 400,000 miles on the odometer. Something is going on with him. He and David both have been as secretive as schoolgirls lately. Of course my stupidity in sleeping with the man who betrayed their trust and friendship by publicly accusing them of murder, well, no way that is helping whatever complicated situation the two of them are enmeshed in.

At the junction from Highway 101 onto 299, we turn east, away from the driving force of the storm, and climb up into the mountains. The existence of the little town of Blue Lake, off to our left, I take on faith. The rain has let up but fog hangs thick as smoke. The F-150's headlights bounce off the heavy translucence, reflect their beams back at me, shorten my visibility still further. The defroster transitions from making a sound like a diesel truck up into the roar of a jet on takeoff. If we don't drive out of this storm by Lord Ellis at the crest of the first coastal foothill, I'll have to pull over and let the truck cool off.

Next to me, Mark shifts, touches my thigh. His hand is warm against my damp jeans.

"Was that our first fight?" he asks.

There's no mistaking the teasing in his voice. Sure. Let's call it our first fight.

When I don't answer, he digs around in the pocket of his jacket and drops a gold foil-wrapped box with Godiva spelled out in cursive on the top.

"I may need to pull over and let the truck cool down," I say, ignoring the beguiling little box between us.

"Good," he says. "We can make up while the engine cools."

Fat chance.

Halfway up Lord Ellis, the fog thins. I'm celebrating this miracle when the back end of a Chevy Trailblazer with no brake lights rises out of the silvered mist and forces me to pump the brakes while uttering a string of unladylike curses.

"Sorry." I swing around the Trailblazer. "My redneck is showing."

Mark's laughter catches me off guard, slips in under the door of my anger. At the crest of the mountain, I pull into the scenic overlook parking lot. When I turn the ignition off, the engine takes a half minute to register that it can quit. The air is heavy with the tang of pine mixed with the gin smell of juniper. My finger taps a staccato rhythm on the top of the gold-foil box between us. Candy and flowers. He's trying just a tad too hard, isn't he?

I remove the fancy gold paper to reveal four golf-ball-sized truffles. All dark chocolate, which I do not like, and all sprinkled with powdered nuts. God, what was I thinking, sleeping with this man? We know nothing about each other. Hell, I didn't know until yesterday that he's a lying, conniving bastard.

"Yeah. Thanks, but I'm allergic to nuts. Nice thought, though."

He looks crestfallen. "I'm sorry. I didn't know you had a nut allergy."

"No way you could have known. It didn't come up in conversation on our skunk picnic or on our Humboldt House fling."

"Fling?" The pupils of his moss-green eyes expand, the muscles along his mouth tighten just a hair. "You think that night was a fling?"

"What do you call it?"

Jesus, this is like walking in a minefield. There ought to be little white warning flags fluttering in my peripheral vision every minute I'm with this man. I look down, concentrate on the open box of truffles in my lap. Better not to let him see my eyes.

"I thought it was the beginning of our getting to know each other, Sam. I was hoping we'd be doing more of that. Becoming better acquainted."

All I've got to do to keep from giving away the whole plan is to keep my big mouth shut. Dad, David, Letticia, hell even Lefty, told me before I left this morning just to smile, look good, and keep my mouth shut. There's a reason all these people keep repeating the same instructions to me. I do not have a history of being the quiet type.

"Who the hell are you?" The family gene bestowing the ability to smile sweetly and lie through our teeth must have died out with Aunt Mandy.

The guardrail at the edge of the parking lot, preventing a thousand-foot drop into Redwood Creek, is just visible. Its shiny surface, slick with moisture, is a wavering line of darker silver in the midst of the thinning fog.

Mark blows air through his nose. He takes the candy from my lap, folds the crisp white tissue paper with its elegant cursive "G" over the rejected offering, gently replaces the lid.

"You saw the blog." It's a statement.

My voice is shrill, echoes in the cab of the truck, bounces around like a wounded bird.

"You prance into my world, sweet talk me like I'm some kind of gullible idiot. And all the time…." My volume keeps increasing of its own accord, spurred by a frantic beating of wings in my chest. "The whole fucking time! You're lying about my dad. Making up nonsense to slander him, to make him out to be some bloodthirsty monster. When you know damn good and well he's the gentlest man in the world! So, yeah, that's what I want to know! Who the hell are you?"

"Look at me Samantha. You need to calm down. The direction that blog took wasn't my idea. You've got to understand how publishing works. It was my publisher who focused on the idea that your dad and David killed a family of Bigfoots."

My anger is too big for the confines of the truck. I pull the handle, slam my shoulder against the door, step out into the crisp smell of wet evergreen needles and rotting underbrush. Three steps toward the overlook I turn, stomp back and yell into the cab.

"No! No! I don't have to understand a thing. You! You have to understand that you have been identified as a goddamn liar. That's what you have to understand!"

The sound of a city shoulder hitting the stuck passenger door, followed by some fine cussing, follows me out into the fog. I'm at the far side of the parking lot, one foot on the slick rail at the overhang, when the truck door creaks open. In front of me, like a striptease, the higher mountain across the canyon divide slowly reveals itself. Wisps of fog surrender to the sun's heat, lace the green forest with shifting, shadowy swirls of sheerest silk.

"I was afraid you'd see that misguided blog before I could explain."

He's to my left, and about ten feet behind me. Cleverly he's positioned himself out of range for me to toss him over the rail, sending his lying body crashing through manzanita and poison oak into the creek below.

"Look, Sam. I'm sorry. I don't know what else to say. We came into possession of the original film, the footage Patterson showed around the country."

"That isn't the original film, but do go on. I'm dying to hear your warped version of how my dad has been falsely accused and, by the way, put in real danger."

A crow joins the argument, his raucous voice cutting through the cold wet air. The bird is somewhere in the fog-wrapped top branches of the Doug fir off to our right.

"How has your dad been endangered?"

His voice is low, evenly modulated. Mine is loud, pitched high, disturbs the wildlife.

"A bunch of guys came into the bar. One jackass took a swing at Dad. This is after reading the mess stirred up by your blog. Yours! The one with your face grinning like a hyena on the first page. There've been death threats over the phone and some idiot even pasted newspaper letters onto the back of a postcard of Patty, tied it to a brick, and tossed it through Dad's bedroom window."

The shiny black crow hops out of the foggy top of the fir, perches on a lower branch, gives me hell for disturbing the peace and quiet of his little world.

Again with that calm reasoned voice. "When I found that frame, the one with your dad and David and the dogs, it seemed out of place. No one had ever mentioned anyone else being there when Patterson shot that footage. The figures were in the far corner of one frame. They had never been found because the people who evaluated that film looked only at the few seconds that Patterson shot at Bluff Creek. The frames with whatever it was—Bob Hieronimus in a monkey suit would be my guess—those were the only frames previously studied."

My voice actually seems to lift the crow off his needled perch.

"That's because that's all the footage Patterson shot. The rest was edited onto the beginning. Over a hundred-thousand people around the country paid to see that film. The promoters wanted just a tad more to give those folks. They were looking to create some suspense, give the honest people in thirty-three states a little something for their money. What was edited into the beginning of the film has nothing to do with the sighting, has no relevance to the truth of the original footage of Patty."

Mark takes two steps toward me. Still out of reach, but coming into range. He really doesn't know me at all.

A black Nissan Frontier, its side panels streaked with red mud, pulls into the parking lot. The driver leaves the motor running, the heater blasting, while he rolls a joint, doesn't open his window until he draws the first hit. The sweet skunky smell of bud turns Mark's head. He stares at the driver in the A's cap. The guy holds the smoke deep, throws us a friendly wave.

"I feel as though I've stepped into another dimension," Mark says, shaking his head. "Every time I cross that Humboldt County line and pass through the redwood curtain. Wet flannel and faded denim. Fog and rain. Jesus, does it ever stop? People who honest-to-god believe that some mythical creature is roaming the woods, passing from one dimension to another. Have faith strong enough to engage in fistfights, become genuinely irate about the notion that forty years in the past, somebody was in the woods with blood on their hands. Samantha. Do you not see how ridiculous this whole thing is? It's akin to accusing someone of killing the Easter Bunny."

I step toward him with enough energy that he braces himself for the blow I ache to give. The crow gives one last croak of disgust before flying across the canyon and disappearing into the sun-dazzled green of the mountaintop.

"No," I say. "It's like accusing a priest of killing the biological child of Jesus. You come up here, into a world about which, as you say, you know squat. You pretend genuine interest in a local phenomenon. You blatantly lie to me. To my dad and to David. You claim to be seeking the truth, when all you're really after is a few bucks and your fifteen minutes of fame. You have started a holy war, is what you've done."

My fury sprays his face with a drop or two of spittle. He doesn't wipe it off. Arms hang loosely at his sides, his hands open, relaxed, his voice as calm as the surface of the bay at dawn.

"I did not lie to you."

The headlights of a bronze Crew Cab Ram blink once as it passes behind Mark's back on Highway 299. A cage big enough to hold a small bear is strapped in the bed, mournful doggie eyes stare out at me through the heavy mesh. Two men in the cab. But wait now. Is there someone in the back seat? That better not be a feather! So help me God if those two went behind my back and brought Hawk they're going to wish they'd run into the real Bigfoot before I'm through with them.

My stomach rises into my throat. I turn, walk quickly to the cliff's edge, lean at the waist and lose my breakfast over the rail. Evidently I don't handle stress as well as I used to. I've been pukey and tired and cranky practically since this whole stupid thing with Mark started. In the corner of my eye a white fluttering hanky appears. Probably made from cotton woven by Egyptian virgins. I blow my nose, wipe my mouth.

"I'm sorry to have caused you pain, Samantha. I know you don't believe me, but it was never my intent to hurt you or anyone else. It was a mistake to allow my publisher to post that blog. I see that now and I apologize. The idea seemed different when it was proposed over grilled salmon and arugula in the Napa valley than it does now, catching a contact high on this overhang on the cusp between Humboldt and Trinity County."

The sun warms my back, my throat is a little raw but otherwise I feel cleansed, almost believe him. Worse, I want to forgive him. This impulse is just the natural reaction to seeing the sun for the first time in a month. Couldn't be anything but solar-powered benevolence.

He refuses his kitten-soft hanky when I offer it back, smiles sadly.

"Maybe we should call it a day, Samantha. Head back to the coast. I'll hire a guide to transport me to Bluff Creek."

I turn away from him. Redwood Creek is hidden from sight, lies at the bottom of this verdant canyon studded with the exposed pink of bedrock granite. Across the chasm stretches thousands of acres of lush temperate rainforest, wilderness that cares not one whit about the decision I make.

"The worst part is behind us," I say, even as a not-so-tiny voice whispers that I can go to hell for lying as well as for stealing. "Let's get you into Bigfoot Country."

twenty

AT WILLOW CREEK, I turn into the heart of the mountains. The road narrows as the two-lane winds and twists its way through deep chasms, narrow passes, and along drought-yellowed saddlebacks. Steep, verdant mountains block the sun. A ragged slice of exposed sky directly overhead is cloudless and blue. I roll my window down a few inches, breathe deeply of the crisp air, the green tang of fir mixing with the primordial scent of fallen foliage, fecund and ripe with rebirth.

The Eureka Garbage Company is blaring from a boom box on the seat between my hip and Mark's. The lead singer's raspy voice screams something indecipherable through the tinny speakers. The CD ends.

I hit eject, take a few minutes to enjoy the silence before asking, "Did you interview this guy?"

Mark looks shell-shocked. He's been staring out the passenger window for the length of the CD. Good deal. Gave me time to regroup.

"What guy?" he asks.

"Josh Clark. The guitarist we've been listening to since we topped Lord Ellis Mountain."

His forehead wrinkles. "I'm lost here, Samantha." His frown crinkles the corners of those amazing mossy-green eyes. "Why would I interview a guitarist in a local band?"

"Because Josh and his brothers are the grandsons of the man who made the area's first Bigfoot sighting. Fritz Brockmueller. He and his Indian partner, Bud Ryerson, are the guys that were building a logging road along Blue Mountain. Back in 'fifty-seven. They were camped just east of the construction site, heard what Fritz described as 'ungodly noises' coming from the area where they had their Cat and grader. You didn't look into this when you did your research? First newspaper account of a Bigfoot in the local *Times-Standard*?"

"The only name I found connected with the reported incident was Bud Ryerson. The newspaper didn't mention Fritz… what was it again?"

"Brockmueller. This whole area weaves in, around, and through the Hoopa and Yurok Reservations. The way it worked back then is that white men partnered with Indians in order to wild cat all through here. Small logging operations."

The sun crests the mountain. From pleasantly cool, the temperature in the cab rises to suffocating heat before I can get my window cranked all the way down. I'm pulling my hair back out of my face, searching the ashtray for a scrunchy, steering with my knees, when we come up on a hairpin turn that requires me to shift from third down into first. Scrunchy in my mouth, I downshift. When we pull out of the turn my hair is secured in a high ponytail and I shift back up into second in preparation for the upcoming bend in the road.

I hum Gretchen Wilson's "Redneck Woman," my arm resting on the window sill when I notice Mark's face.

"What's the matter?" I ask.

"Just contemplating my chances of surviving this trip."

My heart seizes up a little. He can't possibly suspect anything. Can he?

"Don't know what you mean." Denial. That's my best option.

"I'm just hoping you don't plunge us both down an embankment before I make it back to my own car."

Ah. My driving. Again.

"Oh. Sorry. I had to get my hair out of my face."

"You didn't kill us and, on the bright side, this is the most I've prayed in years."

This prank would be easier to pull off if he wasn't so good at pretending to enjoy my company. Or if he were ugly. Ugly would help. Or if he didn't have that streaked, butterscotch hair and those warm, green eyes. Well, the devil comes in many disguises, that's the thing to remember.

"Ah, yeah. So, tell me what your research told you about Ryerson's 'fifty-seven sighting on Blue Mountain Road?"

"Back to business? Just when we were starting to make nice?" His dreamy smile, the way his left eyebrow cocks up just a tad, reminds me of our night at The Humboldt House. Bad thought! Look away from the dreamy man. The lying, scheming, but, God help me, dreamy man.

I glare across the bench seat, remind myself of Dad's startled face when that kid in the bar took a swing at his grizzled chin.

"You are laboring under the false assumption that just because we're continuing this little adventure, I have forgiven you for slandering and endangering my dad."

There, that ought to let him know where he stands without mucking up the plan.

His soft mouth turns up at the corners. Why are his eyelashes thicker than my own? Stop this! Don't look at him.

"All right. I capitulate." He takes a small notebook from an inside pocket of his jacket, unclips a fountain pen. "The topic is the area's first recorded sighting of Bigfoot. Ryerson is the name that appears in all the reports, but you say there was another man there too?"

"Brockmueller. Fritz Brockmueller. Grandfather of Josh Clark, who still lives in Humboldt County."

He writes something down. "This is a sighting that produced casts? Right?"

"That's right. Dozens of footprints were found. A lot of different sizes, too. Like a group or family of Bigfoots had milled around the area. Dad and David have several of those casts." My orneriness will not stay down. "Probably both men would've been happy to show them to you if you hadn't accused them publicly of murder."

"Again. I can only apologize and reiterate that the blog was my publisher's idea."

"And yet it's your face and name on that blog. I guess things work a lot different in the city than they do in the country."

This is good. Just talking about the blog, remembering that idiotic cartoon image of Dad raising his rifle again and again—the Bigfoot, Patty, looking over her shoulder as he aims—keeps me in touch with my anger.

In an unfortunate side-effect of getting in touch with my inner rage, I press a teensy bit too hard on the accelerator. The truck slips coming out of a turn, does a small fishtail. I momentarily gain a good view of the gorge with the sun glinting off the river far, far below. Okay. Fine line here between justifiable anger and killing us both.

Let's just pretend that never happened. Good time to finish my story.

"Yeah. Ryerson and Brockmueller were building a logging road. They'd set up camp a few hundred yards from where they left the heavy equipment. Heard all this commotion in the night, grabbed flashlights and rifles, and ran down the road toward the site.

"Brockmueller is who I heard tell this story. Years ago. When I was just a kid. 'Course, the whole deal had happened years before, but even after all that time, there wasn't any mistaking the man's fear. When the two men got closer to their machinery, Brockmueller said a smell like skunk cabbage mixed with rancid meat stopped them in their tracks.

"Mister Brockmueller was an old man when I met him. He'd had one leg amputated by then, was in a wheelchair, age-spotted, and nearly bald. But when he got to this part of the story, I watched, with my own eyes, the hairs on his skinny-old-man arms stand straight up. His whole stooped body shivered like a goose had walked over his grave."

"Where'd you talk to him? Is he some kind of relative?"

"Not blood kin. No. But do you not, even now, understand that all true, washed-in-the-blood believers are one big squabbling family?"

The crushed gravel ends abruptly and the truck bounces over packed dirt. The guardrail along the cliff edge on the passenger side of the road disappears. We're coming into Indian country.

"Jesus!"

Could be he's praying out loud now.

I slow some as the tires slip on the last of the loose gravel.

"The old guy died in Grenada Convalescent Home," I say. "Dad used to go and get him sometimes. Bring him back to VD's. He drank Evan Williams. Straight. No back."

"Not to anger you Samantha, because God knows that is not my intent, but has it occurred to you that Mister Brockmueller fabricated stories in order to escape the nursing home for the day?"

I grin over at him.

"Damn. You *are* cynical. And, to answer your question, I always look for motive. But Brockmueller and Ryerson reported this when it was downright dangerous to their reputations to do so. In fact, that's one of the reasons you won't find Brockmueller's name in any of the old references to the encounter. Ryerson was about one-sixteenth Yurok. To the Indians he was a white man, but he had enough native blood that he couldn't keep it to himself when The Old Man of the Forest came to visit."

In the rocky gorge below, the Trinity River is a glistening green serpent. We're slip-sliding our way deeper into the V between two mountains.

Mark looks up from his notepad.

"Continue?"

He nods, sums up my narrative. "They race down the road to where they have abandoned their heavy equipment for the night and are, supposedly, assailed by a rancid smell."

He's looking down at his lined tablet, sketching a series of tiny footprints. My glare at his use of the word *supposedly* slides unnoticed down the side of his tanning-salon browned face.

"It was confusing for Brockmueller and Ryerson." I turn back to the road. "As you can imagine. It's pitch dark. Middle-of-the-forest-on-a-moonless-night dark. There are these crashing sounds. Grunts and squeals and deep bellows. The suffocating, dense smell of rotting death. Ryerson said it sounded like a dozen or so bears on a rampage. Brockmueller told Dad he kept praying it was bears, but his gut was screaming for him to get to hell out of there before whatever it was turned its attention to them.

"The two men ran. You won't find that in any written record. But Brockmueller said that's just what he and Ryerson did. Ran back down the newly-made road a quarter mile. Locked themselves in the cab of their GMC truck. Spent a sleepless night. At dawn they made their way back to their equipment."

Our road goes downhill more steeply now. The back tires lose traction coming around a right turn. No good pumping the brakes. I turn into the skid. The F-150's nose stops a few feet from the solid wall of granite on the opposite side of the road. Reverse is sticky and it takes me a few seconds to get turned around and moving in the right direction again.

I steal a look at Mark. He's a little pale, and his mouth is pressed into a thin line, but he's scribbling in his notepad, keeping his mouth shut.

"Sorry," I lie. "I wasn't going all that fast."

"Please, continue distracting me from near certain death with this rendition of the tale."

"True story. But okay. When the two of them got to where they'd left their grader and Caterpillar tractor, they found a real mess. The seat of the grader had been ripped from its base. Remember now, a grader is a huge piece of equipment. There were skid marks in the raw dirt from where the bobcat tractor had been pushed sideways. Fifty-five-gallon barrels of diesel scattered over a quarter mile. The place looked like a cyclone had hit it. All this destruction overlaid with dozens of these giant footprints. All different sizes, but all big. Too big to be human or bear."

Still filling in the margins of his paper with tiny feet, he interrupts. "Are there pictures, photos of any of this?"

"No. Even Bob Titmus didn't think to bring a camera the next day."

"Titmus?"

"A local guy. He'd been talking to the Yurok for years about this giant hairy creature they encountered regularly in the woods around these parts. Bob had come up with a way of taking plaster casts of the prints. Had a good-sized collection of Bigfoot imprints by then. Ryerson knew Titmus. When he saw a dozen or so huge footprints in the middle of all this damage to his equipment, well, Ryerson and Brockmueller hightailed it into Willow Creek and reported everything to Titmus."

"I researched him." He squints out the windshield into the sun, refuses to look at me. "Detractors claim it was him that perpetrated most of the Bigfoot hoaxes in this area."

I slow the truck to a near stop as we swing through a section of the hard-packed dirt that is cantilevered out over the canyon. Heavy rains wash out this patch of road almost every winter.

"Some people'll make up just about anything to convince themselves that we live in a simple, comprehensible world," I say. "Folks'll tell you the apostles stole Jesus's body and faked the resurrection. Never mind explaining the life-changing effects of the Holy Spirit or why on earth the followers would have used a lowly woman to report this hoax."

"You continue to compare Bigfoot to religion. Why do you find it necessary to do that?"

"Because it is a faith. You can't prove Bigfoot's existence one way or another. Every encounter, and there have been thousands. Each one only really affects the person who gags on the rotting smell. Feels their hair stand on end. Makes eye contact with a being from another world."

The road gets sketchy now and I'm busy down-shifting, gently pumping brakes, and easing around badly canted turns. Halfway down the gorge and the river is a widening beacon of dancing light. We pass a nearly invisible gash in the underbrush on our left where it has been recently penetrated by a four-wheel-drive vehicle.

Once past the fresh tire tracks that disappear into the obscurity of bruised poison oak bushes and snapped, wrist-thick manzanita trunks, I say, "Just back there. That's the entrance to Blue Mountain Road. Where Ryerson and Brockmueller had their encounter."

"Why are we not going to Blue Mountain, instead of Bluff Creek?"

I lie blatantly and, I hope, convincingly.

"The road's been gone for a decade or more. The whole area was clear-cut back in the sixties."

He looks confused.

"Clear-cut." It's amazing how much local vocabulary has to be explained before an outsider can follow a simple conversation. "Lumber companies used to take down every tree. Wildcatters, especially, weren't long-term business planners."

He shakes his head, his brow still wrinkled.

"No trees means nothing to keep the mud and silt, basically the entire treeless side of the mountain, from washing down each winter into whatever streambed is at its base. The road's gone."

"So we can't gain access to the area on that road?"

"Sure we can. But we've got to have horses. Or mules. The way I'm taking you, we can get to Bluff Creek with a hike of just a few hours. Seemed a better idea for your first excursion into Bigfoot country. Besides," I do my best to set the hook, "this area, between Bluff Creek and Blue Mountain Road, has had over four hundred Bigfoot sightings and encounters since Brockmueller and Ryerson had their road-making equipment strewn along the mountainside. Our chances of running into one of the big guys isn't great. But we've got better odds than winning the lottery. Or of your book ending up on the *New York Times* Bestseller List."

twenty-one

HERE WE ARE, all alone in the big wide woods. He's pretty much at my mercy from this point on. Deep in my vengeful soul, a little spark of glee ignites. The air is dense with the smell of Doug fir, pine, and some recent, small death. Leathery black buzzards hop from branch to branch in the pine to our left, sending showers of brown needles to the ground.

"You need to lighten that pack before we start." I give him a look.

"I got it. Don't worry."

He balances the weight on the tailgate, backs into the straps, and slips the monstrosity over his shoulders. My Northface is settled nicely against my back, and I'm anxious to get on the trail. Dark clouds roll in out of the west, and the hairs on the inside of my nose twitch with a premonition of an electrical storm headed our way. The weather's going to complicate everything. And what about Dad and David? Those two are too old to be slogging up the muddy side of a mountain or crossing a rising creek on horseback. I should have insisted they tell me where they were going. Respect for age and privacy be damned!

"Its past lunchtime, but I'd rather put a few miles behind us before we stop—if that's okay with you." I amble off for the trailhead without waiting for an answer.

"After the ride here, I don't believe my stomach is quite ready for food."

No way to get an overview of this storm under all this tree cover. Hopefully I'm not overestimating how much time we have before the weather hits.

The trail follows a saddle between Blue Mountain and Bear Peak. An hour or so in, we'll work our way down toward Bluff Creek itself. We could have driven what's left of Blue Mountain road, dropped down the mountain, and ended up within a quarter-mile of where we're going to camp tonight. But what would be the fun of that? Besides, we'd have run smack-dab into the rest of my crew.

Within a half-hour the sky is menacing, black and heavy with rain. God, I hope Dad has taken cover, postponed the hunt until this blows over.

"What do you like to sing?" I call to the huffing man behind me.

"Sing?" It sounds to me like he's got all he can do to breathe.

"Ah, yeah. We're coming to the end of the trail here in a few minutes. Be on mostly deer and bear paths down to the creek. Early October. Black bear are filling up their bellies for winter hibernation. Couple of nice fat backpackers be just what an old mama bear needs to top her off before the big sleep."

"I am finding your sense of humor less and less enjoyable."

My cackling laughter bounces off the trees. I skip backwards a step or three, make sure he sees my full-face shit-eating grin. My city boy is already straining under that pack, his breath short and face an unhealthy mottled red. His eyes admit defeat before his words.

"I'm afraid you were correct about the weight I'm carrying."

"A storm's coming in. We need to strip that ridiculous thing down and get moving or we're going to be caught on the mountainside with no shelter."

He struggles out of his pack and I quickly discard several hundred dollars' worth of useless gadgets. The battery-operated coffee grinder follows the coffee pot and two pounds of Ethiopian coffee. I stack these next to enough aluminum pots to cook a seven-course meal. A telescoping fishing pole and tackle box. Cans—actual *cans*—of food. Smoked oysters and fois de gras. Tins of European crackers. Three cans of shrimp, two of real crab meat. A pound of raw brown rice. Twelve little tins with assorted spices. A bottle of champagne.

"We'll pick this up on the way back. What in the hell were you thinking? Why would you bring all this crap?"

"I was thinking you and me alone in the romantic woods. Me surprising you with a lovely meal. You falling gratefully into my arms and forgiving me for my association with that offensive blog."

"Yeah. Well." The mention of the blog pisses me off all over again. Plus, I'm beginning to think it would have been wiser to cancel this entire prank. Wait for the weather to clear. "Just surprise me by making it to the creek without breaking your neck."

I retrieve the largest pan and a wooden spoon. We store the rest of the paraphernalia in the hollow of a Doug fir long ago blackened by a lightning strike. Its early afternoon, but the sky is dark and brooding. If it weren't for my watch, I'd judge the day to be almost gone. Opening the Northface, my yellow slicker is the first thing I touch. The smell of old wood smoke greets me when I pull it on. I shoulder my pack and start walking. Fast.

When we leave the trail and start down the steep mountainside, I begin beating the aluminum pan with the wooden spoon. The noise is intrusive, irritating, an assault on my ears and a disruption of the bountiful quiet of the forest. Which is good. We're traveling a path made by animals significantly larger than us. Grumpy mammals with large teeth and sharp claws who've been known to maul a quiet hiker. I keep banging on the metal pan every tenth step or so.

Behind me comes the unmistakable sound of someone sliding downhill through manzanita brush. When I turn around, Mark is lying on his side, blood from a small but deep gouge at his hairline already dripping into one eye. He's just above me on a steep slope, fifteen feet to my left. By the time I work my way to him through the heavy brush, he's standing. The pack has slipped sideways, the belly strap hangs cockeyed. He wipes at the blood with his jacket sleeve.

I step behind him and ease the burden of the pack off his shoulders.

"Sit on your pack. Let me see what you've done."

A wad of gauze and a couple strips of tape from the outside pocket of my pack is all it takes to stop the bleeding.

"You'll live," I tell him, passing him a bottle of water. "How do you feel?"

"Not great. I seriously underestimated this whole venture."

The first raindrops, fat and filled with cold intent, hit our heads. I pull up my hood, help him to his feet. "Drink and talk while we walk. If we don't make the shelter at Bluff Creek before this slams into us, we are going to get a whole lot wetter."

We weave our way back to the deer trail. I hope it's a deer trail. Back a quarter-mile or so I did see a good-sized pile of berry-seed-laced scat and, twice now, I've heard movement behind us. The soft swish of ferns. The snap of a carelessly placed foot on a manzanita limb. Once, the unmistakable plop of heavy rain from a low-hanging branch disturbed by something passing by.

Looking surreptitiously back up the hill while I taped Mark's cut, a large shape moved in the thick green pines. My guess is a curious bear is keeping an eye on us. Not likely it'll get much closer, but I keep beating with the wooden spoon every few steps. Off to the west the sky rumbles. No lightning yet, but it's coming.

Mark's just behind me now, seems to be placing his feet into my footprints.

"You gotta back off just a little," I tell him, "If you fall again, you're going to take me with you."

"My goal is to *not* fall again."

"Good goal. But you still gotta back off. I'll slow down some. But I'm getting nervous about this storm. It wasn't supposed to hit this far inland. Around here, weather that surprises the forecasters is generally wicked bad."

An hour later, we're still a couple miles above Bluff Creek and our shelter. While walking east, the bulk of Blue Mountain provided some shelter at our backs. When we turn north, we're less than two miles from the small cave I hope is going to be our night's shelter. But we're beyond the protection of the mountain now, walking a small jut of land that protrudes out like a witch's nose between the two mountains. Our path is almost straight down, no switchbacks to be had, and we're completely exposed to the wind and driving rain. This is the section of trail I'd hoped to cover before the storm hit.

twenty-two

A BEDRAGGLED, OVERBURDENED, very wet mule—that's what Mark reminds me of when I turn to see how far behind he's fallen. Rain has already soaked the branches of the pine and fir trees we're weaving our way through, one slippery step at a time. The thick, needle-laden branches droop, heavy and wet with cold menace. Each gust of wind shakes water free so that it falls in heavy plops onto the forest floor. Still over a mile from our night's shelter, our trail is quickly turning to muddy slush. We step sideways, place our feet carefully at each step, brace our weight and, whenever possible, grab a handful of tree limbs or underbrush in the hope of breaking a fall.

The cold wind-driven rain is a nuisance, but in the distance, thunder rumbles its way directly at us. This time of year that can only mean an electrical storm, and bolts of lightning hitting tall pine and fir can be a downright danger to an unsheltered hiker. I'm less worried about a direct hit than I am about a widow-maker—a two hundred pound, thirty-foot limb crashing through its sisters to land on our heads. I'll feel safer in the cave above the creek.

The sky is solid black, a low menacing mass just overhead. No way to tell how far-reaching this storm has become. Lord, I hope Dad and David are holed up somewhere warm and dry. Two mountains to the north, near Happy Camp, is my best guess as to where the two ancient yahoos were headed. Several Bigfoot encounters had been reported there this summer.

Damn that stubborn old man for insisting on this last hunt. Why can't he stay home with a blanket over his skinny legs and a hot toddy in his hand like other men his age? It's not as though a fanatic would have a hard time following a two-ton truck painted with a life-size picture of Bigfoot, and once Dad and David are in the woods, well, there's never a shortage around here of thick forest and heavy underbrush for any stalker, man or beast, to hide behind.

It's the sound that draws my attention, turns my head from looking down at my carefully-placed, wide-planted feet, upward, toward the sliding screams. Mark doesn't go far. The scaly trunk of a thick pine breaks his fall nicely. I grab a handful of sword ferns and pull myself uphill. Enough is enough. We need to make it to the shelter and get a fire going. Soon.

He unhooks the belly strap of his pack, leaves it on its side in the muck of the forest floor. On his hands and knees he slips around on wet leaves and black mud until he gets a good grip on a pine branch and pulls himself to his feet.

This is bad. My intent was to scare Mark, teach him a lesson for being such an ass and slandering Dad and David. Plus, it felt like the bastard connived and tricked his way into my panties. And, all right, maybe I was pissed off because my own bad judgment led me between the Egyptian cotton sheets of that elegant bed at The Humboldt House. But, this—this shaky, panting, hypothermic man—this was never my intent.

I open his backpack and start slinging the contents. "Here." My small pack slides off my shoulders easily. I lengthen the straps and hand him my Northface. Another thirty pounds of the contents of his pack are soon scattered around us. A stainless steel compass, alarm clock, and radio combination peeks from under a deep green fern. Two cans of smoked salmon roll down the hill.

A boom of thunder meshes with an immediate strobe of light that illuminates the hill above us. The air shimmers with electricity, raises the hair on the back of my arms, and pours adrenaline into my tired, wet body.

I blink. Squeeze my eyes together. Hard.

What is that?

Just up the mountain, nearly hidden by underbrush and the red scaly trunk of that Manzanita. Bear? Too tall. Must be a bear. The same one I thought I saw earlier? The thing has been following us all this way? Another crash of thunder and flash of silvery blue light. Whatever the creature was, it's gone. Maybe it was nothing. My imagination playing tricks.

I shorten the straps and sling the big pack up on my back. "We gotta move. *Move.* Follow me and do *not* fall again."

"I can carry my own pack." His insistence would be more convincing if he wasn't still trying to catch his breath. I can almost feel the pain each gasp costs him as he drags the air into his lungs.

He takes two limping steps toward me before I turn and start back downhill.

I crab walk in a half squat, do my best to lower my center of gravity. "Look, this is my bad judgment that's put us here. I knew you couldn't carry that much weight. I give you credit. You've schlepped the thing a lot farther than I thought you'd be able to."

He's a couple yards above me, at that point of exhaustion when shivering and weakness is just about to whisper in his ear that he needs to lie down and rest. Just for a minute or two.

The wind howls in the tree tops, the rain blows sideways—icy daggers on my face and drenched jeans. Another flash of airborne electricity and I look up, search for whatever is behind us.

"Something may be following us." Maybe a shot of adrenaline is just what Mark needs to drive him down this mountainside. "I heard it just as we turned off the main trail and, when you fell this last time, I thought I saw something."

His pale face is streaked with mud, that gash on his forehead has started bleeding again. He pauses in an awkward side step, shakes his head a little, and meets my eye.

"I don't need this now, Samantha. If you're trying to kill me, just take out that gun I know you've got there in your belly pack and shoot me."

I actually have enough energy to laugh. Surprises me.

"I'm not jerking your chain. Something, probably a curious bear, is dogging us." Sure, a bear. That's what it is. Probably the rain and cold overtook my imagination when I saw it looking at us from behind the tree. Easy enough to mistake a six-foot bear standing on its hind legs for an eight-foot creature whose head seemed just about twice as wide as any black bear I've ever seen.

"Look, whatever it is," I yell up the hill, "it's not going to have any easier time getting down the mountain in this rain than we are." That's a bald-faced lie, but it sounds reasonable. "Just keep moving. We're almost there."

For a city boy, he's got grit, I'll give him that. With my lighter pack, he keeps up with me, step for step. By the time we get to the creek, both of us are running on ice-cold desperation. Our boots fill with water, but we stumble across without falling. I lead him up the chalky cliff, work my way along the rock face until my searching hand hits empty air.

The cave!

Thank you, Jesus and Mary. Thank you, Aunt Mandy and anyone else who was listening to my fervent prayers.

The entrance is low enough to make us duck, but once inside, the ceiling rises gradually so that toward the back we can stand without bumping our heads. Twenty feet inside, at the rear wall, dry wood is arranged in a haphazard, leaning tepee with additional wood stacked to the left—hands down the best gift I've ever received. A small smile curls my half-frozen mouth, this messy but match-ready fire a much better gift than flowers.

I take my pack from Mark, find the watertight tin of matches in the right side pocket where I've kept it for twenty years. Bubba's gift catches on the first strike. Quivering blue flames ignite the curls of wood tinder and quickly catch the scattered kindling.

"Take off your wet clothes."

I struggle out of my jeans and reach in my pack for a tightly-wrapped black plastic garbage bag with my dry clothes inside. Turn my back on him, strip and change into dry jeans, a T-shirt, sweatshirt, and soft wool socks. When I turn back around, the fire has caught the larger chunks of wood and the den is already warming.

Mark is still wearing his dripping clothes, struggling to remove his hiking boots. I don't like the way he's shaking. The idea of this outing was to scare him, teach him a lesson. Not kill him. I kneel, push his awkward hands away and untie the laces, remove his expensive new boots.

This is trouble. Both gray wool socks are stained brownish red across the length of his toes and in a wide dark curve at each heel.

"Stand up. Now!" I drag him to his feet, unzip and strip him of his pants. His shorts are those long-legged ones that hug him tight, made to show off his man parts. Right now they're wringing wet and those very parts are pulled deep, seeking life-saving warmth.

"Get those off! Wet clothes leach every bit of warmth out of you. Take off everything. Move!" Damn. Hypothermia in the middle of the forest on the first stormy night of the season. Could this trip get any worse?

I rummage in Mark's pack for his dry clothes. He hasn't protected anything with plastic, but his pack has done a decent job of wicking the rain away from the contents. I scrounge out a pair of almost dry pants and toss them to him. The fire seems to be reviving him somewhat. He's moving a little faster. A wet undershirt, soggy sweatshirt, and damp socks that didn't fare as well, I arrange on a pole stuck in a crevice of the cave wall so that it extends out over the fire.

His sleeping bag is tied to the bottom of his pack. It's wet. But the advantage to spending several hundred dollars for a quality bag is that the thing really does resist water. The inside is dry. Once he's hopped and struggled into his dry pants, I have him sit almost on top of the fire and wrap the bag around his chest and legs.

He whimpers when I tear the socks from his feet.

"Why didn't you tell me you had blisters? I have moleskin. Bleeding feet are not something to ignore on a hiking trip."

My disgust with his failure to ask for help masks a growing concern that I may have carried this prank a bit too far. All right, way too far. And we haven't even gotten to the good part of the plan yet.

twenty-three

NOTHING I LOVE more than being safe and warm while a storm bites at the edges of my world. Usually. But tonight feels different. I'm jittery. For no reason at all, I'm frightened. Dad would say a goose is walking on my grave. Mark and I are wrapped together in both sleeping bags, our backs against the rock wall, feet extended to the warmth of the flickering fire. The mouth of the cave gapes black, roars with wind and rain. A strong, sweet-rancid smell laces the air, the identity of which drifts up from my subconscious almost to within reach and then disappears again, a hair's breath before I recognize the scent. Maybe all this anxiety is just a case of being in the right place with the wrong man.

"I hear skin-to-skin contact is the best way to keep warm." Mark's voice is close. His breath warm on my ear.

"The only reason I'm in these sleeping bags is to keep you from dying of hypothermia. Don't push your luck."

Hawk and I have been coming to this den since we stumbled into it on a camping trip six years ago. Everything about the place reminds me of my first love, even the damp, musky smell, mingled with wood smoke and ancient cougar urine. All of it, God help me, makes me ache for Hawk's touch, yearn for the sound of his voice. Lord, I am a mess. What kind of woman gets turned on by the smell of cat piss?

Tonight the scent of a slightly decomposing and carefully-placed carcass is also wafting gently out into the wet night air. This added odor should put a hidden smile on my face. Instead I have the heebie-jeebies. Keep staring out into the black night, the hair on the back of my neck lifting with the sense something is standing just outside, peering in at Mark and me as we lie exposed, illuminated by the sputtering fire like prey in a spotlight. Of course this feeling is nothing but paranoia. The mouth of the cave is a full eight feet above the creek bed.

Mark stretches one of his legs over mine, brings me back to a more immediate issue.

"Ah, Samantha. You talk tough, but you were downright gentle when you were tending to my feet and feeding me whatever that freeze-dried concoction was you spooned into my mouth. By the way, what was in that little foil package in your little pack? The one that smells suspiciously like chocolate?"

"Don't read anything into my treating your blistered feet. I just don't want to pack your dead body out of here come morning. And, keep out of my chocolate." I slap his hand away from its slow journey. "Swear to God, if that hand moves another inch, I'll leave you here to fend for yourself."

His low chuckle is a good sign. Time to get out of here and do what I can to end this prank. I slide out from under the sleeping bag.

"Come back." he whines. "I'll be a perfect gentleman. Scout's honor."

The sleeping bag moves over his earnest cross-my-heart gesture, but his eyebrows wiggle naughtily above those dark green eyes.

Yep. He's pretty well revived.

I dig around in my Northface, careful to bypass the foil-wrapped square Bubba contributed, and remove a Ziploc bag of venison jerky. The second the blue zipper slides opens, the peppery smell is released. One leathery chunk in hand, I zip the plastic bag shut and throw it to Mark.

"Eat some of this. Be right back. Potty break." I bundle up, grab my flashlight, ready to go out into gale force winds and pouring rain.

"You can't just pee in the corner? You'll get soaked."

"Nervous bladder. Can't be helped." I'm already at the mouth of the cave. "Don't move until I get back. Gnaw on a piece of jerky and stay warm. It'll just be a few minutes."

I work my way along the slick face of the cliff, hug the shelter of the small overhang as long as I can. I've got to put an end to this scheme of revenge. Hell, maybe Mark's even telling the truth and all he's really guilty of is being a spineless wannabe-famous jackass.

I edge around a curve in the cliff. Less than fifty yards from where Mark lies waiting, the light from our campfire is invisible, swallowed by the depth of darkness of this primordial forest. With the slick rock face to my left, I keep my head down, place one foot in front of the other until I've gained five hundred feet or so. My flashlight points downstream toward the path where three men and a dog as big as a pony should be hunkered down waiting for my signal. I turn the light on and off three times.

No answering signal.

My light off, I slip it into the pocket of my coat. I really do have to pee.

There's something primal about squatting in the dark, wind slashing the trees overhead, relieving myself on a narrow ledge, urine splashing below into the fecund, rotting cycle of life of the forest floor. Nobody can possibly see me here in this private moment. So why do I feel like someone is watching?

Finished, I stand, pull up my jeans, can't help squinting into the pitchy night. If those guys are out there hiding I'm going to skin them alive. I smooth my T-shirt, sweatshirt, readjust the poncho, and refasten the clasps closed before turning my flashlight back on. The feeble cone of manmade light is all but swallowed by the forest night.

No answer to my signal flash.

Again.

Where are those three? They've got to be here. Bubba laid the fire. One of them even thought to cut a sturdy limb and leave it leaning against the wall so I'd have somewhere to hang the wet clothes. Why don't they show themselves? I don't want to leave what small protection I have under the overhang to go and look for them. No way I'm crossing that creek again. I just got my boots halfway dry.

The storm is a roaring beast in the dark night. Wind rips through the tall trees, lashes me with icy pinpricks of rain. Maybe they're sitting in Bubba's truck a half mile from here, sipping coffee, waiting for the rain to let up.

Wherever they are, I've got to get back inside. It's too wet and cold out here to stand around flashing lights into empty darkness.

Like a gunshot, the stone bounces off the cliff at my back, ricochets over the incline, and tumbles into the creek ten feet below me.

Finally. The guys are here. Why are they tossing rocks instead of answering my signal? I swing my flashlight up. Move it in an arc along the length of the creek bed where the rock came from. Why can't I spot them?

From the backside of the mountain, over near Blue Mountain Road where Bubba's truck should be parked, a howl rises above the roaring wind, pierces the night. The wail is that of a nightmare banshee. Or a very big dog terrified by something not of this world. Jesus, where are those guys? Rattled, I stumble sideways, ready to return to the safety of the den. Feet slipping, my flashlight tips, points high above the creek bed.

Red eyes stare back at me.

Holy Mother of God.

The first set of eyes has to be nine feet from the soggy ground. The second, and for some reason most compelling pair, stare back from a position just to the left and a foot or so lower, maybe eight feet above the earth. Then, as the thin beam of my flashlight twitches in the black night, there's the reflection of one more set, lower and directly in front of the others. Three sets of eyes in a lopsided T shape.

I jerk away from the impossible.

My boot slides on the slippery rock and I'm falling. Light strobes on swaying treetops, bear-sized boulders, a flash of a shaggy moving mountain. Something big and hard slams into my chest. The flashlight flies from my hand. Darkness is on me in an instant. I gasp, try to remember how to inhale. My first ragged breath fills my lungs with an unmistakable putrid-sweet smell. I scramble to get my legs under me, reach wildly in the dark for something to grab onto and pull myself upright.

The woods are as dark as a grave. I can't see my own hands. On my knees I flail blindly, the suffocating smell like an invasion that rubs against my skin, pushes down into my lungs, becomes a part of me. Panic gnaws at my mind, terror quickly overwhelms me as my hand closes on something warm, something hairy. I wrench myself backward, and I'm falling again. End over end, in cold black space, until my head smacks something hard and the world ends.

twenty-four

I OPEN MY eyes to the rosy gray of false dawn. The wind is a mere rustle in the treetops, the creek a muted roar off to my left. I run my hands over my body. Nothing seems broken. My belly pack is intact, the small, hard weight of fully-loaded and completely inadequate metal presses against my middle. I'm not ready to move just yet. Still trying to take stock. Figure out where I am.

The air is rich with spent electricity. Gentle rain, like a final blessing, scrims the low wall of underbrush around a flattened bed of soft ferns where I lie. Rubbing my fists into my eyes, hoping to wake up, memories of last night flood my senses. The smell! It's heavy on my hands, triggers a morning-after flashback. Those eyes in the night. Hands lifting me, being carried in the dark.

Did that *really* happen?

The swollen creek, blackish green with runoff from the night's storm, is a dull growl a few feet below. How did I get here? I jerk my head to the right, search the rugged face of the cliff.

I'm less than ten feet from the entrance to the cave.

This is not where I fell.

Cold morning air hits the bare skin of my waist as I sit up. My poncho, wrapped carefully around my sleeping body, flops open. Didn't I fasten each clasp after squatting to pee last night?

A flash of memory like a forgotten dream invades my mind. Giant creatures. Surrounding me. Touching my body with huge, gentle hands. Something warm and calming pressing between the heat of their rough palms and some seeking emptiness deep inside me, a center I never knew existed until those gentle touches filled the void.

I tear my sweatshirt and T-shirt away, lift them high enough to expose my belly. A reddish brown imprint of a wide hand conjures a bone-deep shaking. Nausea roils my empty stomach, produces nothing. I struggle to my feet, wipe clammy sweat from my face, and work my way through the wet underbrush around my night's bed. The cliff face, reflecting the diffused light of dawn, is a soft glow of peach-tinted light, the entrance to the den a darker, blood-red slash in the rock.

I hurry toward that yawning mouth.

Inside is the gray ash of a dead fire. Mark's clothes hang limply from the pole where I draped them. Two packs lie side by side, their contents strewn throughout the cave. Crinkled wads of empty red and silver foil packets of freeze-dried food shine in the dim light like bizarre decorations. An empty traveler-size tube of toothpaste is half hidden under the aluminum top of my open match tin. The sleeping bags, still zipped together, are a crumpled, empty heap.

I drop to my knees, unzip the bags, run my hands along the cold flannel. Body heat is long gone. Mark didn't just step outside. A neatly folded square of chocolate-tainted tinfoil reflects the morning light back at me from where it lies on the packed dirt floor of the cave.

No! Mark ate Bubba's brownies? This is bad. This is very bad.

Where the hell is that clueless city boy?

Something is coming. Something making a lot of noise and whistling Dixie. Thank God.

I'm firing off questions before they're even inside the cave.

"Where the hell were you guys?"

It's Bubba I see first. He ducks his big head and steps inside. My God, but he is beautiful. I'm up and stepping into his surprised embrace when Hawk stoops under the low entrance. Lefty strides upright through the portal and joins the ragged circle.

I pound on Bubba's wide chest, cry in relief at their appearance.

"Where were you? Mark's gone! The Bigfoots took him I think. Last night. I saw… three… a family. They. Carried. Me. Made a bed in the ferns and left me there. My coat was opened. Touch… They laid hands on me. "

"We had our own encounter." Hawk's soft voice draws me. It's as though deep inside I'm scattered with shards and filings of the past, magnetized over twenty-eight years by rubbing up against this man. My attraction to him feels inevitable, a quiet force of nature. Bubba's arms release me to my chosen fate.

The telling of the night's events on the other side of the mountain unfolds around me. Events so bizarre I should be shaking, crying, doing something more than breathing in Hawk's piney smell, resting my head on his shoulder so that my mouth is pressed into the soft, delicate skin behind his ear.

"Them monsters run off Caroline's dawg," Lefty reports. "Big ass freakin' hairy damn things. Come up all around us. Was like they was herdin' us."

Hawk's voice is low, reverent. "Forced us to the truck. Every time we thought to get out of the cab, one of them would charge. Always just out of sight, they'd shake the truck. Made clear we were to stay inside."

Bubba's deep bass sounds plain pissed-off. "Muddy handprints, bigger'n a grizzly bear, all the hell over my ve-hicle. Truck was rockin'. Was a second or two, I thought I saw eyes like I ain't never seen before. Like as they could stare down into my soul. And the smell. Sumbitch'd take your breath clean out of you. Weren't no way we could get ourselves over here to you."

A thought occurs to me. A question I've heard discussed at dozens of Bigfoot Hunter Meetings. "Did any of you think to fire your weapons?"

Hawk seems shocked at the suggestion. Lefty doesn't appear to have heard the question. He stares out the ragged entrance of the cave, won't meet my eye. Bubba looks like I've slapped him.

"Lord almighty, Sam. I was plum desperate to get over here to you. Knew good and well you was in trouble." Are those tears in Bubba's eyes? "But I never thought of using the Glock until right now this instant."

"Ah, yeah. Nobody does, Bubba," I reassure him. "The big mystery has always been, with so many armed rednecks traipsing through the woods, how come nobody's ever taken a single shot at one of the creatures. After last night... I understand the phenomenon. For me anyway, from the time I saw those three sets of eyes in the dark, my mind wasn't exactly in this world."

I step back out of Hawk's warmth, lift the layers covering my upper body, expose the proof of my own night's encounter.

Lefty takes a step away from me, his eyes round, mouth slack.

Bubba pushes toward me, edges Hawk out of the way, almost lays his hand on my belly before remembering himself and letting his arms fall to his sides.

"You all right, Sammy?"

Hawk closes the two-step gap Bubba has created between us, a look on his face like awe. His hand is cold against my skin. The tips of his tapered fingers end well inside the elliptical palm print. The wide blunt digits of the reddish print extend around my waist, end just short of my spine.

My voice catches in my throat. The words choke me in my need to get them out into the cold morning air.

"I fell. Hit my head. I think one of them carried me. I'll show you. Ferns were trampled into a bed. They didn't hurt me. When I woke up, this... muddy handprint was... here."

"That ain't mud." Bubba's voice is low and raspy, like he's whispering in church or sneaking past the devil. "That there is blood."

Whose blood?

"Mark!" I moan. "He fell and hit his head on the hike in. There was a little blood. But not this much. Nowhere near this much. Would they take him?"

"They have him," Hawk says, statement of fact, no hesitation. "Can't you smell that they've been here, inside the cave, and not that long ago?"

"That might be me." I say. "God knows I can smell it on myself."

I don't share the realization that I'm no longer repulsed by the odor. Somehow what I at first identified as the smell of rotting death now seems filled with promise. I have an uneasy feeling I'm going to crave that smell for the rest of my life.

"We don't know that the Bigfoots took Mark," I insist. "Maybe he wandered off and got lost. Could be that's what happened."

I'm clutching at straws here. This was supposed to be a simple prank. I drag Mark's city ass through the woods. Feed him a marijuana-laced brownie. Play a small joke. Bubba, Lefty and me—we thought of everything!

Bubba even put nuts in the brownie so my allergy would give me an excuse not to eat the dessert laced with Humboldt Gold. Once Mark ate the chocolate square and the marijuana kicked in, I'd signal the guys and they'd make a racket, toss a stink bomb of doe urine near the mouth of the den. Lefty would release Caroline's mastiff and the monstrous dog would make a run for the cave, drawn by the smell of the turkey carcass the guys planted earlier. An irresistible treat for Rufus, the men had pointed out while they laid the fire, letting the dog build up a powerful longing for turkey before dragging him away, dripping slobber.

A big joke. A gotcha. Revenge for the slanderous blog and what I perceived as Mark's betrayal of me. His stirring up of a holy war against Dad and David. Now everything has gone horribly wrong. Mark's missing. A bloody handprint is stamped across my belly.

Fifty years of chasing Bigfoot and the closest Dad and David ever got to the creature were a few dozen footprints, a strong whiff of decay blown on a distant breeze, a stone thrown into a campsite. The four of us drag a clueless writer into the woods intending harmless revenge and a freaking herd of the creatures show up and muck up the works but good.

"Oh Lord," Lefty groans. "I went and lost Caroline's dawg."

"I lost a person!" I yell. "I lost the guy writing the book about the very creatures that have dragged him off into the woods. Imagine what he'll write about Dad now!"

"We'll find him," Hawk promises. "Bigfoot has never harmed a human."

Bubba's stare is cold and hard. Something is going on between him and Hawk. The big man has always deferred. Always been the faithful follower.

"My heart near about beat itself out of my chest last night." Bubba says. "I suppose that don't count as harmin' a fellow. And Samantha's got a palm print on her belly, stamped in blood, and spent the night exposed to the rain and storm. That don't count as harm either, I guess."

"Okay. So. You think it could be dawg blood on your belly?" Lefty interjects. "I hate to think of ole Rufus being hurt."

Three of us exchange a look. We're hoping, praying it is dog blood. I can't think of a better alternative, and I doubt Bubba or Hawk can either.

Outside we find a cluster of giant footprints where several of the creatures went into the creek. Bubba lays his boot beside one of the smaller tracks. The bare footprint is just an inch or two shorter than the length of his size fifteen boot, but almost half again as wide.

I squat in the wet gravel beside the muddy patch of tracks. Seeing the impressions, more proof, this confirmation of what my shattered nighttime senses insisted was happening—the shaking returns. The rational part of me would have preferred to discover that I had simply hallucinated the entire experience. Some kind of explanation for the handprint will, eventually, present itself to my mind. Rather be crazy as a bed bug, maybe, than admit I encountered something unknown and, maybe, unknowable.

I force myself to relay the facts. Just the facts.

"There were two sets of eyes that were eight feet or more off the ground. Another pair much lower. Maybe five feet high. It happened fast. Was dark. But… I think—I'm pretty sure—there were three of them. I think they were … I think they were a family."

Bubba kneels at the creek, wets a red handkerchief. "Here Sam, clean that blood off yourself. I can't bear to think of them critters puttin' their hands on you."

"It wasn't like that. What I remember… they were gentle. Looking back at it, I'm not sure they meant to hurt me at all."

"Leave the print, Sam," Hawk orders. "I think they meant it as a kind of blessing."

Bubba glares at Hawk, points to my middle, and offers me the wet cloth.

"Tell you what, Chief," Bubba says to Hawk. "When you're the one with a bloody handprint on your person, you get to decide if it stays."

"Hey! Hey, over here!" Having inched his way across the creek balanced on a moss-slick pine log, Lefty is less than twenty feet into the woods. "I found him!"

The three of us splash across the cold water. The creek, no more than calf-deep last night when Mark and I crossed, is at mid-thigh before I realize how hard it's pushing me sideways. Bubba grabs my elbow a second before

Hawk's arm slips around my waist. Four steps and we stagger out on the other side of the stream, my heart a jackhammer in my chest.

Mark!

Let him be alive. Please Lord, let him be alive.

Water sloshes in my boots, each stride creates a cold breeze against my drenched jeans. Silhouetted against a backdrop of blue-green pine trees, Lefty's back is to me. He's standing wide-legged, perfectly still, his head cocked to the left in a position I recognize as his way of studying on something.

This can't be good. Why is he just standing there? Why don't I already hear Mark's voice, happy to see us, maybe even forgiving me for dragging him into this mess? Or screaming in rage and threatening to expose us all as the dumbest rednecks on the face of the planet? Just let him be alive.

I pull up short just behind Lefty, stare at the object of his concentration.

"Caroline's gonna be glad to see you, fella," Lefty coos.

Now that backup has arrived, Lefty picks up a long leather lead trailing into the brush, careful not to get between the dog's teeth and the remains of the turkey carcass.

twenty-five

"TAKE THAT DAMN turkey carcass away from the dog!"

Disappointment in finding the dog and not Mark makes me angry. Lefty is a handy target.

"Don't you know anything about taking care of an animal? Turkey bones'll kill a dog."

"I ain't getting between that dawg and food." Lefty waves his barely-healed hand in the air. "I know that damn much."

We're standing in a clearing created by the dying branches of an ancient wind-felled pine. The log, rich with speckled fungi, smaller trees already rooted along its length, has nearly completed its life cycle. The forest floor is thick with dark, rotting wood, and dead pine needles. The dog has nestled into a bed of young sword ferns which are flourishing in the death-rich soil. One huge paw pins the remains of the carcass to the deep-green forest floor.

My anger propels me forward. With no thought whatsoever, I push the dog's jowly head to the side with my boot, lean down and recover what's left of the turkey. A two-hundred-pound dog is a little like a dinosaur. It takes a second or two for his thoughts to get from his brain to his giant feet. But, before I'm standing upright, the rib cage of the bird dangling from my hand, Rufus rolls to his back, exposes his belly, tail tucked firmly between his legs covering his vulnerable male parts. His whine, a heartbreaking whimper of submission, startles us all.

"That there dog is scared about half to death of you." Bubba points out the obvious. "It's the smell of them critters on you, is what it is."

"Get up, you big baby," I say to the whimpering animal. "I'm not going to hurt you."

Rufus is not reassured. He crawls out to the end of his lead, peers out from behind a young manzanita, putting as much distance as possible between me and him.

"Enough with the dog," I scold. "Mark's out here someplace. Because of us. He's got to be cold and wet and scared half out of his mind."

Please, Lord, let that be all that's wrong with him. Let the blood from the handprint not be his. I'll go to Mass every Sunday. Well, I don't want to promise something we both know I'm probably not going to be able to follow through on. But, you wouldn't punish Mark because of my sins, would you? A loving Father like you.

Dad!

How did he survive the night's storm? I wish I'd talked to him more before the two of us stomped off into the woods on fools' errands. Something is going on with his health. And something Letticia said the other night has been nagging me. How could my mother have lived at VD's for only a few months? Did she leave after she got pregnant and then come back just before I was born?

I didn't push Letticia for an explanation because I didn't want to know the answer. Still don't. Dad and me, the two of us are just alike. Both as stubborn as Missouri mules with just about half as much good sense.

Salmonberry bushes and manzanita brush pull at my wet jeans. Hawk and I are on point, Bubba right behind me. Lefty, with a whimpering Rufus straining at the end of a leash, is in drag position. We weave our way uphill, on a fresh trail. An occasional broken branch or trampled toadstool gives hope, but we're just as likely to be following a bear as tracking a family of kidnapping Bigfoots.

"Have you heard from our dads?" I ask Hawk.

"No cell service on the mountain. I meant to hike up to the ridge and try to get a call out from there, but we got a little busy with our visitors."

"You think the two old fools had enough sense to hole up at a nice warm motel for the night? Ride out the storm in comfort?"

Hawk doesn't bother to answer me. We both know they spent a wet night in a leaky tent.

The sun is a welcome stranger as it peeks through a deep cleft in Bear Mountain to the east. Its warmth instigates a smile on the faces of three of us. Lefty has fallen behind. I can hear him muttering to Rufus. Little snippets of grumbling about *damn fools with no brains whatsoever* and *dawg's got more sense than anybody else in this crew.* My grin widens. I can't help it. No matter what's going on in my life, a moment's sunshine and the company of these three men make it better.

When they're not making it worse.

Nobody's said it yet, but if we don't stumble on Mark within the next hour or two, one of us is going to have to hike out and get help. People die of exposure in these mountains every year. The man has to be found before dark.

At the crest of the ridge, the backside of Blue Mountain falls away. Folds of deep green fir, fiery red of poison oak, and the burnished gold of dormant maple pepper the slope. The sun slides past the cleft and vanishes behind Bear Mountain while we stand in a haphazard line along the saddle and watch a ragged shadow reclaim the land below us.

"Look over yonder." Just before the sun disappears completely, Bubba points to a glint of light off to our right.

The reflection's gone before we can walk twenty feet toward the shimmer of hope. I stop, squint into the shadows. Bubba and I re-spot the glint at the same time. Hanging by a strap, on the lowest limb of an ancient fir, is Mark's stainless steel GPS, radio, and compass combination.

I turn it in my hands, shake it as if, with encouragement, it will talk to me, tell me what happened, how it got here.

"His pack was too heavy." I tell Bubba what we all knew before I left VD's yesterday morning. Was that yesterday morning? Just over twenty-four hours ago? "I had to lighten his load on the trail. Coming down the other side of Blue Mountain." I point with my chin at the shadowed mountain behind us. "Mark fell twice, was staggering under the weight. I tossed a bunch of stuff."

"What's that?" Lefty shouts from behind us.

Hawk's already sidestepping down the mountain, headed to a small hoard of pilfered camping gear. Mark's telescoping fishing pole leans against a lightning-blackened oak stump. The tip is broken and dangles loosely in a patch of flame-red poison oak. Shiny aluminum pots, last seen nesting in a neat stack on the other side of the mountain, are scattered among maidenhair ferns, half hidden beneath a rotting pine log. A dented can of salmon lies on its side beside the waxy paper remains of a pound of butter.

The shaking begins at my center and radiates out in waves. I don't know I'm falling until Bubba's hard chest is against my face and my boots dangle from the crook of his arms.

"When's the last time you ate?" he drawls.

Yesterday morning? Half a sesame seed bagel with jalapeño pepper jelly that I shared with Dad. A chunk of jerky last night when I left the cave.

The granola bar Hawk hands me is wrapped in some indestructible wrapper that my shaky hands don't seem able to open. Bubba stands me on my own feet. My legs buckle a bit, but hold me upright. He rips open the green foil.

"Knock it off now, Sam," Hawk says. "You need to pull yourself together. This wilting violet act isn't helping anyone."

Leaning against Bubba, I feel the muscles in his belly tighten, know what the flexing of his right arm means an instant before Hawk takes the punch.

"Look here, hoss. I been right damn patient with you. But, son, you ain't got the good sense God almighty give my grandma's Christmas goose."

Hawk staggers on his feet, his eyes glazed with surprise. He shakes his head, rubs his jaw, and clenches his fists as testosterone turns surprise to anger.

Bubba stands wide-legged between us. He faces Hawk, but he talks to me. "Go on now. Please, Sam, get over there and sit yourself on that log. Me and Hawk, we're gonna have us a come-to-Jesus-meetin'."

"You hit me again and I'll kick your peckerwood ass all over the side of this mountain." Big talk for a man half the size of the giant he's trying to intimidate.

From the corner of my eye I can see Lefty being dragged down the mountain, skidding sideways, Rufus at the end of the leather lead, in full pursuit of God alone knows what.

What has happened to us in the last twenty-four hours? We've had an up close and personal, impossible to reason our way around, encounter with not one but an entire family of creatures that, until late last night, I wasn't even convinced existed. An encounter that has left me with ambivalent feelings ranging from shaking terror to mystic faith. Like Mary turning her face in fear from Gabriel and his message, I am both terrified and filled with grace.

In the middle of all of this, Mark is missing. Based on the smell in the cave and finding his discarded camping gear on the opposite side of the mountain from where I so nonchalantly tossed it, someone or something has carried him off into the woods. If the blood on the hand that pressed itself against my belly was Mark's, than there is a good chance he's dead or dying. And, because of me and my stupid, irresponsible idea for revenge, he's drugged on a marijuana-laced brownie.

Lefty has disappeared down the backside of the mountain, dragged on a long leash by a slobber-afflicted dog as big as a bear. Dad and David, accused of a decades-old murder, are stumbling around in some undisclosed woods seeking a meeting with the very creatures who have chosen to entangle themselves, to one degree or another, with every single person on this little hoax gone wrong.

And now, because things aren't peculiar enough, Bubba, the most softhearted person I know, has slugged Hawk. An occurrence almost as hard to believe as a family of Bigfoots carrying me gently through the night and watching over me while I slept.

This can't be happening!

I'm going to wake up any minute and the rain's going to be creating a chimera of swirling gray at my bedroom window. I'm going to hurry downstairs, breathe in the familiar smell of moldy wood and stale booze, and put on a pot of coffee, anxious to recount this amazing, ridiculous dream to Dad.

I blink my eyes. Keep them squeezed tight as I inhale slowly, blow the breath out through my open mouth. Open my eyes to dark, brooding clouds over thickly forested mountains. Air heavy with the next storm is already easing its way over the mountain, winter's hostile takeover of a short-lived autumn.

Bubba's wide back is to me, his thick arms loose at his sides. His voice is slow and calm, reminds me of Dad when he's gentling a riled horse.

"Just stay right there." He soothes Hawk. "Think on it."

All I can see of Hawk are his stiff legs. He's rocking on his heels. Probably gauging his chances of getting in one good lick before the big guy lays him out. This is just what we need in the middle of trying to rescue Mark. These two circling each other like mad dogs while Lefty thrashes through the bushes below trying to keep up with that damn dog.

Bubba's voice is low and so rumbly I half-expect to see the leaves tremble on the maples that ring this small clearing. "She's been sick to her stomach for a couple weeks now. Tired all the damn time. Falls asleep in the middle of a work shift. Just the smell of food makes her upchuck. Now she's been carried off into the night by giant damn fur-balls. Hairy-ass critters strong enough to lift my one-ton clear up off the ground. Y'all need to open your eyes, my man… figure out what's going on with your woman. Else someone else is gonna step up and you're going to be left out in the cold, wondering why you was so damn stupid."

Oh my God. No!

Tired, pukey, even more emotional than usual. Jesus, Mary, and Joseph. Could I be?

The crunchy granola bar rushes back up, spatters on the toe of my right boot. I'm counting backwards. I've never been real regular but that can't be right. I had a period two dart nights before the Bluff Creek camping trip when something hurled rocks at Hawk and me. My mind, or something lower, flashes on orange campfire flames backlighting Hawk's naked glory. His muscled arms spread wide in welcome as the rocks fell around him. My view from the sleeping bag of his sculpted ass.

Concentrate, damn it! This is no time to be envisioning Hawk's fine ass. How long ago was that? Four, no, five weeks ago. My last period was two weeks before that. Seven weeks ago!

I'm pregnant with Hawk's baby?
No. Oh, God no.
Unless I'm pregnant with Mark's child.

twenty-six

THE UNDERBRUSH BREAKS, snaps, gives way before the animal charging up the mountain directly at me. Bubba and Hawk, squared off to each other on my right, turn their attention to the crashing noise. I stagger on my feet, the remains of the granola bar still steaming between my boots. The animal thrashes his way through the last of the tangled manzanita, salmonberry bushes, and poison oak. He skids to a stop, like a cartoon mule when he sees me, drops down and exposes his belly, whimpers deep in his doggie throat.

Lefty's yell echoes, bounces off tall trees and dense underbrush, comes to us ragged and thin. Rufus eases himself to his giant feet. Strings of drool hang from his lowered head. His lethal tail swipes from side to side, whacks into the scaly trunk of a fir. He turns, plods two steps back down the mountain, stops to look over his shoulder at me. The dog's eyes are muddy pools beseeching me to follow him.

Hawk and Bubba are already crashing through the brush, on their way toward the sound of Lefty's calls. I follow Rufus. By virtue of my earthy smell, I seem to have become his feared and beloved pack leader. The dog is a good trailblazer. His size and power clear a narrow path the two of us skid down, Lefty's voice becoming clearer with each jarring impact of our bodies against exposed rock, fallen branches, and unbelievably hard manzanita trunks.

I'm bone cold in wet jeans, can't feel my toes. Blood trickles into my right eye from where I rolled through a patch of Himalaya berry bushes. Half a pine cone and a goodly portion of a poison ivy vine are smeared along my left side. I slide another twenty feet on my butt.

One thought blots out all others.

Let me not be hurtling down this mountain to find a dead body.

Rufus stops, slinks under the branches of a flame red maple, whines, and cuts his droopy eyes to me.

Lefty kneels, statue-still, in the open end of a horseshoe-shaped clearing. I half expect to see The White Witch with her magic wand as I step out of the woods. Instead, a silent family stares back at me.

The Bigfoots are on the far side of the U, along a curve of tall pine trees. The male is almost black, with bits of pale green moss and dark fern stuck to his hairy legs and belly. Mahogany-red hair covers the female. She brings one arm across her pendulant breasts, splays her hand across her belly. A dark brown youngster peeks around her massive body.

Immersed in a fog of terror and awesome joy, I drop, as though over a cliff, from my ordinary world into a swirling mist of possibility. Confronted, in broad, indisputable daylight, with the unbelievable, I am freed from expectation. The moment seems to stretch around me, expand beyond my preconceived notion of time and space.

Bubba and Hawk crash through the brush between me and the creatures, stumble into the clearing.

My eyes flick to the men.

When I look back, the forest is empty.

"Sam." Bubba's low voice beckons me. " Ya all right?"

They're gone! Wet, cold, and scared, I am bereft.

"Ah, yeah. I'm here."

A cold nose tickles my hand, Rufus's warm bulk presses against my side.

Lefty rises dreamily from his kneeling position, turns toward me. "He dead?"

What?

"Mark's here." Hawk moves fast to the north edge of the clearing. Bubba turns from me and follows.

I move through a viscous mist of confusion, my brain reorienting itself to a new reality. Part of me knows they've found Mark, that we've discovered the object of our frantic search. But I'm still scrambling to connect the dots as to why this matters.

Why anything in this wet world matters.

At Lefty's side, I ask the only question that seems relevant at the moment. "Did you see them?"

He turns away. Shakes his head violently.

"Sam!" Hawk stretches out his long legs, turns his back on Bubba, closes the distance between us.

I sink into the wood rot smell of the forest floor, my butt flat on the ground, legs stuck out in front of me like those of a broken doll. The dog crouches beside me, growls at Hawk's approach. The rumbling warning intensifies and the man squats five feet in front of me, coos low and soft like a mother to a fevered infant.

"Snap out of it now, Sam. We all need to concentrate."

How do I tell him what I saw?

"Bigfoot. Three. Father. Mother and a child."

That tells him nothing. Doesn't explain the connection I felt. The fear-streaked joy. Peace tangled with awe.

"You've been touched. White Feather calls it 'marked.' But it's really a kind of blessing and curse rolled into one. It's a special gift from the forest people. But you've got to come back now, Sam. Return to your own world. And quick. We've found your city boy. They stacked his gear all around him like tokens. He's alive, but unconscious. We need to get him out of here. Now."

Hawk's voice is a tiny beacon of light at the far end of a long tunnel. I focus on it, but it's going to take me a while to make my way through the dark. A second voice, deeper, honeyed with concern, penetrates the fog that swirls around me.

"No more Indian hokum. Lefty, get this damn dawg out of here. Sam, listen to me now. We're strippin' off your wet clothes. Y'all stay right here with us. We done found a satellite phone hung on a branch over the head of your city slick.

Them furry-ass critters brought 'ever last fool thang over the mountain. Stacked it all around like if he was an Egyptian on his way to glory."

Through the warmth of Bubba's voice, my boots drop away, wet socks and pants are peeled off, something warm surrounds my numb legs. Rough hands rub my feet.

"Globalstar GSP-1700. That there phone is a natural wonder. Help is comin'. Whirlybird out of Redding. You hear me, Sammy? Stay right with us. We dumbass men be lost as chil'en without you now."

Overhead a crow caws. I picture the sleek bird's shiny black feathers against the deep green of the fir needles. The air is thick with moisture, rich with the smell of decomposing fir and pine needles, fallen branches, and a scattering of red maple leaves.

Someone is chanting.

I sink into darkness as welcoming as home after a long journey.

Then the air is filled with a sound like a mighty wind. I'm bouncing in someone's arms. A voice I've come to know and love argues, demands to stay with me. Strange hands pull my arms over my head, peel off the rest of my clothes, wrap me in blessed warmth.

twenty-seven

THE AIR STINKS of sterilized death. The potent mix of ammonia, alcohol, and desperate fear stings my nose, warns me I'm in a hospital.

"Is she awake?"

"Coming around, I think. It's a mystery to me how these idiots traipse around in the woods hunting for some ridiculous monster and then expect us to fly in and drag their asses out of the woods and patch 'em up."

"You flew the helicopter yourself, did you? And I don't recall Dr. Patel allowing a nurse's aide into surgery when he was operating on her dad. Watch your mouth. I've told you before, folks coming around hear more than you expect."

"Yeah, well. I don't much care what the other old guy says, it ain't like that's her dad, neither."

Dad? Surgery?

I open my eyes to a narrow rectangle of bruised sky, turn away from the light and toward the voices.

Tiny dancing monkeys swim into view.

A woman in fanciful scrubs is fluffing my pillows. Is that a bird's nest on her head? I blink. Her pimply face swims into view. An orange butterfly clip holds her greasy hair in a hodgepodge of henna red and burnt orange strands.

"Here you are, hon. How're you feeling?"

Why is she talking to me in that high-pitched singsong voice, as if I were mentally impaired? Have I sustained a head injury?

"What hospital? Where am I?" I lick my dry mouth and she lifts a Styrofoam liter of water for me to sip through a flex straw.

"Weaverville."

This is bad. I'm in Our Lady of Misery. I need to snap out of this other worldly dream-state and get myself out of this tiny, much sued hospital before they kill me!

"I'm feeling better," I slur and attempt to sit up. "Did you say something about my dad?"

Dancing monkey nurse glances at a woman in pink scrubs who leans against the door frame.

"Told you she was coming out of it." Pinkie shakes her head, turns, and walks away, her dyed black ponytail bouncing with each quick step.

The bed whirs and lifts me into a sit. My head becomes a helium balloon. I expect it to float up off the scratchy sheets.

"Well, hon." Monkey-nurse smoothes my pillow, holds my wrist in her hot hand. Taking my pulse or restraining me, I'm unsure which. "Let's get you caught up on the happenings around here."

That kindergarten teacher voice is chalk on the blackboard of my soul.

"Where's my dad?"

Could he have found out I was here and come to me? Did I hear someone say surgery? And what about Mark? What's happening with him? I need to get out of this bed and get some answers.

"Let's just calm down, shall we?"

Why is she stalling? Fidgeting with the TV remote, adjusting the box of tissues on the metal nightstand, fussing with my pillows. Anger is more effective than smelling salts for snapping me back into my body.

"What's going on? Where's my dad?"

"My goodness, hon. No need to get yourself in an uproar. He's recuperating nicely. We have everything under control."

I am possessed with fury, adrenaline charged, healed of weakness. My hand comes off the bed and grips a fistful of cavorting simians.

"Tell… me… now! What is going on? Where's my dad? What's happened to Mark, the man they brought in with me?"

"Miss Foster?" A dark man in a white coat steps quickly to the bed and gently eases the baby-talking aide out of my grip. "I'm Dr. Patel. I treated you in ER. Happy to see you're awake. I understand you have questions."

"She said something about my dad." I glare at the woman backing away, smoothing the front of her scrubs.

"Mister Victor Foster. You speak of him as your father?"

"Ah, yeah. He's my dad. Is he here?"

"Mister Foster is here. Yes. We are giving him good care, I assure you."

The loose-weaved thermal blanket and a messy bundle of scratchy sheets hit Dr. Patel in the chest as I kick my way out of the bed. The room moves in a sickening swirl, darkness crunches in from my periphery. I have just enough time to put my head between my bare legs and suck in poorly sanitized air. Then firm hands are laying me back into the smell of bleach. A whirring noise and the hard bed flattens under me.

"Miz Foster?" The voice of Dr. Patel. "Am I going to have to tranquilize you to keep you in this bed?"

"Naw. You just gonna have to fill her in on the details about her ole man. I expect she's a might curious about the flower-bearer too."

"David?" I bawl like a frightened child.

He crawls onto the narrow bed beside me, pulls me against his bony, old man chest.

"Please," I beg. "Just tell me."

My fear hiccups in my chest, steals my breath, and shakes my body like a giant with a ragdoll.

"Hush now. I'll tell you everything. But you've gotta calm down, Samantha." David waves away Dr. Patel and the big-mouthed nurse's aide. "Your Dad's going to be fine. I promise you that. Take a deep breath and relax. Victor will skin me alive if I get you so riled that grandbaby of ours comes to harm."

Bubba was right?

I'm pregnant. But not necessarily with a burnished brown, dark-haired beauty. The baby could just as easily, right this minute, be encrypting butterscotch-blond hair and mossy-eyes.

"Really? A baby?"

"The rabbit died. Yep. At the scene, when they hauled you onto the helicopter along with your gym-toned hiking partner? Somebody wouldn't turn loose of your hand until the medics knew you were 'with chil'."

"Bubba?"

An image strobes into my mind. Being lifted onto that rocking, shaking, ear-splittingly loud machine. A giant hand being peeled from mine. A deep voice shouting over the noise of the spinning rotors. A helmeted pilot yelling back as we lifted off the tiny meadow, "Turn loose, man. We'll take care of her."

"Bubba would be my guess." David smells of horses and the woods of home. "The pilot said it was some guy big as Bigfoot and just about as ferocious."

"So you were here when they brought us in? You and Dad, both of you?"

"I'll get to that. Promise. Just ease yourself back down here. Let an old man tell the story his own way."

If Dad was in danger, David wouldn't be pussyfooting around the tale. Would he?

"There you go. Settle down and snuggle in here. You got any desire to know what's going on with your writer friend?"

The man I almost got killed? The one who might well be the father of this baby swimming around inside me?

"Yeah." I pull my arm from around his back, roll away just enough to lay the flat of my hand on my belly. "I've got some curiosity about Mark. But, for now, tell me about Dad!"

David pulls back a bit, studies my hand, raises his eyes to mine. Left eyebrow lifts a fraction.

I'm no good at keeping secrets. Never have been. I'm afraid he's going to ask a question for which I have no answer, but he seems to think better of it.

"I'll get to your dad. Let me tell it my way. Your friend was awake an hour ago, with an interesting tale to tell. Was in shock when he got here. Some hypothermia. 'Bout the same as you."

"The Bigfoots, they took him from the cave."

I try to push myself up, need to move, stretch my muscles and get out of this room. For a scrawny old guy, David is surprisingly strong. He rolls me against him, his hands making increasingly smaller circles on my lower back.

Those circles sooth me for some reason. The tension drains from by body and I let myself be comforted by his horsey smell.

"Used to do this with you when you was a babe. Had bad colic. Your dad and I, we'd take turns walking you around VD's, painting these little circles on your tiny back. Now. Tell me what happened with the writer."

"I didn't see it. Where we found him. But I think I remember Bubba saying his expensive gizmos and gadgets were stacked around him like he was an Egyptian king on his way to paradise. I got to the clearing first. I... I saw them. Three. A family."

Thinking of the encounter, letting my mind float on the warm muck of belief in the impossible, a calm center expands in my chest.

"You saw them before then. How else did you get that bloody handprint?"

"Yes. No. I didn't see them. I fell. They moved me, I think. Laid me gently in a bed of ferns they'd flattened. Put me right back almost where I started."

"I got pictures when you came in. Was there in the room when they pulled off your shirt and found that print. Made them take scrapings for a DNA test, too. You might have done it, Sammy. You just might have brought back the proof your dad and me been looking for all these years!"

He could be right.

But right now, if he doesn't tell me why dad was brought into this weak excuse of a hospital, I'm going to flip his bony ass off this narrow bed and go get the answers myself.

"Dammit, David. I'll tell you everything later. In detail. I'll write you a damn book. Right now, tell me what happened to Dad. Did he take another fall?"

"Not exactly."

Jagged shards of detail and blade-sharp scenes unfold as David pins me to him and speaks in a voice of calm and reason. My mind allows the story to penetrate in bits and pieces.

"We went in at Redwood Creek. Drove the capture van as far as the entrance to Tall Trees Grove. Let the horses pick their way through four decades of clear-cut slag until we got to Redwood National Park. Then we slowed, rode in single file."

In my mind I watch them, two men on horseback in a slow procession through a small doomed cathedral of two-thousand-year-old trees with their dead crowns proof of the need for community in all living things.

"At the bottom of the valley we re-crossed Redwood Creek at Cougar Gulch, worked our way up the backside of Elk Point."

"Where were you when the storm hit?"

I settle into the smell of damp, horse-infused flannel, do my best to breathe slowly. I have a bad feeling about the ending of this story.

"About three miles below the fork of the Trinity, it commenced to pour rain. We were a touch wet by the time we got to Little Fish Lake and struck camp.

"The thing was, both your dad and I thought something had been following us all day, but never saw anything. An occasional scatter of loose rock or the snap of a dead tree limb. Always coming from our right, up above us, and never closer than a quarter mile. 'Course, we should have paid more attention, circled back and waited. But the storm was moving in fast and mean and, truth be told, our old bones were begging to get un-straddled of the horses and into a dry tent."

"Just tell me what happened to Dad!"

My voice is muffled against his flat chest. More and more I'm convinced that those strong hands rubbing circles on my lower back are less about comfort and more about restraint. One deep breath expands his skinny chest. There's a protracted pause, as though he's deciding whether or not to exhale. Then warm breath is blown onto the top of my head. His grip tightens.

"The storm hit with a vengeance as we were setting up the tent along the west side of Little Fish Lake. We were hoping the mountain would provide some protection from the wind blowing in off the coast. Your dad was settling the horses, pulling 'em in under the protection of a narrow ledge."

"I know the campsite. Skip the details. Tell me what happened!"

"You're a good bit stronger than you look, Samantha Jean." His wiry arms are a vise. If he doesn't spit it out soon, I'm going to suffocate against all this steaming flannel.

"All right. Here's the gist of it. Old fools that we are, we were hoping the commotion above us throughout the hike was Bigfoot himself, come to welcome us back one last time to his domicile."

My struggle to break free and beat the truth out of him is met with a breath-stealing squeeze.

"Can't... breathe," I pant.

He does not loosen his hold.

"Someone followed us in. Took a shot at your dad while he was securing the horses."

If I could break free, I'd be running on shaky legs, bare feet on worn green hospital linoleum, on my way to Dad. With no hope of that, something at my center clicks off, escapes back into a fugue state where nothing can harm me, there is no need of worry, time simply ceases to exist.

"Samantha? You stay with me now."

"I'm... here. I'm... okay."

Both partial truths at best.

"Honey, now. He was hit in the shoulder. Clean shot. Missed the bone. We got lucky and the shooter had one of those satellite phones, like your city boy. Something to be said for technology. Anyways, we had him medivacked here within a couple hours of the time he was hit."

"How...?"

"Your dad might've had his hands full with the horses, but I had both hands free. Shot the bastard. Used his fancy phone to call for help."

"Why? Why shoot Dad?"

"Probably the same fanatic that's been calling the bar. The one sent that threat. What's important now is that the doctor's patched your dad up just fine. He's weak is all. Lost a bit of blood. But the docs are saying he's going to pull through this okay. Right now they're scurrying to find AB blood. Your old man could use a transfusion."

"What about me? Dad and I must be compatible. Get them in here to take my blood."

David's arms have slowly eased their pressure. Now he sits up on the edge of the narrow bed, one hip cocked crookedly on the protruding stainless steel rail. He strokes my tangled hair from my face. Frightened as I am about Dad, part of me is just happy to be able to draw a full breath again.

Flying Monkey-woman is back. Must have been leaning on the door jamb, eavesdropping on our conversation.

"Why didn't you tell me my dad needed a transfusion?" I ask the squeaky-voiced snoop.

"Wrong blood type," David answers. He glares at the nurse's aide. His jaw tightens, eyes narrow.

"Is this about me being pregnant. Is that why you won't use my blood?"

"Got nothing to do with that," David insists. "You're O-positive. Not compatible blood types."

Monkey Nurse snorts.

I know I'm projecting my anger onto this ratty Florence Nightingale, understand that pissing off an inept aide in a hospital infamous for life-threatening mishaps is a very bad idea. Still, I simply cannot keep my big mouth shut.

"What is your problem?" I demand and, even to my ears, I sound snotty, challenging this health-care amateur to some kind of inane pissing contest.

"Honey." The kindergarten teacher voice is gone. This is The Wicked Witch of the West releasing the flying monkeys. "With those blood types. There ain't no way that man is your daddy."

twenty-eight

THIN TUFTS OF fluffy white surround his head like a feathery halo.

I smooth his hair away from his forehead the way he always did when I was a kid and had a fever, or a hurt of any kind, really.

His skin, under my hand, is cool as marble.

Plastic tubes carry various liquids in, and out, of his still body. An oxygen line hisses softly. Monitors click, beep and, occasionally, bleat some warning upon which no one comes to check.

I hate all this paraphernalia attached to him, have an irrational and unshakable conviction that the machinery is shrinking him from the giant of a man I've always known to this small, shrunken, gray soul barely big enough to make an impression under the dull white hospital sheets. He doesn't even smell like Dad anymore. My face, in his upturned palm, gives me, not the sour tang of old Winstons overlaid with Bay Rum, or even the honest smell of forest dirt. Instead, my nose fills with the sting of rubbing alcohol and the coppery scent of blood.

I could leave Dad's side right now, open the door of the room directly across the hall, and stare down at the face of the man who sighted down the barrel of a . 22 and sent a bullet through cold air to pierce and tear at the warm flesh of the only man I've ever loved unconditionally. The way I understand it, David's shot clipped the lunatic's upper thigh, missed any major arteries.

The shooter was able to explain, in great raving detail, why he felt compelled to stake out two harmless old men and follow them from a rain-blackened street in Eureka to a dusty gravel parking lot north of Orick. David said the man ranted through the entire thirty-minute helicopter ride, telling how he tracked them through the forest until the whispering voices in his head told him to shoot the man who, forty years ago, stood in a clearing above Bluff Creek with blood on his hands and a dog in a bright red harness straining at the end of a long lead.

Hawk's dad just about rubbed a sore spot on my back, moving circles with his rough hand, chanting over and over again that none of this was my fault. Mark, or as David called him, "That Snake," would have posted that blog deal no matter what, had nothing to do with me spending time with the man. Of course he can wear the skin clean off me with good intentions and it won't change the fact I slept with the enemy. May even have conceived his child.

I don't believe I told Mark anything that he could have used to harm Dad. I don't! Been over it and over it in my mind and no family secrets were exposed. So why do I feel like this is all my fault?

Two images are stuck on a loop in my tired brain.

Borrowed high-heeled pumps framing the face of a green-eyed, smiling man.

Dad's arm rising endlessly, mechanically, taking aim at the Bigfoot we've named Patty looking back over her shoulder at him in bewilderment and fear.

This endless tape has an audio, too. The voice of the Wicked Witch gloating. "Ain't no way that man is your daddy." Awash in my own little tidal wave of self-pity and guilt, I miss the moment Dad's eyes open.

"Told you I'd be fine." His voice is a scratchy whisper, tiny animal claws on a wet canvas tent.

Tears swell my throat, cover my face with wet heat. I have just enough strength to lean forward and lay my head gently on his chest.

"Daddy."

His hand makes slow circles on my back. I can tell the moment he realizes I'm wearing, not street clothes, but a thin hospital robe over a butt-flashing cotton gown. His hand on my back stills.

"I'm good, Dad. Not hurt, just worn out. But… things didn't exactly go as planned when we got to Bluff Creek."

"Ah, yeah. I'm not surprised. Hawk came by after you left. Bubba and Lefty filled him in on the prank. When he found out you were going to be camping in that cave, that's when he insisted Bubba bring him along."

I sit up while he presses the button to raise the head of the bed. He sips ice water from a striped straw. His dark eyes sparkle. He wiggles his eyebrows. A lopsided smile emerges from behind the giant Styrofoam cup.

All these I take as signs that Dad has returned. I haven't lost him after all. My grin is wide, but I can't stop the hot tears.

He really is going to be all right. Shrunken gray man is banished. Dad is back. "You ever have occasion to talk to Doctor Bernstein about what he calls 'portals'?"

My throat too swollen to talk, I shake my head.

"Well, you ought to listen to what he has to say. Has something to do with that string theory physics he teaches down there at Berkeley. Portals in time and space. I believe that cave you and Hawk found might be one."

He points to a pack of tissues and I blow my nose.

The bed whirs halfway down. I adjust crinkly pillows behind his back and head.

"You need to rest, Dad."

He nods, points to a squished bag of dark red liquid. I follow the tubing to the needle in the back of his wrist.

"Turns out one of the nurse's aides is my blood type."

"Not the orange-haired woman?"

"Ah, yeah. I believe that's her. Scrubs covered in some kind of somersaulting animals as I recall."

Huh. Well damn.

"Dad? We need to talk sometime about that transfusion. Okay?"

His eyes are shut but he nods his head. "Need to rest. But tell me you saw Bigfoot." Like a kid asking for a bedtime story.

"I did. Saw three. They were different than I ever imagined. More terrifying. Awesomely beautiful in a way I still haven't quite worked out."

His breathing has slowed and I think he's fallen asleep. But when I lay my hand on top of his, he opens his eyes and gives me that lopsided smile.

"Tell me."

"Later."

Right now I'm happy to sit in a hard-backed chair, weak sunlight and strong wind making a kaleidoscope of light from dancing branches of the blue spruce outside the window. His snores lull me to sleep like the lapping of playful waves on a stone- strewn beach. I dream of the safety of warm arms in dark woods, imagine love strong enough to transcend time and space.

Hands as wide as a bear's come over my shoulders, thick fingertips meet at my clavicle. Still half asleep, I lean back into the welcome girth, luxuriate in the warm rot smell of rich black forest dirt, spiced with a hint of marijuana resin under the fingernails.

"You near 'bout scared the life out of this ole boy."

The stink of sterility rushes in with the fluorescent light when I open my eyes. I want to go back to sleep. Had just about forgotten Mark is lying somewhere in a hospital bed pretty much exactly like this one. I need to talk to him, find out what happened to him out there on Blue Mountain. Oh yeah... and tell him I'm pregnant. Still haven't told Hawk. How will they react? Whose baby is this growing in my belly? How am I going to raise it alone? Have I messed my life up so completely that I'll never get out of VD's? Never see any other part of the world?

Somewhere deep inside me, a levee breaks. A wall of stubborn anger, cemented with guilt and trembling fear, is breeched.

I bawl like an abandoned child. Bubba squats down, pulls my hiccupping, howling body against the comfort of his deep chest.

"Your daddy's gonna be finer'n frog's hair. I talked to the doc what patched him up. Be just another story to tell at them Bigfoot meetin's."

"I... know... that." I cannot catch my breath.

Can a person drown in their own bad choices?

"You still discombobulated, Darlin'. That there's all that's wrong with you. Come on back to bed. You got to think of the little one now."

Another wave of grief pours itself all over Bubba's shirt front. That stupid, wicked, lifeblood-giving nurse. What if Dad isn't my real father? What if, on top of everything else, my whole life's been a big fat lie?

When the wailing has decreased from wolf pack on a full silver-mooned night to the whimpering of a frightened pup, Bubba pulls away and slips out of his shirt. Kneeling in front of me in a black cotton XXXL T-shirt emblazoned in curlicue pink with the proclamation "Y'all are looking at a Fine Georgia Peach," he turns his flannel shirt wrong side out and hands it to me.

"Blow," he instructs.

I do as I'm told.

"Tell your daddy bye for now. Let's get you back to bed."

The tent-sized shirt clutched like a security blanket, I lean in and kiss Dad's forehead, whisper in his ear.

"I love you. I didn't get a chance to mention. You're going to have a grandbaby. And I've messed things up as usual and need your help to get everything straightened out."

Bubba's arm around my waist, I'm halfway to the door when I remember something else.

Back at Dad's bed, I stand tall, make the announcement straight up and out loud.

"There was a handprint on my belly. We've got a picture of it. David made them take DNA samples before the nurses washed it off. You maybe have proof this time. Undisputable scientific proof of the existence of Bigfoot."

I trace Dad's exposed wrist with my finger, kiss his whiskery cheek one more time. "I need you to help me sort through what I saw. What I felt looking into those eyes."

The blubbering swells up again and I'm crying like a frightened child.

"Lord have mercy, gal. Let the man get him some shut-eye."

Bubba leads me like an invalid, past the uniformed cop asleep in his hard-backed chair in front the shooter's door. We're almost to my room when I hear angry voices that snap my head up. I stare down the hall.

Hawk and his dad are leaning into each other. David is animated. He sways, his hands moving along with his words. Hawk is as still as a stone, back ramrod straight, hands deep in the pockets of his jeans.

"You so sure it's my kid?"

"You telling me you're not going to step up on this?"

Like the low growl of some kind of large animal, Bubba's voice is an irresistible command.

"Keep movin'. Now ain't the time for this nonsense."

Under the scratchy sheets again, Bubba wedged into a folding chair pushed close, my shaky hand encapsulated in his paw, my breath finally evens. Calm settles over me. I'm in the eye of a hurricane.

It's not over, I know that. But the first hit is already a psyche-preserving blur, and my mind is not yet ready to recognize that the second wall of the storm always hits harder than the first.

Almost asleep, I'm suddenly compelled by a need for confession.

"Bubba?"

"Right here."

"Hawk's right. I don't know whose baby it is."

My hand flutters as he tightens his grip for the barest second.

"I ever tell you why I left Georgia?"

The cloud-shrouded sun leaks weak light through the window blinds. Slats of watery light mark Bubba's face. On the edge of exhausted sleep, this moment has the feel of returning to a childhood dream.

"Nope," I say, "you just walked into VD's five years ago."

His voice is pitched low and tinged with the vibrato of a private man sharing a long-held secret. "Got my diploma from up in Athens. Come on back home to Noisy Creek and was working construction, thinking on startin' my own company. Had me a woman. Elizabeth." His eyes never leave mine. "Lizzie… she… got pregnant." His thumb strokes my cheek. "I went out and bought a ring. Little diamond chip weren't no bigger than the twinkle in my eye got us into the situation to begin with. Had it all planned out. Dinner at The Plantation House. Down on one knee."

"What happened?" His beard is rough under my palm.

"Turns out what I saw as a surprise blessing, Lizzie saw as a temporary inconvenience."

"I'm sorry, Bubba."

"Ain't nothin' for you to be sorry about. As for that little one of yours? Don't fret. I know whose chil' it is."

"How could you…"

He leans forward. His face inches from mine.

"She's your baby, Sam. Ain't nothing else matters."

I fall asleep with the image of his shaggy head and wonderful grin imprinting itself on my exhausted soul.

twenty-nine

"YOU COME TO my hospital room to finish the job you and your pack of hicks started when you dragged me into the wilderness?"

"First of all, we weren't in the wilderness. Didn't the helicopter get you here in less than twenty minutes? And we never meant you any real harm. Just wanted to scare you some. Teach you a lesson for that ridiculous blog which, just so you know, got my dad shot!"

My intentions are good. I just want to check on how Mark's doing. Make sure he's not suffered any permanent damage. Guilt at my involvement in what happened to him nags at my conscience.

Dad says I have an overactive sense of responsibility. Maybe. But it was me boot camping him down the slippery muck of Blue Mountain.

Besides, I'm dying to hear about his encounter with the family of Bigfoots. There aren't that many people out there with whom I share this experience. Did he react the same way I did? Is he still overwhelmed with awe and terror? Does he wake from dreams with his heart beating its way out of his chest and want, more than anything, to return to the very image that nearly ended his life with fright?

Also, while I'm here, I figure I'll mention that he might have fathered a baby with this Humboldt County hick.

"I've already spoken to my publisher. We're suing you. All of you. You're all being charged with attempted murder. Reckless endangerment at the very least. There'll be a civil suit as well."

"What are you ranting about? All we did was take you on a walk in the woods. A hike you asked to go on, by the way. I didn't tell you to pack an entire sporting goods store of crap with you. There was no way I could have known you were so ignorant you would risk hypothermia by not protecting your spare clothes from the rain that falls, let's see, pretty much every day of the year in this county."

He buckles the lid on one of those carry-on pieces of luggage. The ones with little wheels so they can be pulled like reluctant children through airports. All three of us are checking out of this deathtrap of a hospital this morning. Dad, Mark, and me. The shooter is taking his chances at Our Lady of Misery another day or two before being transported to the Humboldt County jail.

Since Mark didn't come looking for me, I decided this might be my last opportunity to talk to him before he disappears back into the wider world outside my circle of knowledge. Outside VD's, in other words.

Bag packed, he sits on the side of his hospital bed in black slacks with not one, not two, but three prissy little pleats, and a sweater I'll bet anything is some kind of extra super-duper virgin cashmere. The sweater is the same color green as his eyes. Damn his hide. How can he possibly look this good?

Since the medical folks cut me out of what was left of my clothes when I checked in, and since I do not have a publisher to FedEx me five hundred dollars' worth of fancy duds, I'm wearing what Bubba could find at the Weaverville General Store.

Jeans a full size too small. Bless his heart for believing my ass was that small, but the denim is cutting me in half in an area I don't generally abuse in that manner. My fluorescent orange sweatshirt has an embossed image of Bigfoot. The right arm is reflective and, each time I shift positions, the appendage moves up and down in a continual wave of greeting.

I like the sweatshirt a lot.

Reminds me of that stupid blog with Dad's arm rising again and again to site down the rifle barrel at Bigfoot, keeps me in touch with why I'm angry with the undeniably sexy man sitting across from me with one adorable ass cheek perched on the narrow hospital bed.

"I can't believe you did that to me, Samantha. Do you have any idea how I felt? Hallucinating after eating the brownie you made a point of showing me. Knowing, as hungry as I was, I'd eat it. Bubba in that monkey suit packing me through the woods in the dark. Was that you in the other suit or was it your Indian? And Lefty playing the part of the young Bigfoot?"

He thinks we did this? Faked the smell? Gathered up his electronic crap and packed it over the mountain? Carried him through the woods in the middle of the night?

"Do you hear yourself? We didn't do anything except leave you alone in a warm cave with a marijuana-laced brownie I specifically told you not to eat. You hiked down that mountain. What kind of strength do you think it'd take to pack a grown man up the same grade and back down the other side? In the middle of gale force winds. In the pitch dark. No moon. Just knowledge of the woods."

The Wicked Witch/blood-giving angel lingers in the hallway. Eavesdropping again. Today she's draped herself in purple scrubs, leering orange jack-o-lanterns tumbling from the neckline.

"You're denying you did this? Sticking with the claim that a family of non-existent monsters kidnapped me? You know, Sam. I think I'd have forgiven you the whole thing, scary as it was, if you hadn't felt the need to do the examination."

"What now? Examination?"

Sun breaks through the clouds and floods the drab green room in glorious pale yellow light. Without thinking, I lean back in the uncomfortable chair, open my arms to expose myself more fully to the blessed warmth.

"Don't pretend to be stupid, Samantha. Which one of your goons put his hands all over me?"

The sun disappears again. I get out of the chair, walk to the window. Nothing but low, dull gray clouds.

"Did you have prints on you? When you got here, did you think to have somebody take pictures of them? Preserve anything for DNA tests?"

"Of course not. It was a hoax. A prank that came close to killing me! A dangerous joke for which you and your buddies are going to pay dearly."

"For an educated man, you're not thinking clearly. Look at the facts. I know you won't believe me, but I spent the night passed out from a fall down the cliff. The same family of Bigfoots that took you carried me through the woods and put me gently in a bed of ferns. Not ten feet from the mouth of the cave. I must have been there when they passed by with you in their arms."

"Stop the lies. God, I can't believe I actually cared for you. Well, my mistake. You fooled me into believing you and I might have a real relationship. But I'm not stupid enough to let you convince me that Bigfoot exists."

A lunch cart rattles down the hallway. Dad will be dressed and ready to check out, wondering where I am.

There's no point in asking this particular doubter to plunge his fingers in the bloody side of a living faith. People choose to believe. Or not. Time to tell Mark what he needs to know and get on with the rest of my life.

I walk back across the room, lower myself into the chair, and lean back. With no thought at all, my arms wrap protectively around my middle. A deep breath in, I push the air out through my nose, look across the four feet of faded linoleum, force myself to meet his river-green eyes. Funny how close anger is to desire, the narrowest of gaps in a synapse-firing brain.

My right arm uncurls itself from my flat stomach, is on its way across the divide when he clears his throat, puts his tasseled loafers on the floor.

"I think we're finished here, Samantha."

Standing, so that I'm forced to tilt my head awkwardly to meet his eye, he straightens the pleats of his trousers, taps a Cordova-leather loafer.

"No." I stay seated, don't trust my legs to support me. "I need to talk to you about something else."

He rolls his shoulders, shakes his head.

"This has nothing to do with Bigfoot."

His sigh is a statement of exasperation, but he sits back down on the edge of the bed, folds his arms across his chest. He won't meet my eye, but at least he's not walking away. Yet.

Two ways to rip off a bandage. I never have been much for prolonging the agony.

"I'm pregnant. Could be the baby's yours."

The wood laminate door swings open. Dr. Patel is in the tiny room. He sweeps his muddy brown eyes over the two of us. The tension seems to physically repel him back toward the hall.

"I'll release Mister Foster first," he tells Mark. "Be back here to sign your paperwork in ten minutes."

The heavy door makes a swish as it closes.

The sun once again plays peek-a-boo with the steel-gray clouds. Dust moats are suddenly exposed in the pale gold light, beautiful floating specks of dead tissue.

"*If* you're pregnant."

His stress on that first word swells my throat. I swallow hard. There is no way in hell I'm going to let him see me cry.

"And that's a huge *if*. There's no way it's mine. Let's cut the crap here, Samantha. Be honest for a change. Maybe you could even stop the naïve act and we could talk about how careful we were to use condoms."

"Ah, yeah. All four times."

It hurts to force words out into the astringent air. What I want is to go home, crawl in bed, and stay there until I wake up and the last six weeks never happened. Well. Time enough to give that a try.

"Look, Mark. You believe what you want. I don't want anything from you. Just thought you should know. I am pregnant. The chances are four-to-one it's your baby. I've never had unprotected sex in my life. Well, once when Hawk and I were sixteen and seventeen. Our first time."

What am I saying? Shut up! Just tell him goodbye and get out of this suffocating room that smells of sanitized death and betrayal.

Get up! Go!

My legs try to buckle under me, but cleansing, empowering anger kicks in some much needed adrenaline. Finally. I turn my back on him, don't need to see his jaw set hard enough to break a bleached molar. My legs hold my weight, carry me five steps to the door. The stainless steel handle is cold in my palm.

"Get a paternity test." His voice is low, tiny fissures along the hard edges of each word. "If it's mine, I'll have my attorney get in touch. We'll work something out."

I hold the door open with my foot. Dad's blood donor is lingering at a magazine cart, pretending to straighten ten-year-old *Readers Digest*s and coverless *Field & Stream*. My smile in her direction is the best I can do for a twin apology and thank you.

I know just the Anglo-Saxon word to throw back over my shoulder at the green-eyed man watching me go. Can feel the curse building like a hot volcano of bile. Instead, I let the door swish shut behind me. My restraint has nothing to do with any new-found manners. I just don't have enough strength right now to walk and cuss at the same time.

thirty

IT RAINS NON-stop for three days.

The first day, a howling banshee of a storm roars down from up around Barrow, Alaska. Pellets of steel-blue rain blow sideways off the bay, pound against my bedroom windows. Wind, an endless 'Om,' tears shingles from the roof, litters the wet asphalt with tree limbs, the improperly secured sleeping bags of the homeless, and the white soapy foam of whitecaps from the thrashing waters of Humboldt Bay.

I spend the morning under the covers. Refuse to do more than peek my head out of the quilt and monitor the slow movement of the day's meager lavender light across my trembling windows.

Just after one o'clock, Bubba and Stacey invade with tomato basil soup and vegetarian sandwiches from Nooners. Bubba clears the nightstand of wadded-up balls of Kleenex, three half-empty glasses of Diet Cherry 7-Up, and a dog-eared Jodi Picoult novel that is supposed to be helping me see that other people have it a whole lot harder than me. It's not working. The *I was sad because I had no shoes until I met a man who had no feet* deal is only making me wonder how long before my own metaphorical feet drop off. Contrary to common belief, misery does not love company.

"I have a headache," I moan. The top sheet is trapped under my butt. It takes me a minute of pulling, tugging, and cussing to figure out this simple fact.

"Coffee headache," Stacey says.

She and Bubba exchange a look at my struggle with the sheet.

"Can't have any caffeine now what with the little one."

"Who are you two? Emissaries from Doctor Oz?"

Both ignore me.

They tuck into the food. I pretend to sip at my soup. We listen to the howling of the wind as it finds a path around hundred-year-old brick buildings, swoops up and over improvised roofs and poorly envisioned renovations. Rain-blasted windows shimmy eerily.

Bubba finishes his meal first. I offer him my untouched sandwich.

"Nope. I understand you're dealin' with a mighty heavy situation here. But that chil' can't grow healthy on worry. You have to eat."

"Bubba's right." Stacey stretches her arms in the air, yawns like a sleek cat. "Shit happens. Get up and start shoveling."

I jerk the covers higher on my chest, glare like Carrie at the prom. My fiery stare has no effect whatsoever on Stacey.

She smiles at me. "You stay in bed all day like a child trying to avoid a math test, people going to start treating you like one."

"Ah, yeah. Well. You just run the bar till I get back on my feet."

"Already got it covered."

She stuffs three tomato-and-mustard-stained bags into one, holds the crumbled bundle against her chest with both hands. Her parting shot as she goes back down to run the bar I'm supposed to manage, "Your dad's asking for you."

A sudden blast of salt-laden wind slams the windows. I throw off the quilt, wrap myself in scruffy chenille. The storm draws me to the windows. The sky is a brooding mass of roiling black streaked with the shimmering silver gray of an electrical storm.

From behind me, Bubba's deep rumbling voice seems part of the weather.

"I wish I'd've seen them."

Lightning reveals the dark bay. Swirling whitecaps top a confused sea pocked with troughs as big as hills. In the darkness after the flash, my reflection stares back. Arms crossed, robe cinched crookedly, pale face framed in stringy hair.

"Yeah. Bigfoot doesn't seem like the right name for them, somehow." I turn from the window, finger comb my greasy hair. "You believe I saw them though. Right?"

"Yep. I smelled them good enough. And I felt them 'round the truck. I been wantin' to talk to you about that."

The mattress bows under my weight when I sit on the edge of the bed. I keep my wool socks flat on the wood floor, lean forward so my head is inches from his, and clasp my hands above my knees. The space heater kicks on. The air is dense, too filled with moisture to be drawn properly into my lungs.

Bubba rolls his shoulders, a mountain shaking off the night.

"If I'd had any idea in this world that you was in trouble on the other side of that mountain, you know the devil himself couldn't've kept me in that truck."

It takes only the smallest movement. His cheek is smooth against my mouth, tastes of the alcohol in his aftershave.

"I'm beginning to look like Bigfoot," I say. "Going to take a shower and then spend the afternoon with Dad. You up for dinner tonight at Marcelli's?"

At the door to the bathroom, the belt of my robe already untied, I turn to see him standing, a smile that goes all the way to his eyes lighting his face.

"You think we should ask Lefty to come?" I ask.

In this light his eyes are the speckled blue-green of beach-polished turquoise.

Why have I never noticed that before?

"Naw. That boy'll likely be busy with Car-o-line. How's about tonight it'll just be you and me?"

"JEEZ, DAD. IT'S hot enough in here to roast a turkey."

His room behind the bar has narrow windows, set high like gun slots along the south-facing wall. He's up and dressed, settled in his duct-taped recliner, a pole light throwing fluorescent blue on the red plaid blanket across his lap. He puts a finger in John Green's *The Best of Sasquatch*.

His cheek is smooth when I lean in for a kiss, but he hasn't showered yet. Too weak yet to stand that long is my guess.

"I'm an old man. Injured, too. Soon enough I'll be cold."

It takes a few minutes to clear the only other chair in the room of topography maps, much read books, and Bigfoot periodicals.

"How come you keep talking about dying? Is there something you're not telling me?"

My voice is calm. Mostly calm. No way he can hear my heart pounding.

"You first. I hear rumors you have some news of your own."

He's as stubborn as me. Or I'm as stubborn as he is. Either way, if he's sick, he's not going to tell me until he's ready.

The humming light magnifies the deep wrinkles around his eyes and mouth.

Please God, let him hear this as good news.

"Mark and Hawk. I slept… had sex… with both of them. Same month."

The words hang in the room's sticky heat and near darkness.

"I… um… I'm pregnant."

His eyes react first. Their sparkle seems to pull the corners of his mouth up into a wide grin. Every wrinkle deepens as he bestows on me a look that I do my best to memorize, flash freeze for barren moments down the road. Moments I know are coming, when I will need this warmth to sustain me.

Then the Sasquatch book is on the floor, buried under the fallen wool blanket, and he does an old man jig across the rag rug that separates us. He sweeps me into his arms and I'm bawling, dancing, my arms around his skinny waist.

thirty-one

IN THE NIGHT, the weather turns bad. Real bad.

Just after dawn the *Lucky Eight*, a trawler out of Portland, disappears off Trinidad. Two local women in their seventies, beachcombing below the lighthouse, watch as the forty-eight-foot fishing boat races up the mountainous edge of a rogue wave and never re-surfaces on the other side.

Seventy-five-mile-an-hour winds tip an ancient redwood at the Duck Street entrance to Sequoia Park. The two-hundred-and-forty-foot giant falls across a block of power lines. The hoary tree takes out three of its brethren, the detached garage of Mr. and Mrs. James Ambrosini, and electricity to two hundred and sixty homes.

I spend the morning in the bar. It's amazing how much work there is to do when Stacey has a day off. I believe the girl plans it that way.

Dad's snuffling snores are reassuringly loud through the open door of his room. Bubba is off on some mystery meeting, the details of which he refused to share with me last night over dinner. He showed up at six o'clock in clean jeans and a freshly ironed flamingo-pink shirt. He'd even brushed the mud off his Timberlakes.

David, nursing a draft at the bar, gave him a hard time about the new shirt. Accused Bubba of giving tailoring work to Omar the tentmaker.

It's just after noon and two regulars, mail-carrier brothers Eric and Junior, are having their usual lunch—boilermakers and salted peanuts. I fill the maraschino cherry tray, pop two in my mouth, one sugar sweet circle for each cheek. For a bar that serves mostly beer, we go through a phenomenal amount of cherries.

The door opens and a wall of icy cold collides with the overheated air of the bar.

It's the haircut that draws my attention first. A hundred-dollar razor cut over a balding forehead. I work my way down the apparition. Square, steel-framed glasses protect the eyes of a weasel. Predatory eyes, tiny, programmed to seek perpetually for advantage. Gray, three-piece suit tailored over small, sleek body and a plumb-line straight, purple bowtie under a short gray beard.

"I'm hoping you're Samantha Jean Foster."

He slides his narrow butt gingerly onto the bar stool across from me. His extended hand hangs in the air between us. Mine is sticky with cherry juice so I go ahead and offer it.

"You are?"

"James William Stewart." He leans in, drops his voice as though he's revealing a priceless secret. "Of Pope, Smith, and Stewart. Literary agency."

Ah. Mark Neilsen's good buddy.

I stab the pointy tip of a paring knife into a ten-pound bag of peanuts, empty the salted contents into a cracked wooden bowl at the end of the bar.

He rubs the tips of his fingers together, looks around for something to wipe the sugary red contamination from his hands.

Since my encounter in that U-shaped meadow, I've spent a good bit of time convincing myself that something inside me has been altered. Be it pregnancy or communion with another species or parallel universe, my usual underlying anger seems to have subsided, replaced with a sense of peace, a calm acceptance of what I cannot change.

Watching the man whose idea it was to slander Dad by accusing him of murder, of sacrilege, I understand this revelation for the self-deception it is. Far as I'm concerned, Mr. James Williams Stewart is as responsible for my dad being shot as the man locked up in the Humboldt County jail awaiting trial. I may be more at peace overall, but evidently I'm still capable of being angry enough to kill with my bare hands.

"You the guy whose idea it was to post that blog?"'

His ferret eyes blink.

"If I may? It was never my intent to cause any harm with that bit of publicity. If I'm at fault in any way, I suppose it could be said that I misjudged the fanaticism of simple folk, overlooked the potency of the symbolism of this mythological mountain creature."

Six inches of maraschino cherry juice remains in a gallon jar behind the bar. It flashes blood red, calls to me. I unclench my fists, watch as both my hands lift the sticky jar, pour a quart of the sweet liquid into the lap of the man who got my dad shot.

"I believe," I say, "you have once again underestimated the fanaticism of us simple folk."

The weasel is still sitting, watching the crimson syrup soak into his gray suit. I can see the tiny wheels turning in his little rodent brain.

"Young lady, I can understand how you might think I deserved that. You may, however, wish to hear me out."

My palms are pressed against my thighs. Twin slamming pulses resonate through my core.

"Get. Out."

"Miss Foster. I'm here to offer you a sizeable advance to persuade you to write a book about your experience in the woods the other day. I understand DNA samples were taken?"

"Get... out... of... my... bar. I ain't never been a lady. Your mistake. Go now or I'm going to see if your pointy little rodent head will fit inside that empty gallon jar."

Two hours later, I'm on my hands and knees cleaning the customer bathroom, when Dad pokes his head in to tell me I've got company.

"Who?" I raise up to my knees, the toilet brush pointing upright and slightly away from me like a magic wand.

"The law."

He's grinning, so I'm not worried. Much.

I strip off rubber gloves, scrub to my elbows until the water heats to scalding. The mirror over the stained porcelain sink shows a youngish woman with no discernible pregnancy glow. The skin around my eyes looks bruised. My hair pokes out in yellow tufts from the edges of the red handkerchief I've tied around my head. I untie the bandana, finger comb my hair. Maybe it looks bedroom messy. Sexy. But I doubt it. More like "interrupted cleaning the ill-aimed piss from the sides of a toilet bowl" messy.

Ah well. Life ain't always a bowl of cherries. Or cherry syrup either.

The Humboldt County Deputy District Attorney sits at the bar, a thick white mug of steaming coffee warming his hands. I catch his eye in the mirror and motion him to the table under the one-eyed bear.

He's wearing soft jeans, a white shirt open at the neck, and a black blazer made from the wool of decrepit sheep sheared one last stop before the house of mutton chops.

"Afternoon, Bobby."

"You look good, Sammy."

I snag the seat facing out into the bar. Bobby pulls a chair around next to mine. Both of us with our backs firmly against the wall.

"I smell like Lysol and toilet cakes. You didn't come all the way across town to give a girl a compliment."

"No. No I didn't." Is he blushing?

"Let me help you out. You had a visit from a little weasel in a sticky three-piece suit."

"Uh-huh. And a writer friend of his who claims you and a couple of friends tried to kill him."

"Mark was there?"

Now I'm blushing.

Dad's long legs are stretched out in front of him. An hour ago he had Bubba drag the stuffing-leaking recliner from his room to his favorite spot at the back of VD's. With the recliner kicked up like that, customers are going to have to squeeze sideways around him to get to the courtyard. The *Times-Standard* is open in front of him, but he's not reading.

The District Attorney nods. "Mark Neilsen? Blond guy? Nice teeth? He was there, yeah. Those two had quite a story to tell."

Against all natural inclinations, I keep my mouth shut.

Dad rattles his newspaper. The Deputy District Attorney clears his throat, pulls his left foot up to rest on his right knee.

"The writer claims you had the aid of three individuals whose names he didn't know but who he described as 'a giant', 'a smaller guy,' and 'some kind of Indian.'"

I meet his eye, keep my face blank. Everybody in the county knows Hawk and I have been an item since grade school, and Bobby plays darts against Bubba and Lefty every Thursday night.

Finally he looks away, sips at his coffee.

"Anyway… Mister Neilsen maintains that you tricked him into going on a hike for which he was improperly prepared."

A memory of Mark staggering down the side of Blue Mountain, slipping and stumbling under the weight of his pack, is quickly replaced with a vision of me standing in the parking lot telling him the damn thing needed to be lightened. Okay. I didn't insist strenuously, but then, he's a grown man. Plus, I was good and angry at the time. I believe I may even have chuckled a little internally with the knowledge that he was going to pay for his bad judgment.

My resolve to keep my big mouth shut tears, top to bottom.

"If there's a law against being stupid, it'd be him that'd need to be arrested, far as I can see."

"Well, but the man also claims he was drugged, kidnapped, and terrorized."

Dad's snort lifts him clean out of his chair. The footrest of the recliner slams shut and he crosses the bar and settles himself in the chair across the table from us. His glare at the DA is a challenge that brings to mind an old bull elk, shaggy with age, head lowered, strips of velvet hanging from wide antlers, standing firm, protecting his herd from the encroachment of some sleek young interloper.

"You got any actual evidence any this took place?" Dad asks.

Bobby sits up straight, both feet flat on the floor.

"No sir. As I explained to both these fellows. Seems to me the entire alleged episode is his word against Sam's. He wants to look foolish and bother some attorney to file a civil suit, nothing I can do about that, but far as I can see, there's no evidence of criminal action."

His work done, the old bull wanders back to his ancient recliner with nothing more than a backward glare. Bobby and I study each other in the mirror over the bar. He buttons his blazer. Opens it again. When he turns his chair to face me, his back to the door, I know he's ready to spit it out.

"Couple other things."

I wait.

"First off, just to satisfy my own curiosity and, hell, because it'll make a damn good story around the courthouse, did you really pour a gallon of cherry syrup on the guy's two-thousand-dollar suit?"

"Was closer to a quart and, you've known me for years, Bobby. Would I do a thing like that?"

We grin at each other for a second or two, couple of rednecks happy as pigs in shit to be who we are, right where we need to be. He watches Stacey come in the front door, tie on her apron, draw drafts for three fishermen leaning over the bar cussing the weather.

"This guy, Mark Neilsen?"

I nod, know what's coming.

"Neilsen, uh, he also maintains that you're accusing him of being... of fathering a child."

"It's a possibility."

I'm pretty sure that's confusion I see in his eyes. It actually looks like betrayal, but that seems unlikely. Bobby comes sniffing around occasionally when Hawk has disappeared on one of his drunken escapades. But the two of us have never been any more than friends.

"How? I mean, why'd you...? Really, Sam?"

"You had to be there. Plus, aren't you the guy that, in high school, fell in love first with Mary Ann Cushner? Nicknamed Hummer. An affectionate term given by the football team? And when Mary Ann, in a move diametrically opposed to her nickname, got pregnant by the shop teacher, you moved on to Susan Hacker. The brunette whose daddy kept rattlesnakes in the trunk of his car and, correct me if I'm wrong, once shot up the grill of your truck when you brought her home an hour late?"

He shifts in his seat, rolls his shoulders before managing a small smile.

"Okay. I get it. Lust is blind." He sips at his cold coffee. "How's Hawk dealing with the news?"

"Don't know. Not well is what I hear. He's avoiding me."

"Well. My daddy always said water takes the shape of its container. Not much new there, huh?"

I don't like him trash talking Hawk and open my mouth to tell him so when he interrupts my train of thought.

"Want me to send a sheriff to pick him up? I'd be delighted to do so. Knowing Hawk, finding a legal reason to run him in wouldn't be much of a challenge."

Do I want to see Hawk? It suddenly occurs to me that it's been well, okay, not days, but a good long string of hours, since I thought of the man. I mentally poke at my feelings. Huh. Scab seems to have dropped away. Shiny new skin is tender as new love, the pain when I press too hard steals my breath. I decide not to poke it.

"Bubba already offered to drag his ass down the mountain. I believe I'm gonna just let Hawk sort himself out on his own this time."

He shrugs.

"Your choice."

I change the subject. "What's happening to Mitch Simpson? How come he's not in the Trinity County Jail in Redding?"

"The guy that shot your dad? Trinity didn't want him. Right on the border there, no telling which county the shooting took place. Mr. Simpson's here in Eureka, in Semper Virens. We'll plead him out. Mental. Won't do any good to throw him into the general prison population. I've already talked to your dad and David about this. Their best defense against this latest group of fanatics is to organize a blitz of the nighttime radio shows like *Coast to Coast AM*. Get themselves on the internet with their own side of the story."

The footrest of Dad's recliner slaps down like a shot fired in the shadows. He pretends not to see me, limps dramatically to his room. So he knew the shooter was going to be let off with some psychological counseling and a steady supply of mind-altering drugs. Didn't say a word to me about it.

Bobby clears his throat. I imagine he's uncomfortable getting in the middle between me and Dad. Between me and anybody, probably. For reasons unclear to me, I have a reputation for having a short fuse and a long memory.

"The guy? Mitch Simpson? I'm the one booked him. He claims to have seen Bigfoot. Actually, what he's spouting to the headshrinkers is that he communes with them on a regular basis."

"So I heard. Fine line between unshakable belief and fanatic insanity."

Which helps explain why I'm still praying the DNA from that handprint on my belly comes back inconclusive. Amazing how tempting it is to deny a life-changing truth when acceptance will align me with a group of people I've loved for years, but from whom I've always held myself apart. Apart, hell. I've thought of myself as being above them, smarter than them, less in need of an elusive, manmade entity. To align myself with the crazies is scary stuff. And yet, I cannot deny what I saw for those few seconds across that grassy meadow.

Bobby's voice pulls me back to this dark bar.

"So," he asks. "Off the record. What the hell happened up at Bluff Creek?"

I shiver, shift in my chair to get the blood flowing in my legs again. I haven't quite cleared the fog from my head. I'm right here, my butt in a hard wooden chair in VD's. And, I still stand at the edge of a deep green woods, look across soggy grass, into the eyes of creatures from another world. I rub my hands over my face.

The lingering smell of toilet cleaner snaps me right back into this reality.

"Remember senior year? Miss Conner's class. Advanced English. First class after second-period lunch. We'd all be half asleep watching the minute hand of that black-and-white clock tick away our youth? She made us memorize that poem by Robert Burns. Only line I remember is, *The best-laid plans o' mice an' men, Gang aft agley*. That's what happened on that mountain."

thirty-two

THE WEATHER HAS returned to normal. A perfectly ordinary silvery sheet of rain falls straight down from a low, dense blanket of bruised clouds. The calming presence of cold fog, once again, obscures the bay. The space heater is cranked up to bake, Letticia's handmade quilt is snugged under my chin, and if God has any mercy on fools, Stacey will be stomping into my room any minute now, the cup of coffee I begged for in hand.

Ah, yeah. Footsteps on the stairs. Lord, the woman must be wearing her combat boots.

"Get yourself up out of that there bed."

Bubba hands me two venti grande Starbucks containers.

"One's a decaf caramel latte. Other cup's got green tea. With the chil', you need to cut out the caffeine, but the trick is to ease into it."

"Who are you? Some deliverance-style midwife?"

I remove the top from the best smelling cup. The latte smells almost as good as caffeinated. I'm not touching that green tea.

"I ever explain to you how I got three younger sisters? Twelve nieces and nephews? Swallow the tea when you're done with the good stuff. The caffeine in it's a might peaked, but it'll stave off the headache you got goin'."

I pat his hand. Long as he stops first at Starbucks, he can order me around as much as he pleases.

"Soon as you're done there, go shower," he says. "Put on somethin' nice. I'm fixin' to carry Hawk up here in about two shakes of a lamb's tail."

"He's here?" Hot foamy coffee splashes over my hand.

"I done told you not to remove them lids."

I lick the sticky stuff from my palm.

"Hawk doesn't want to see me. He avoided me in the hospital. And now how many days have I been home? He can't walk up seventeen steps to talk?"

Dark miles out over a turbulent ocean, thunder rumbles.

"Ain't open for discussion. You got thirty minutes. Then the man is gonna be sittin' in that there chair, fixin' to hold a polite conversation with the woman be carryin' his chil'."

"Might be his child. Might!"

Bubba's already closing the door gently behind him when lightning bounces between cloud and fog. The source of light miles away, its reflection speeds along the dimpled surface of the water, bares the room for a flash, exposes an avalanche of used Kleenex, a lopsided mound of dirty laundry. I throw the quilt off, knock over a half-empty bag of corn chips and the remains of the fudge bar I ate just before going to bed last night.

Ten minutes ago I thought I might never leave my bed, be like that ancestor of mine who took to her bed for ten years. The woman yet another example of my family's propensity for lunacy. Six children that had to be pawned off on other relatives. The kids were brought to their bedridden mama each day for an hour of cuddle sessions and group reading, then whisked away so as not to bother the poor invalid. Set right here where VD's now leans into the wind, the house caught fire when the youngest child was fifteen. Jesus performed a miracle and my ancestor, poor soul, got right up out of her sick bed, gathered up her jewelry and her Bible, was waiting patiently in the middle of First Street when the pump fire truck finally arrived.

Yolanda. That was her name. She's starting to seem downright clever. Or she was, until Bubba announced Hawk was on his way up here. I'd just as soon not contemplate on the likeness of that man to a house fire. There's a common thread there, though. Both destroy everything you own and yet you can't help standing in the cold night, drawn to their flash and crackle, lustful as a pyromaniac for their consuming heat.

Missing him is an ache like when I was seven and broke my arm on the high slide at Highland Park. Back then, I couldn't help probing with the tips of my fingers, trying to determine just how much pressure the break could bear before the pain shot up my arm.

In this case, the throbbing seems connected directly to my gut, which clenches at each memory examined. And to my throat, which swells shut as though I've swallowed ground glass every time I twist and turn an old conversation, hold old words up to a new light, strain to resurrect some hope.

The funny thing is, what I want most isn't for him to recognize that I might be carrying his child. The child seems mythical. It's Bigfoot that's real. My greatest need is to talk to another true believer.

God that sounds crazy. All these years of listening to Dad's stories, hearing the fervent longing of seekers. At best, I was an agnostic. Even after waking in a bed of ferns with a bloody handprint across my belly, even then, my brain scurried through crooked tunnels of confusion. Like a twitchy mouse in a maze of dead ends, I repeatedly bruised the tip of my rationality on the dead-end of logic, frantic for an explanation that didn't involve faith in that which cannot be proven in this world.

That handprint was curse and blessing. It left me changed, allowed an opportunity for a peek into a reality more beautiful and more terrifying than my own. But the slice of time at the edge of the meadow, when I looked across an expanse of nettles and yellowed grass into the eyes of a family of creatures that we name Bigfoot—that was the defining moment of my life.

Dad and David are true believers. There is no doubt of that. But neither of them has gotten closer to Bigfoot than a strong stink blown on a hillside breeze. Both have placed their hands in the deep muddy imprints left by a giant forest creature. But neither has looked into the creature's eyes.

I wake night after night from dreams of being cradled against a hairy chest that is both alien and familiar. So, crazy as it is, my need to see Hawk is more about a desire to be with another member of the inner circle of believers than about talking to a man who might be the father of my baby.

In truth, his refusal to talk to me about Bigfoot seems a more unforgivable betrayal than does his denial of the child.

Hell, while I'm being honest, might as well admit some small part of me still hopes the DNA test of that print is going to come back human. Or bear. Anything that would allow me to shut down my belief and free me to go back to the land of logic and normalcy. There's a longing for some loophole I could use to turn my back on the experience, convince myself it was some sort of hallucination or breakdown. Crazy I can get over, revelation demands change.

God help me, I am a mess.

After a quick shower, I step into my favorite jeans. The soft denim slides easily over my legs, but the metal button at the waistband is tight. The brass zipper closes when I suck in my belly and bounce on the balls of my feet. But I'm not going to be able to sit down in these pants. Hell, I can't move in these jeans. The realization that my life has changed forever hits like a blow. I fumble with the button and zipper, slide the pants down, hang them in the back of my closet. In white underpants and a too-tight sports bra, I stand in front of the closet mirror, hands overlapping across my bare stomach.

A baby is growing inside me.

A real, honest to God child. Not some possibility for the future. A baby. Growing. Now. Right here, under my hand.

I twist a pale blue towel around my wet hair, wrap myself in my soft chenille. Under a pile of old towels and discarded scarves and stocking caps, the wood of the cigar box is warm and smooth against my searching fingers. I hold the gift in front of me, arms slightly extended. In the silvered light from the windows, the room is ethereal. Dust motes float in warm sunlight. The smell of caramel from the latte is both comfort and blessing. My robed and turbaned shadow along the back wall is that of a lone magi, lost somewhere in time.

Cross-legged in the middle of my unmade bed, I open the box and take out the photo.

Her hair still floats, suspended in time, a golden nimbus around her smiling face. But, it's not the image of the woman I examine. For the first time, it's the face of the man that draws me. A man whose dark hair is streaked with a good measure of gray. A man whose smile I have always read as longing for the woman. Now it appears to be more concern for the child. His dark hand protects the baby's pale back. It's possible that he is turning, not toward the woman, but away from her, beginning a turn that will position his body between the dancing woman and the child in his arms.

Letticia's comment that she only knew my mother for a few months, the nurse's gloat that my blood type and Dad's are not compatible—these clues tip the balance on a lifetime of subconscious knowing. The woman in the picture was already pregnant when she got here. The man who has always been my dad took her in, married her, raised the child as his own when she left.

Footfalls on the steps announce Hawk's arrival. I don't get up.

He's in the room seconds after the knock. I drop the picture back in the box, close the lid gently.

"Bubba said he told you I was coming up."

He sits on the edge of the chair in front of the windows. His face backlit by the stormy sky, he avoids looking at me, focuses on the pointy tips of his cowboy boots extended in front of him.

"Let's not talk about the baby," I say.

Over the years I've seen his eyes sparkle with fun or smolder with passion, but mostly I've seen in them the acceptance of a friend. Tonight I look into gray ash, any fire he ever felt for me smothered by my betrayal of a trust he didn't deserve in the first place.

It's an odd truth, but the death of love isn't hate at all. It's cold, dead, grief.

I pull the robe around me, tie the belt in a hard knot.

He studies his boot tips.

"When it's born, I'd like a paternity test. If it's mine, I'll do what's right."

"The baby's not yours Hawk. I already know that."

His eyes open wide, boots pull back. He leans forward, elbows on bent knees.

"It's the writer's? You're sure?" Relief makes his voice almost giddy.

"Not his, either." My right palm cups the spot where I imagine the child is floating, growing strong in her warm, safe world.

His forehead wrinkles, for an instant panic returns, then he shakes his head.

"God, Sam, I don't know who you are anymore."

My laughter is genuine and laced with relief and acceptance.

"You're right," I agree. "You have no idea who I am now."

We sit in silence while a weak sun pours lacey light through ragged clouds, the room a dull reflection of ever-shifting grays. After a time, the heavy clouds thicken, lower and become one with the swirling fog on the surface of the bay. The room is in near darkness. Neither of us makes a move to turn on an artificial light.

Finally I swing my legs off the bed, press my feet flat on the cold wood floor.

"Did you see them Hawk? Bubba and Lefty heard them, smelled them, felt the rocking of the truck. But they never looked in their eyes."

His soft mouth curves up at the corners. Not quite a smile, but interest, maybe.

"I felt them, know it was them, but, no, I never saw them. What about the writer? Mark Neilsen? He's the one that had the most contact."

"Ah, yeah. Except he doesn't believe it was real. His theory is that the whole thing, dragging him from the cave, packing him through the woods, stacking his useless, expensive equipment all around him… he thinks it was us that did all that. An elaborate hoax."

"There are none so blind as those that will not see," Hawk says.

The streetlight on First and B, triggered by the morning's thickening darkness, switches on, covers us in a nimbus of bluish light.

"Seeing them destroyed my old world, Hawk. I'm terrified. Filled with joy. I keep thinking of the rosary. Hail Mary, full of grace. That's how I feel. Filled with a terrible, awesome grace."

He nods his head.

"I feel the same and I never actually saw them. This whole scare with the baby? It threw me for a loop when all I wanted to do was disappear into the woods and think about what happened with that encounter."

This whole scare with the baby? Even as his words confirm my belief that he will never be dad to this child, an edge of anger creeps into my voice.

"Ah, yeah, well, I imagine you're still a working professor at the college. Instructing young minds on the joys of anthropology? That right there would prevent you from doing any forty days in the wilderness, right?"

"Sure." He bounces his knee, taps his index fingers on the arm of the chair. "I just meant, it's been a distraction, you know." The twitching stops. He leans toward me. "I just always thought you and I would be together. Not in any conventional marriage kind of arrangement, but just there for each other. It's disconcerting to think of you as a mother. Your life going in a direction that leads away from me."

"Well. Woman's virtue has always been man's greatest invention."

He twitches again.

"What are you saying?"

"I'm explaining to you, in the gentlest way possible, that your good-hearted woman is done putting up with your narcissistic crap. I've always been there for you, Hawk. You've been there for me only when it was convenient."

His face jerks away as though I've slapped him. He lifts himself from the chair, arms loose at his sides, walks out of the room, and shuts the door gently behind him. I sit in the glow of the streetlight, move my hand in slow circles across my belly.

thirty-three

DAWN COMES SOFTLY.

A warm breath of west wind smooths the surface of the Pacific. Caught between storms, the ocean rests.

Bubba and I stand, side by side. Fishing lines tug in the outgoing tide.

"About time you came fishin' with me."

"Ah, yeah." Neither of us take our eyes off the sun-glittered river. "About time I did a number of things."

A Boston Whaler just this side of the mouth of the Mad is singled out by circling seagulls. Someone has a fish on.

"How'd you and Hawk leave it?" His voice is just a tad off plumb line, an edge tilting his emotions off center.

I glance across at him. His jaw line is set a bit hard for a casual morning's fishing. My eyes return to the Whaler. Someone in a bright orange Elmer Fudd hat, hard to tell from here if it's a man or a woman, is going to lose that fish. They're pulling too hard, too fast. In the excitement of the hit, they've forgotten to let the fish run, tire itself, then ease it to the boat.

"I'm always going to love Hawk. No way around that. I think, for the first time, I'm also able to accept him just as he is."

The orange hat jerks backward as the fish pulls free, releases the salmon to fight its way upstream, do its best to spawn.

"That there mean you and him are still together? Just takin' another little break?"

"Nope. Just the opposite. It means Hawk's been telling me for years he's not a commitment sort of guy. I finally heard him."

He smiles over at me. "Fish ain't bitin'."

"They're not interested in feeding," I say. "The run's late. Rains inland are early. Not much time to get where they need to be."

I push back the hood of my sweatshirt, turn my face to the morning sun. The air is rich with the smells of home. The tang of the ocean, the muddy, fishy smell of the river, the steaming wet rocks of the jetty, a thick stew, spiced with a hint of marijuana smoke drifting from the fishermen a few boulders down from us.

"I tell you I'm getting' out of growin'?" Bubba asks.

A tug on my line, a bump, not a bite.

"How come?"

"I'm gonna be an uncle. Right? Bad example to set. Me growin pot."

"You've got nieces and nephews back in Georgia, don't you?"

"I do. But I'm hopin' to be a mite closer to this here youngun."

The tip of Bubba's pole dips, then snaps upward. The whir of nylon filament running fast and smooth ends our conversation. I reel in my line, step back, and get out of his way, glad for the chance to observe, mull over his last words. Funny how we miss what's right smack in front of our face. As Dad says, "If it had been a snake it'd've bit me." Bubba is the man who has been there for me. Distracted by lesser men, I took for granted his support and love and his calm, steady presence.

He plays the salmon beautifully, never applies too much pressure, lets the fish pull out just enough line at each run until, in the end, the flashing orange-and-silver fish seems to leap from the river of its own accord to lie flopping at his feet.

He slips the single hook gently from the salmon, grins at me over its arching body, returns it gently to the river.

I smile back. "You skunked me. And the fog's rolling in. You ready to head back?"

"Y'all didn't want that fish, did you?"

"Lord, no. Dad's got a freezer full. How would VD's fishermen drink if I didn't accept crab and salmon in lieu of greenbacks?"

He insists on packing my gear on the way back to his truck. I sit to scoot down off a quartz-streaked SUV-sized boulder. He sets down the tackle box and poles, lifts me from the stone as if I were a child. I glare at him when he sets me on my feet.

"I'm pregnant. Not crippled. I don't need help getting across a damn jetty I've been fishing off of since I was two."

"Huh." He shrugs, keeps possession of my gear. "My mistake. So. How'd you leave it with the city slick?"

"He's having second thoughts about suing me. Bobby Barellis threatened to file charges against him for inciting mayhem. Because that blog of his riled up Simpson. The shooter. The District Attorney told him the blog fell under jurisdiction of The PATRIOT Act. Said he was stirring up a holy war."

Heavy braying laughter mixes with my unladylike snorts, floats out into the fog, dissipates into whatever dimension sound goes when it leaves this world.

"That there holy war business, we're laughin', but it ain't far from the mark."

"Ah, yeah. Lefty's been helping Dad and David set up their own blog, telling their side of the story. The whole tribe of Tri-County Bigfooters have been calling into *Coast to Coast AM* radio. Our guys have taken the battle to the airwaves."

I pull up the hood of my sweatshirt, match my stride to Bubba's so as to let him block the wind some. Even now, after looking into the eyes of not one, but three, real, honest-to-God, Bigfoots, a large part of me hears this conversation as absurd. I'm uncomfortable talking about it, even to Bubba. My inclination is to keep this foggy world separate from the land where Bigfoot walks. The two realities disparate, oil and water that co-exist but rarely mix.

"I was actually askin' about the baby. What all did the city boy say about the chil'?'"

"His name is Mark." I talk right over his grunt. "He's not interested in the baby. Of course it doesn't help that I don't know for certain it's his. Still, given his attitude, I don't want him around."

"That's right, man can't love that little girl like the gift from God she is, be better off stayin' out of her life."

Fog has reclaimed the beach, returned my world to its rightful luminous shades of gray.

"How come you're so sure I'm having a girl? Could be a boy."

We're in the cab of the truck before he answers, the heater blasting cold air, doing its diesel best to warm. The fog piles up on the ocean, a soft blanket settling gently back into place.

"I believe I'm gonna go on record as predictin' baby girls. Twins. I had me a dream awhile back. Had me two little baby girls, one in the crook of each arm."

He folds his arms gently across his massive chest. A rogue wave of longing washes over me. I slide across the bench seat, snuggle up under his arm, don't say a word until the cab is warm and the rolling ocean is completely hidden under its protective quilt.

"Twins would be all I need. Don't even think it, Nostradamus."

"Can't help it. Wait and see. Twin girls."

The feeling comes back into my feet. I wiggle my toes. Push my hands against the dash vents to warm my hands.

"Did you know Stacey's leaving us? Wants to go back to school full-time. Be an elementary school teacher. She'll work one or two nights a week, but with Hawk selling out, too, I'm looking for a full-time bartender. You know, one like Stacey who'll do most all the work and pretend I manage the place."

He is very still beside me. I like the comfort of his warm arm around my shoulder, the slightly fishy, spicy smell of his flannel shirt. His voice rumbles his chest.

"I'm lookin' for work."

"That why you been getting all dressed up lately? Showing up in pressed pants and new shirts?"

"One of the reasons. I was sort a hopin' you'd figured out the other one. The most important reason."

The fog has made the whalers, aluminum skiffs, and other assorted fishing boats invisible. I imagine myself in one of those boats, surrounded by water of one kind or another, hoping to make the correct choice of direction when it's time to bring the boat in across the bar.

"How about you working at VD's? Be my general, all-purpose bartender, bouncer." I hesitate over the next words, take a deep breath, and pray my internal compass has finally found true north. "My... friend. Like always, but maybe we're ready for a deeper kind of friendship."

He shifts against me, tightens his touch on my shoulders.

"That sounds good. For now. But you got to understand, I ain't one of them ole boys is lookin' for a California-type 'friends with benefits' deals. And, whatever you decide in the long run, I am gonna be right here for you and for them baby girls of yours."

thirty-four

DAD SITS UNDER the one-eyed bear, a cup of coffee cradled in his hands.

VD's is packed with newcomers. The Bigfoot mobile parked out front, coupled with the last few days' newspaper articles, draws them in like flies to… well, recent events pull in the customers.

I kiss Dad's smooth cheek, the bay rum and Winstons—a balm on an already fine day.

He winks at me. "You call that gentleman Doctor Bernstein recommended you speak with?"

"I did. He had some interesting ideas." I'm not ready to talk about this yet, have something else altogether on my mind. "Can I talk to you in your room, Dad? Something I've been meaning to ask you."

"Ah, yeah. Got some talking of my own to do."

He gets up, carries his coffee with him. I stop behind the bar, fill a shot glass with maraschino cherries, take a Diet Cherry Coke from the refrigerator. Blue smoke floats in the air of his room, shot through with meager light from the high, narrow windows along the outside wall.

"You first." He lowers himself into his duct-taped recliner.

I take the rocker across from him. "I'm not quite sure how to say this."

"This about your mom?"

"Not exactly."

He blows a smoke ring. Watches it hang in the still air. "You're wondering about our blood types, yours and mine, being incompatible."

"I think I already know why that is. But, with being pregnant and everything, I guess I'm just curious. Wondering if I'm right."

It's been a while since I've been in this room when there wasn't rain playing a symphony on the roof above us. Today's quiet is disconcerting, adds to my anxiety.

"I never meant to mislead you, Samantha. Never lied. I just never sat you down and told you the whole truth."

I get up from the rocker. "Scoot your skinny old man butt over. Plenty of room for both of us in that awful recliner."

I end up with one butt cheek squished up on the hard arm of the chair, my head on his narrow chest.

"Your mom was about six months along when she came in here the first time."

He rubs my arm, his chest stills while he waits for my response. It's what I expected so I don't know why my throat closes and tears well up. I nod my head against his chest, hug him hard.

"I was a beat-to-hell fifty-three. She was a beautiful twenty-six. Wasn't exactly a match made in heaven. But she needed help and I took her in. She worked the bar for a few nights, but it was hard on her being on her feet. I moved a cot out into the bar each night. Gave her my bed."

He points with his chin to the double bed in the corner. The bowed-in-the-middle, lumpy mattress I've been trying to get him to replace for a dozen years.

"Came a night when she persuaded me to stay here with her. Not much of a story there. Old fool. Young, desperate woman. I was already more than half in love with her anyway. Asked her to marry me a month later. We married January fourteenth. You came along March twenty-seventh."

I tilt my head up, want to see his face. "So she stayed until I was born, and then left six weeks later?"

"Almost right. Middle of March, I came in here after the bar closed, found a note saying she was on her way to San Francisco. To a Rolling Stones concert. Eight months pregnant and she's going to a rock-and-roll concert. As scared as I was, I had to smile. You got that from her, Sam, that stubborn refusal to be stalled by reality. The need to plow ahead in the face of any challenge and be just who you want to be."

I shake my head. "I'm nothing like her. I got that stubborn streak from you."

His chuckle shakes his chest and is followed by a coughing fit that brings me out of the recliner and back into the rocker. He hasn't fully recovered yet from his ordeal in the woods. Acts tough, but his color isn't good, frightens me by being closer to the gray of cigarette ash than his usual olive brown.

The coughing passes, he sips at his cold coffee. "She had the baby. Had you. While she was in the city. Came back here a week after she left. You a tiny little thing, beautiful, wrapped in a pink blanket I'd never seen before."

"How'd she get between here and the city? Did she take your truck?"

He shakes his head, never takes his eyes from mine. "That's a mystery. No idea how she left or how she returned. Letticia has always claimed she saw her, the night she left, getting into a navy blue Mercedes in front of the Eureka Inn. Doesn't seem likely to me but, you never know."

I lean forward, lay my head on his bony knees. "All these years, Dad, I've been so busy grieving over her leaving, that I didn't appreciate as much as I should have, you staying. Especially if I wasn't even you—"

His voice is sharp, angry, a retort that freezes the words in my mouth. "Don't say it! Don't you ever say you're not my daughter. You've been mine since before you were laid in my arms the first time. You used to fuss at me when you were a child, asking about if I missed your mom, if I thought of going after her. Truth is, the only feeling I ever had about her once she left was fear of her coming back. Trying to take you from me."

His rough hand soothes the side of my face. "You going to be okay with this, Sam?"

"Ah, yeah. You're my dad. Always have been, always will be."

We watch the dust motes float in the smoky air. The noise from the bar is building. Bursts of laughter, shouts of greeting are punctuated with the occasional nervous shriek.

"Before we go back out there," his voice is soft, too soft maybe, "I've got something needs telling."

Fear captures my breath. The world shrinks to this wrinkled old man in his silver duct-tape throne, his feathery hair a soft crown, his quavering voice about to deliver a proclamation I do not want to hear.

"Doctor says I got a little problem with my heart. They're wanting to do an angioplasty surgery. Go in somehow and sort of Roto-Rooter out my arteries. Maybe put in a stent."

This feels like slow motion. I see his calloused hand move toward the white-and-red pack of Winstons. Watch as he shakes out a cigarette. Brings it to his mouth. Runs his thumb along the raised Marine Corp emblem on the Zippo. His face lit by the tiny blue-and-yellow flame. The red glow at the tip of the cigarette. He draws smoke into his expanding chest. All this seems to take place outside of time, someplace where he didn't just tell me he needs major surgery to go on living.

Then my breath rushes back, reality pushes in around me.

"When are you having this surgery?" I sound angry. Not scared. I don't sound scared.

He blows smoke out into the air. "Well, that's the thing. I'm not sure I'm going to let them operate."

Now the anger catches up for real, overtakes the fear. I stand up from the chair so fast it rocks back, skitters across the wood floor.

"Hang on now, Samantha. Let me explain. They can't operate until I quit smoking and, at my age, I just don't know if I can do that. Maybe be better to take my chances without the surgery."

The glowing tip of his Winston burns my hand when I snatch it from his mouth. I snatch the red-and-white pack from the pocket of his shirt, remove each cigarette and crumble it in my fist, one by one. Still not sure what to do with my anger, I throw the empty pack on the floor, smash it under my boot toe. Throw open each and every cupboard in the room. Jump up and down on the carton of death when I find it on the counter next to the Lay's potato chips.

I am a child in the middle of a tantrum. I am Shiva destroying the universe. I am frightened right out of my mind.

David sticks his head in the door.

"I guess you told her."

"Don't you dare!" I rant at Dad. "Don't you even think of giving up. I need you here, damnit. You have smoked your last cigarette. I don't give a good God damn if we have to lock you in rehab. You will stop smoking, have that surgery, get better, and be here a good long time more."

"This here." Dad sighs. "This reaction. It's why I didn't tell you sooner. I'm a grown man, Samantha Jean. You're my daughter, but you don't get to make this kind of decision for me. Smoking's my one vice. I'm not giving it up."

My vision tunnels, black with flashes of red along the curve. I may be having some kind of stroke. I cup my hands at my belly, lower myself into the rocker. Breathe. In and out. Slowly.

"Here's the thing, Dad. I am at least as stubborn as you are. And I'm a lot younger. With bunches more stamina. We'll go to the doctor and get you a patch or something. But you have smoked your last cigarette."

He pushes back against his recliner, crosses his scrawny arms, kicks up the footrest, puts a little more distance between us. It's David he glares at.

"Told you I shouldn't tell her."

"Aw partner, that's precisely why I insisted you do it. Now get your butt out here. We've got an anniversary meeting to preside over. Best anniversary meeting ever. DNA results are back."

thirty-five

OCTOBER 20TH. VD'S is closed for a private party. Anniversary of the making of the Patterson tape in 1967.

Dad and David are freaking me out. It's like they're in one of those Disney movies where the teenager's body is inexplicably switched with that of the parent. Two old guys in their late seventies, one with his arm in a camouflage sling, both of them bouncy with excitement. David keeps rising up on his toes like a manic ballerina, flinging his hands in emphasis as he recites the tale to a rapt audience.

Dad is ensconced in his duct-taped recliner. The thing has been moved back and forth between his room and the bar so many times in the last week that Bubba is threatening to put it on wheels to save his back. Dad hasn't used a sling or slowed down a notch since his first day home from the hospital, but, showman that he is, tonight he's stretched out like a prop. Except he can't quite pull off the poor, old, victimized codger act. He keeps popping the footrest to the floor, leaping out of the chair as if a spring is attached to his bony ass.

A sparkling glass jar with a yellow-and-red sticker identifying it as an empty gallon of Beaver Mustard is already half-filled with bills. The instructions in front of the makeshift cash register are Stacey's idea. All drinks are free today. But, as the card says, donations are mightily appreciated.

Between the shaggy head of a bull elk and that of the open-mouthed, one-eyed black bear, David has hung a nicely framed poster of my belly. It's a fine shot. The giant handprint is clear, between the waistband of my dirty jeans and the bottom of a filthy, once-white, sports bra, the palm print and five distinct fingers seem to jump out in 3D. On a table below the belly photo, a stack of papers—the evening's centerpiece and highlight. These reports are secured with a Littlefoot cast whose new white plaster glows in the dark bar, catches the light, draws the eye.

Lefty wears a T-shirt imprinted on the front with a miniaturized version of the hairy image he painted on the Bigfootmobile. The back of the shirt advertises his new business—*Lefty's Trompe L'Oreal. No job too big or too small.* Caroline, in a matching shirt, is right beside him. They carry refills from the bar to a cluster of old-timers hiding in the courtyard, hoping I won't notice the heavy blue smoke already floating into my bar like an unwelcome, and smelly, ghost. Caroline's dog, Rufus, is glued to my side. Almost literally. The animal drools continually and his slobber is the consistency of resin. Somebody should bottle the stuff.

Stacey, who usually avoids these Bigfoot affairs like the black plague, started the evening hovering along the edges of the crowd like Margaret Mead observing the cannibals of New Guinea. She's catching the spirit, though. Drawn into the inner circle by the old-timers, her long legs and high boobs are increasingly difficult to spot, obscured by old flannel and aged testosterone.

Bubba, in jeans and another new shirt, this one the amber of the flecks in his blue-green eyes, is acting as Dad's gopher. He's up on a ladder putting the finishing touches on a string of fairy lights around the framed picture of Patterson's frame 352—Patty looking over her shoulder, her expression as mysterious as that of the Mona Lisa. Job done, he folds the ladder, passes behind me close enough to lean into my backside, and whispers in my ear.

"You doing all right?"

"Finer'n frog's hair."

His laugh is like happy, braying goats.

Hawk, from his position as guardian at the front door, turns and looks our way. I smile, wiggle my fingers in his direction. He looks relaxed, comfortable with himself, clueless as to the happenings in anyone's life but his own.

Letticia, installed on her stool at the end of the bar, takes this all in, crooks her finger at me.

"So. Rumor has it Hawk's selling you his share of VD's?"

"Ah, yeah. He wants to concentrate on anthropology. He does, after all, have that doctorate."

"Uh-huh. A bar has never been a good place for that boy."

I let that pass, concentrate on the art of pouring a draft beer with just the right amount of head. The trick is the angle of the glass.

"New outfit?" I can't help but hear a note of slyness in her voice.

"Getting too big for my old britches."

"Gonna get a whole lot worse before it gets better."

"I expect so. Dad tell you what the sonogram showed?"

"Are you kidding? It's been an hour-and-a-half since you found out you were having twins. I believe your father's putting up a billboard to reach the few souls he hasn't been able to contact."

She sips at her beer, runs her eyes over the old cowboy bringing the skunk smell of marijuana into my bar from the courtyard.

"You know the sex yet?"

"Not yet. Bubba swears its girls. If so, I'm thinking Victoria and Dharma."

Ronald Hanks, reporter for the local *Times-Standard*, motions for his cameraman to get a shot of Dad and David flanking the poster. Maybe two or three people who don't get the paper or own a TV will wake up tomorrow morning and not have seen my bare belly.

"I hear you and the man from Georgia been seeing each other."

"Bubba and I been seeing each other for years. We're friends."

She stares patiently until I shrug.

"He's going to help me manage the place. We're taking it slow. Maybe I'm going to travel a bit here before long. Plus, for a few months anyway, I want to spend some extra time with Dad. Did he tell you he quit smoking?"

Her beer goes down the wrong pipe. It takes a minute before she can catch her breath to respond.

"He mentioned it'd been an hour-and-a-half since his last cigarette. So he's going to have the angioplasty?"

"Did everybody in town know he needed that operation before me?"

"Everybody he wasn't afraid, once they knew, was gonna make sure he never had another cigarette."

At the door, Hawk backslaps a small man in leathers who's just arrived at the party with a larger, slightly younger man in tow. I slip out from behind the bar to give Dr. Bernstein a hug.

"How's the world of string theory?"

I had in mind to ask Bubba to set up a fan to blow the marijuana smell from the courtyard back outside, but one good whiff of the physics professor and I know it's a losing battle.

"Ah. The world of possibilities and chaos continues to delight." His dark eyes sparkle, he adjusts the crystal at his throat, slips past me to slide his arm around Letticia's ample waist, and gently pinch the side of her boob.

Talking with Bernstein is like falling down the rabbit hole. The man is his own best advertisement for an alternate universe. He throws an arm toward the newcomer at his side, wiggles his bushy white eyebrows.

"Samantha Jean Foster, I'd like you to meet Casey Cowan."

I offer my hand to a man in black wool slacks and a charcoal sweater with a black collar showing at the neck, all of which looks like it's been bunched up under a pair of riding overalls for well over five hours. His dark hair is plastered to the sides of his face as though he's been riding in a wind tunnel.

I offer my hand. "Rode up on the back of the Harley, huh?"

He merely nods. I assume his face is still too cold to function properly. I mix him a hot-buttered rum, heavy on the rum, shake my finger at the prankster PhD.

"It's storming out there. You couldn't have driven the Jaguar and brought me an unfrozen man?"

The physicist and Letticia are catching up on old times. Both ignore me completely.

"It was my own fault," Casey says. "I could have driven my car, but was hoping to impress you by arriving with Berkeley's famed Doctor of Physics."

I mix him another hot-buttered rum. Halfway through this one, he gets to the point.

"Have you given any thought to our conversation?"

"I have. Tell me again about your company."

"I own a small—let's say boutique—publishing house in the city. We specialize in books about the Pacific Northwest. Local Indian culture, area histories, a good many scientific publications as well as a few books a year that are actually entertaining to read. This last group, when we're lucky, keep us afloat."

"You published Doctor Bernstein's book?"

"*Untangling String Theory*. We did, yes. It did quite well."

Dad and David prepare for the main event. Bubba has been dispatched to the courtyard to round up the old-timers. The younger hunters reassure themselves that their glasses are full enough to last through the speechifying.

"Mister Cowan," I say, "I'm intrigued, but I'm afraid you've made an uncomfortable ride for nothing. I don't write."

"Sure you do." He's warmed up now, downright animated. "Doctor Bernstein tells me you have your dad's gift of storytelling, and you have the story of the decade. An actual encounter with Bigfoot." He shrugs, smiles mysteriously. "Besides, I have a bit of a soft spot for Patty myself."

All eyes are on Dad now. He and David have bookended the belly handprint poster and the table with the mysterious stack of handouts.

"We're going to tell you what we've got." Dad does his best to drop his voice down in pitch, hide the excitement that seems to leak out his ears, fly from the tips of his feathery hair. "Then we're going to pass around copies of the proof. A keepsake of tonight's historic anniversary meeting of the Tri-County Bigfooters."

David, still bouncing on his toes, cuts in with the speech he's been practicing since the results of the lab tests came back.

"In just a few moments I'm going to call Victor's daughter, Samantha, up here to tell you about last week's monumental events. But first, let me start this evening with some proof of what this brave young woman is going to relate to you."

Bubba, an immovable rock in pale golden-brown chamois, stands to Dad's left. I roll my eyes at him and he grins across the room, winks at me. Hawk sits at the table by the front door, his legs stretched in front of him, pointy-toed boots pointing at the ceiling. He wrinkles his forehead at this interchange between Bubba and me, tilts his handsome face in what I take as a question. "Really? You and *this* guy?"

My smile widens.

"After her encounter with the Bigfoots, Samantha was medevaced by helicopter to Our Lady of Mercy hospital in Weaverville. Why she had to be air-lifted out of the wilderness is her story. It's a good one, but I'm going to let her tell it. My part of the tale only concerns what happened when she got to the hospital."

Mr. Cowan leans across the bar and confides to me, "Roger Patterson drew crowds all over the country. Over sixteen thousand in Salt Lake City alone. He had under two minutes of footage. No scientific proof."

I'm starting to catch on. I lower my voice, whisper in his ear like a conspirator, "Roger Patterson died a poor man."

"Indeed he did. He was a clever, extremely lucky man, but he had no business sense whatsoever. I've been assured that is not the case with you."

David is ready for the evening's big news. "I was, fortuitously, already at the hospital when Samantha arrived."

Dad can't keep himself still. He throws himself into the recitation. "The fortuitous event that brought him there being me getting shot and damn near bleeding to death."

The laughter rears up, releases tension, and then dies quickly. This crowd wants to hear what David has to offer.

"When the doctors cut off Samantha's shirt in the emergency room, I saw this handprint and knew immediately we needed to preserve as much as possible as evidence." David extends his arm toward the poster of the bloody handprint across my belly. A carnie inviting you to step right up, have a gander at what's in the tent. Or a priest raising the body of the living Christ high above his head in worship and awe. All depends on your point of view.

The crowd sucks in its breath, one entity awaiting deliverance.

"This photo, among others, was taken by me. I also had DNA tests run on the material that composed the handprint."

No exhale. They're poised on the brink of discovery or oxygen deprivation, whichever comes first.

"Those DNA tests were sent to three different laboratories. The results of those scientific examinations are now available."

The crowd shifts. Get to it David. These folks can only live on tiny sips of smoky air for so long.

He removes the plaster Littlefoot cast, picks up the top sheet of paper, makes a production of turning it over to read. The crowd leans forward as one.

"Snell labs in Berkeley, California, reports that the handprint consists of '*Blood of non-human female primate. Does not match that of any known great ape.*' Hanger laboratory, Portland, Oregon. '*Blood of female, unknown primate, indications that blood is menstrual.*' Polk lab, Phoenix, Arizona. '*Blood, of unknown female primate.*'"

The noise in the bar has reached Pentecostal-revival level. Enough people to shut us down if the fire marshal drops by, all of them on their feet, stomping work boots, arms raised, hands clapping.

My heart stops beating. One long flicker of hesitation. A moment when my choice is frighteningly clear, wondrously revealed. Begin the long, slow death of denial, or take the first step toward acknowledgement and transformation.

Led by David, the old-timers have joined arms in an uneven circle of stiff movement to internal music. Stacey is pulled into this celebratory dance. Someone shouts "Hallelujah" and the crowd picks up the cry. Four women Bigfooters are in a hand-clapping circle around a fifth who is up on a table, kicking her combat-booted heels, sending the table tilting precariously toward the floor. Rufus leaps up and plants his big feet on my shoulders, his warm, wet tongue no more appealing on my face than I expected it to be.

Caught up in the energy, I begin a journey for which I've been, unknowingly, preparing my whole life. Holding Rufus's shaggy paws in my hands, my body sways. I dance for joy in the knowledge of who I am.

Bubba and Lefty move among the congregation, hand out copies of the proof. Bubba ends his dispersal duties at the bar, steps around next to me. I lean against him for an instant, his big hand warm and dry in mine. I shout up at him, but the distance is too great for him to hear over the noise. He picks me up gently and sits me on the bar, my back to the crowd, facing him. I could gain fifty pounds with these babies and still feel like a little bitty girl next to him.

"This is Mister Cowan." I point my chin toward the publisher. "He wants me to write about what happened. Travel all over the country for a few months. After the twins are born. Promoting the book."

"You could do it. Been fussin' about wantin' to see more of the world." His breath is warm in my ear.

"I'd feel better about saying yes to the book, if I knew you'd be here. Keeping an eye on the bar while Dad and me and the babies are gallivanting around the country."

"Sounds like we got us a plan."

The whoops and shouts of the old-timers turn to wheezes. They collapse onto available wooden chairs. Dad claps his hands, gives a shout like he's calling hogs, collects everyone's attention. He doesn't say a word until the bar is as quiet as a church.

"My daughter, Samantha Jean Foster, will now talk to you some about what happened out there on Blue Mountain." Dad points at the poster. "We old guys got enough sense to know that's what you came for tonight."

Bubba lifts me down from the bar. Impulsive decisions have not worked out well for me lately. I figure I'm due.

I reach across the bar, shake hands with Mr. Cowan.

"I've got a lawyer owes me a favor. We'll sit down and work out the details."

It's a long walk through a sea of smiling faces. People I've known my whole life part around me. A rolling wave of hope and desire for belief, they create a passage through to the other side of the bar. Gentle hands touch my arm, my belly, reach across the room as though their combined need can push me along my chosen path.

I take my position between Dad and David. My fate now sealed, my voice is calm.

"I know you came to hear what happened in the woods above Bluff Creek. But I've got a couple of announcements to make."

A murmur, lapping water over packed sand, washes through the crowd.

"First off, as you know, I'm going to be stretched a little tight here before too long. In more ways than one."

I lay my palms against the curve of my belly. A cheer breaks over the room, temporarily drowns my misgivings.

"Stacey's leaving us to get her teaching credentials. If she runs her classroom like she runs this bar, those kids are going be educated, whether they like it or not."

There is a brief attempt, quickly abandoned, to hoist Stacey up on the shoulders of the old-timers. They settle for grinning happily and rubbing sly circles on her bare arms.

"Nobody is going to be able to take Stacey's place, but Bubba will be managing the bar in his own entertaining and charming way. I'm going to be busy with a project I hope all of you will be happy with, and proud of, when I'm finished.

"What happened to me out there in the woods was so outside my experience, so bizarre and surreal, that I'm having a difficult time explaining it. And I want to tell the gospel truth. That seems to me to be the most important thing. To do that, I need time to sort things out.

"Most of you have known me since I was knee high to a grasshopper." Chuckles, nods, waves of approval wash at my feet. "As far as Bigfoot is concerned, I've been what you might call a hopeful agnostic my whole life. We all, I think, want to believe in something outside ourselves. Most of us would say we don't believe in ghosts and demons. Might be we're a little more open to the possibility of angels and saints. To quote someone right here in this bar tonight, 'If I can't see it, and I can't touch it, I'm not gonna worry none about it.' And yet, how many of you would buy John Wayne Gacey's old house?"

Scuffed boots shift and scrape on the worn wood floor.

"I guess what I'm trying to say here is that, somewhere deep down in our most ancient selves, we all, even agnostics like me, know there's something incomprehensible out there. All around us. Some of you are a lot smarter than me. To believe, you didn't have to stand, exhausted and wringing wet, at the edge of a meadow and look into the eyes of another world. You had faith."

I link my arms through Dad and David's, catch Bubba's eye across the room. The crowd is silent, an ebb tide waiting for moon's nudge.

"Now that I know the truth, I want to get the telling right. No mix-ups and inconsistencies to feed the critics. I have been asked to write a book. A true account of what happened out there above Bluff Creek. I don't want to reveal too much. Like I said, this is an opportunity to get it on record. It needs to be done right and for that I need a little time to sort through my own feelings. I do want to comment tonight on that bloody print, though.

"This is speculation. I don't claim to have any special psychic connection into the mind of Bigfoot. But here's what I think."

The crowd leans forward in their chairs. No one touches a drink. I turn and look at the poster, relive the moment on a soft bed of trampled ferns when I discovered that impression like some holy, terrifying mark. One deep breath of beer, old wood, and hope returns me to the bar.

I smile at the crowd. "I think the Bigfoots knew I was pregnant. Or the female did, anyway. Smelled the pheromones, maybe. That's why they didn't take me, carry me into the woods to examine. Which, as you know, is what they did with Mark Nielson, the man I was guiding on his first expedition into those woods. I think... I believe the female marked me with her life force, blood from her cycle of life. A blessing. A badge of union with the power of females the world over."

I stand silently in front of the crowd. Wait for their reaction.

Ronald, the reporter from *The Times-Standard*, lifts his hand in the air. When I nod his way he asks, "Do you have any ideas about why Mister Neilsen was kidnapped?"

Clever. He knows Mark's saying his abduction was a hoax that I helped perpetuate. Well, might as well take the bull by the horns. Controversy sells books. Least that's what I've always heard.

"Ah, yeah. I think they were just curious. Lord, the man had so many gadgets that I discarded along the hike to lighten his load. Maybe they thought he was molting. Or shedding his skin."

Smiles break out around the room. Bubba lets loose with one of his braying rumbles, and the crowd, eager to stay right with me, laughs along with him. When it's quiet again, I offer another explanation.

"It's not common, but there have been other reports of Bigfoot carrying somebody into the woods to examine. I don't suppose it's much different than us. If we ever capture one of them, I suspect we'll be doing a good bit more poking and prodding than they engaged in."

I grin at the crowd, acknowledge Dad and David by taking their hands, pulling them against my sides. At the bar, Mr. Cowan's grin testifies to his own visions of success.

"Come back next year." I tell the crowd, "Same time, same place. You can buy the first available copies of the book. I'll sign every one of them."

The tide hangs suspended, poised to sweep me to safety, or tumble me to its black depths.

Then Bubba is clapping his big hands, Hawk is on his feet cheering, and Dad pulls me against his bony chest.

"A celebratory round on the house!" David shouts.

That turns the tide.

I wade into my destiny.

PAMELA FOSTER is among the sixth generation of Fosters to be born and raised on the westernmost tip of the continental United States. *Bigfoot Blues* is the first of her Bigfoot trilogy. After over two decades of travel, mostly in Latin America and Asia, Foster has returned to her hometown of Eureka, California, where she wakes each morning to fog draped redwoods, the ebb and flow of Humboldt Bay, and the comfort of finally being home.